Sweetest Fortune

BAMBO DEEN

First Published in Great Britain in 2024 by
LOVE AFRICA PRESS
103 Reaver House, 12 East Street, Epsom KT17 1HX
www.loveafricapress.com[1]

---

1.   http://www.loveafricapress.com

Dedication

To Ify, Omoronike, and Mima (again!)

You were all so excited for this book. I hope it meets your expectations.

Chapter One

The forest at dusk cocooned two women in a gentle embrace. During the season before rainfall, a heaviness often hung in the air, but under the canopy of trees, coolness persisted.

There'd been a time when two women venturing into the woods unaccompanied spelt certain death. The flora surrounding them didn't appear thick—the trees were thin, and vines pooled to the ground—yet, if someone stood a few feet ahead, they wouldn't see anyone. Mercenaries, raiders, and all manner of bloodthirsty men roamed behind the camouflage. Greens, browns, and yellows provided sanctuary for violence to hide and later reveal itself with the element of surprise.

Ewadunni shuddered. She often marvelled at the forest's duplicity. Despite the reassurances of many years of peace and the stronghold that was Kuta, she was no stranger to the wickedness of man.

She inhaled deeply to ground herself and traced her fingers along the maroon bark of the orange-milk tree. Her forehead pressed on the tree's surface, she hummed low in her throat as her eyelids fluttered closed. Humans were nothing like the trees and tender green shrubs marking verdant spaces.

Nuzzling closer to the trunk, she quietened her thoughts and listened, then stepped back.

"This one says no," she announced, shaking her head.

Balanced on a rock behind her, Jomiloju observed her closely.

"Who asks permission before plucking a leaf?" she asked in a teasing tone.

"Students under the supervision of Iya Ogele."

Both of them were healers, trained in dealing with reproductive health and childcare. Ewa was senior to Jomiloju—however, they'd grown close from the moment Jomiloju married into the clan. They trained and practiced following the methods of the matriarch Ogele. While Ewa had learned directly from Ogele, the elder lacked the patience to train Jomiloju and had left her in Ewa's care.

Before she'd found her calling in healthcare, Jomiloju had been a raffia-weaver. Once, she'd apprenticed with the potters, and after that, had earned business as a long-distance trader of fabrics. It was how she met Togun, her husband.

Ewa easily remembered the day her friend's pregnancy was announced. Ogele had known beforehand—she could tell even with Jomiloju's flat stomach. Two months later, a formal announcement was made, and the women of the household gathered to shower blessings on Jomiloju. She was pampered and well taken care of because a pregnant woman couldn't lack in a household that produced warriors.

"Hm." Jomiloju sounded subdued with the mention of the old woman's name. She looked at the purple sky. "At this rate, we shall spend the night in the forest."

"Wouldn't that be an adventure, Jide?" Ewa drew close then squatted low to kiss the child in Jomiloju's arms. She stroked Jide's cheek as she started singing softly. "Ojiji will protect us."

"Ha! You always ridicule us for mentioning Ojiji."

"Hush, you."

Just then, Jide released his mother's nipple to flash a winning grin at Ewa, and her heart clenched gently in response. She began singing.

"Anything my child desires, I will buy."

"You are going to spoil this boy," Jomiloju said, shifting the child at her breast.

"He deserves it."

"He certainly does." Switching her tone to become even more playful, she rubbed her son's belly. "Is that right, my love?"

Ewa stretched to her full height. The sun had continued its descent while they chatted. She had to find another tree willing to depart with the leaves she needed. If they set off in half an hour, they would return home before nightfall.

"We'll be done shortly." Jomiloju looked up with a guilty smile as she burped her baby.

Ewa glanced at her relative. Jomiloju appeared content as she navigated Jide through the stages of feeding.

"Take your time," she said with a small smile.

An old, familiar ache twisted awake in the pit of her stomach. As far as she was concerned, motherhood was one of the most tranquil and beautiful aspects of life. How she wished the expression on Jomiloju's face was transplanted onto hers. If only they could trade places.

Then she reminded herself wishes were useless. Ensuring women and children thrived was her true calling. It was why they were out in the forest, chanting to plants for permission before plucking leaves, seeds, and fruits for medication.

She tugged at her medicine bag. She'd picked the herbs needed to prepare a concoction to ensure Wonu of the Ojise clan gave birth easily. All that remained were the leaves of the orange-milk tree to prepare a remedy to stop bleeding. Returning at dawn was a possibility, but she liked to be prepared. Wonu was due to enter labour any day from now, and Ewa had been with her earlier in the day.

"Before long," Jomiloju declared. "Before long, you'll be carrying your own child."

In the ensuing silence, the sounds of the forest erupted as birds called to their mates. Ewa swallowed her discomfort and didn't solidify Jomiloju's prayer with an affirmation. Instead, she turned to the trees. Behind her, Jomiloju gasped.

"Forgive me, sister." She rushed to Ewa's side, fidgeting with the edge her wrap and with Jide still placed over her shoulder. "I didn't mean to…"

"There's no need to apologise." She swallowed to keep her voice from shaking. "Our elders say that the visitor doesn't take the host along as she leaves. Each person faces her destiny alone."

Jomiloju protested with hurried words as she sought to make amends.

"I have truly upset you now. Your destiny is bright. You're beautiful and talented. You are so kind, and you love so deeply."

Ewa's smile failed to reach her eyes. She quickly drew Jomiloju into a hug. "I'm not upset, aburo, but we must be home before night falls."

"Right." Jomiloju nodded. "The ámùsè nla tree."

"We will have to resume searching for it tomorrow."

Ewa helped Jomiloju secure Jide on her back. Jomiloju then shrugged her own cloth bag filled with herbs over her right shoulder as they began the trek to Kuta town.

There were more plants than humans in the region known as Kuta. Clans lived cheek to cheek in forest clearings, and houses were connected by narrow paths. The forest that shielded villains also protected Kuta and its warriors, in this stronghold forged by mercenaries over a hundred years ago. It boasted ferocious clans of which theirs counted. Kuta stood strong while nearby towns and villages fell to the war. It was a home to men of valour who fiercely defended their homestead.

It was also home to one of the greatest warriors the region had seen yet.

Presently, Ewa led the way home. With a stick in one hand, she pushed aside the detritus, making sure to sidestep the fiery red ants marching in formation to a location known only to them. She let herself wonder how simple life would have been for her if she were an ant. She would only concern herself with eating and surviving, until a careless human squashed the life out of her. She forced out an exhale. She'd told Jomiloju she wasn't upset, yet her heart was heavy with longing.

War had knocked her life over like a potful of water tumbling off a maiden's head. The period of insecurity had stolen her choice to dream and to want. When she'd been Jomilo-ju's age, it had been enough to breathe in another morning, but now she was older, Ewa badly wanted what her sister by marriage had. It was an ulcer in her side.

At nights on her way to the hut she shared with Ogele from the bathing stalls, she encountered happy couples to her left and right. War was over, and the warriors were home to eat and play with their wives and children. That was something Ewa could never have.

The path veered to the left at a cluster of bamboo trees. Behind the tilting stalks was a darkened cove, shrubs covering a hole barely wide enough for one to squeeze through. It was unremarkable and easily missed, but Ewa paused as she always did when in this part of the forest. She glared at the path before kissing her teeth and pushing forward. Jomiloju hurried beside her.

"Sister Dunni." Jomiloju cleared her throat before continuing. "I mean no offence...but have you considered going up there?"

"Never."

Ewa swung her stick down with more force than she intended. She whispered a quiet apology to the earth and started counting her inhales. Every day, she convinced herself she'd accepted her destiny and was content with the small joys that came with it. The pleasures of ferrying other women safely as they crossed death's doors while bringing life, of getting lost in the forest and of listening to Ogele's stories. There were other things that once brought her joy like dancing. However, she had outgrown dances in the square. The last time she'd ventured out at night, the younger girls had gyrated their waists and moved their feet in new moves that had eluded her. They'd sniggered behind their hands at her observance.

"Mother, shouldn't you be at home at this time?" a saucy girl had asked.

And so Ewa stopped going. She stayed indoors dreaming of age group gatherings where she could be unfettered. Women her age were busy juggling their professions, their elders, their husbands, and their children. Ewa only had Ogele and her profession, both easily managed because Ogele was an unnameable force even in her advanced age.

She was at peace with her life. Yet, anytime she passed by this dark corner of the forest set apart from the main road, white hot anger flared under her skin. She hardly got angry.

"I think you should at least attempt to," Jomiloju said earnestly. "So many years have passed."

Jomiloju's weakness was in how she didn't know how to control her tongue. Ogele often warned, *"Your mouth is unstoppable yet you don't know nine times nine."*

"Aburo, don't force me to recall the unfortunate circumstances that brought me here."

Ewa flinched at the harshness of her words. She regretted saying them as Jomiloju sputtered an apology.

"I...I'm sorry. I truly meant no harm."

Ewa conjured up mundane memories of her training and focused on them to let go of her anger. She linked arms with Jomiloju. "When we all came to this world, it was with tears, am I wrong? Eventually, the crying stops, and we learn to laugh."

The entrance to town from this side of the forest took them over the moat with cautious steps over the swaying bridge. A tall post engraved with carvings depicting men hunting and at war marked the entrance to the compound Ewa called home in her adulthood. With several homes containing the twenty-eight women, men, and children of the clan, there was always activity. Children played, co-wives argued, hens clucked, and grains were grounded in the kitchen.

Lit torches were already burning around the compound. Everywhere smelt like dinner, and it wasn't long before her stomach grumbled in longing. Leaving Jomiloju to find her husband, she hurried to the nondescript bungalow set in a far back corner. Ogele's home was a whitewashed building with a wild garden growing to the left and behind its rectangular form.

Ogele had taught her how some plants needed to remain wild while others were content when grown by human hands. The majority of the plants in their garden were the vegetables and fruits the family consumed. Past the garden was a secret path leading into the forest Ogele frequented. Ewa had ventured on it two or three times with the older woman. A wrong turn on Ogele's hidden path, and one could plunge directly into the valley bordering Kuta on the north.

In front of the house, the small clay pots Ewa had set to brew on low-burning charcoals before heading out now stood in ash. She hung her medicine bag on one of the wooden hooks by the entrance and went to check on them.

"I'm back," she called.

Usually, Ogele sat in her favourite chair enjoying the last of the evening air at this time. As the front yard was empty, Ewa assumed the elder was inside.

When she didn't hear a reply, she ducked in to check. Ogele's chambers were built for one person, and she easily saw into the bedroom they shared from the front door. Her eyes adjusted to the interior darkness. It was empty. She shrugged. Ogele was probably out causing a scandal somewhere.

Out in the night once more, she lit a torch and set it a few paces out front. Next, she warmed up some coal and burnt wild basil on it, to ward off the mosquitoes, and spread a mat on the earth below the extended rafters of the thatched roof. Then she carried out Ogele's beloved low back chair for whenever the elder decided to show up.

Finally, she set to work under the light of the torch, sorting out her freshly picked herbal gifts. Among the three leaves she needed for Wonu's upcoming delivery, she had managed to coax a shrub to grant her malaria-curing leaves. She would dry those ones first—it was always good to have anti-malaria concoctions around.

"Good evening, egbon."

Ewa lifted her head as one of the many children that blessed their compound called out in greeting. She flashed her teeth at the young girl, one of those born after the war that had ripped her from the place she knew as home.

"Tope, *iya mi*, my love, good evening."

Tope approached carrying a tray bearing dish bowls, each covered with raffia woven spheres. She placed it on the mat before Ewa.

"We made amala and dried okra soup," Tope explained as she placed the tray down. "Baba returned from hunting. There is a lot of meat."

"Thank you, sweetness." Ewa shifted, reaching for the hidden pocket at her waist, and pulled out a string of cowries. She pushed the money into Tope's hand.

"I shouldn't," Tope said.

"You will upset me if you don't accept." She folded the shells in the girl's right hand. They went through this dance all the time. "Buy something for yourself."

"Thank you!" Tope squealed at the gift. She threw her arms around Ewa's shoulders.

"I have warned you to stop spoiling the children of our clan." Ogele's scratchy voice came from the darkness outside the warm spread of the torch.

Both girl and woman shrieked at the elder's entrance. Ogele walked slowly like a monarch, the long edge of her brilliant white wrapper hanging on her left arm. A woven silk shawl was wrapped around her waist, and she wore the same material knotted over her head in a head wrap. The fabric's dark green colour made the white of her clothes stand out more.

"Welcome back, Mother." Tope knelt down in greeting.

Ogele approached and pulled the girl up into a hug.

"You can't leave me out of this affection," Ogele teased as Tope leapt on her. "Do you love Ewa more than me?"

"I love you best, Iya Ogele," Tope said, her voice muffled in the folds of Ogele's dress.

"Ah!" Ewa shouted, gripping at her forehead with both hands. "So you lied to me when you told me I was your favourite person?"

"No way," Tope objected.

They tittered at the good-natured banter. Ogele had become Ewa's mother and entire family when she'd been transported unwittingly to Kuta. Her journey here had dripped with absolute fear, but now, she covered those dark days up with the positivity Ogele shared with her. It was the price she had to pay, but it wasn't too bad. Ogele never lacked in affection despite growing up in the midst of war-mongering brothers.

As Ogele playfully extracted herself from Tope's grip, she slipped more money to the girl before sending her off. Once Tope had disappeared, Ogele demanded, "What is for dinner? I am starving."

In the light, the contrast of the dark scarifications on Ogele's face and arms against her mahogany skin was mesmerising. Ogele carried tattoos all over her body. Ewa had admired them so much, she'd tried to get designs imprinted on her skin, as well. The pain had proven unbearable, but it was taboo to scream or walk away in the tattooist's compound. That was how her skin had captured a snake on her right side, its tongue extended in a hiss close to her belly button.

Ewa grabbed a hollowed-out calabash and fetched water collected in one of the many large pots lining the outer wall. This, they used to wash their hands. She placed the larger bowl in front of the elder and then went to get smaller cups of the spring water they drank. Before they dug in, each offered a ball of food to the earth. They ate together in silence, with Ogele seated on the chair and Ewa curled on the mat at her feet. When they were finished with their meal, Ewa cleared and rinsed the used dishes. As the night fell deeper, they withdrew into the room.

"You have done well, my dear," Ogele said.

"I pray that Wonu's delivery is smooth." Ewa slipped out of her dusty wrappers and cleaned herself with a damp cotton towel. Then she wrapped a light cloth around her waist.

Iya Ogele lay supine on the bed they shared. One lamp burning in the sconce protruding from the wall provided a dim glow, with a row of lamps waiting to be lit. Iya Ogele never slept in darkness, and her lamps burned till sunrise unfailingly.

"It will be," Iya Ogele affirmed. "Meanwhile, I suspect that girl Arinsoye of the Aperin family is with child."

Ewa frowned as she worked at putting a face to the name. She might have seen Arinsoye dancing at the night market four months ago—the girl was as slender as a pole.

"I never heard that she'd taken a husband or lover," Ewa said.

"You'll see," Iya Ogele replied, smugly. "You should see. I've taught you all I know."

Ewa relied on reading the pulse to confirm pregnancies. Ogele eyed her keenly as she began touching fire to the unlit lamps. With each passing moment, the room grew brighter and warmer.

"Something troubles you," Ogele remarked.

Ewa sighed. She remained silent until she was done then went to lay on the bed. Ogele waited patiently, and now they were face to face, she prepared her reply. Lying to the elder was futile, especially when Ogele locked eyes with her like this. Saying the words out loud was easier than denying it.

"Jomiloju prayed for me while we were gathering," she began. "She prayed that blessings of childbirth would find me. She wants me to seek that man out."

"And?" Ogele prodded.

"And I couldn't affirm her prayer, but I long to carry my own child."

Ewa shut her eyes against a quivering breath.

"You will have them." Ogele sounded like Jomiloju. She placed a wrinkled hand on Ewa's stomach, and Ewa covered the elder's hand with both of hers.

"How?"

"You forget you are a married woman," Ogele began. At Ewa's groan, she warned, "Listen to me."

Ewa prepared to turn her mind away from Ogele's words. Too polite to object or challenge an elder, she was skilled at not listening while pretending to. She was once extremely stubborn.

"Your husband pines for you," Ogele said. "And you, him."

"Did you go up to see him?" she asked accusingly. It would be a betrayal of her trust.

"I'm much too old to brave it," Ogele replied. "But I raised him, and I know him."

A mother was always quick to overlook her child's errors. Not Ewa. She would never reveal her true feelings about the man Ogele had raised to the elder's face. Ewa had witnessed the kind of destruction the region's bravest warrior left in his wake. Such a violent man was no husband of hers, no matter what the elders said.

"You aren't listening," Ogele said.

"I was."

"Alright, what did I say?" At her sigh, Ogele continued. "You see. Do you recall those days when you attempted to run away from this compound? You never did, even after I gave you the directions. Why?"

Because I had nowhere else to go. Because time showed me that my father, his wife, and my sister left me to face war on my own.

The answer came readily, but she refused to voice it. Ogele was primed to lecture her about destiny, that she was in Kuta because she was meant to be, and she wasn't in the mood for this.

She let go of Ogele's hands and turned her back to the older woman.

"I am so tired, Iya," she said, shutting her eyes. "May we sleep to wake up."

"Ase," Ogele replied, softly.

Chapter Two

The tall grass of this part of the forest provided the perfect shield from ghosts.

Lying flat on his back, Makinde was grounded by the earth. The greenery around and the stark blue sky above gifted him a measure of peace. Every once in a while, a breeze came rustling through with the reminder that life continued around him. The stark cry of birds along with the occasional scratch of furred feet against wood let him know he was alive.

A long time ago, his capacity to handle stillness had been a boon. 'Makinde that sits like a rock,' the praise singers trilled. And though there were parts of himself he wished didn't exist, this one was a blessing.

From staring up at the sky, he observed each inhale and exhale. He felt each breath travel through his nose, bringing coolness to his insides. His heart beat powerfully in his chest, and his body was heavy, gravity pulling him down to the earth that will be his final resting place. In a state of calm, he closed his eyes and felt the world around him, the flowing waters of the nearby stream lulling him into a meditative state. Every sound, every sensation, even the lingering taste of the berries he'd eaten for breakfast was appreciated.

This was routine. Every day, he laid for hours. The ground remembered him, a Makinde-sized indention where he chose to enter this state. At times, ants marched over his legs, taking him for part of the forest. Deer grazed in the clearing unaware of his presence. Monkeys swung down from trees to poke at him and confirm if he was alive or not. Of the few things he required in life, there was one he longed for the most: for the ground to open up and swallow him whole like the deities of old.

But he was no hero and certainly not a god. His sins were destined to follow him even closer than his shadow.

A low keening sounded in the far distance, drawing closer. Men and women pleading for mercy, a harsh reminder of the days he wanted to pretend never existed.

His eyes snapped open. He sat up slowly, unperturbed at the ghostly cries as he was prepared to walk to land of the dead, already living one foot in it. The ghosts of his past were never kept in check by the sun. They tortured him more fervently at night in the simple hovel he'd constructed upstream but never here. The ever-blooming tree with violet flowers marked this clearing as a haven. His mother, Ogele, had told him as much when she'd found him in the middle of the forest, a grown man caked in dirt and nearly out of his mind.

"If you don't want to return home, find the tree with the blue flowers and seek peace underneath it."

That had been a lifetime ago. Yet, when he thought time had dulled his demons, they breached his sanctuary. Makinde scoffed. He brushed soft bruised petals off the top of his thighs as he rose. He stretched and rolled his shoulders, bending and twisting to beat his arms and thighs awake.

A twig broke in the underfoot, alerting him. He shifted. Someone was approaching. Perhaps a wild animal. Makinde of the past would have quietly nocked an arrow to send flying in the westerly direction. It would surely hit its mark for his arrow never missed.

His hand betrayed him by reaching to his left side, a habit grown from where his nook of arrows hung. Feeling nothing but grass, he brought himself to the present, tightening his hands until the dry skin around his knuckles cracked, and waited.

The teasing breeze carried a scent of flowers to his nostrils. A woman. Fate wasn't going to give him an easy way out—he should have known this by now. He heard her gasp as she entered the clearing.

"This place is more beautiful than they say." Her voice sounded melodious.

He saw his sanctuary through her eyes. A rough patch of forest he'd made his own without disturbing what he'd found here. The voluminous tree shedding bright blue flowers sat here, and farther down, the tributary stream leading to the grand river which sustained the village meandered. The sun cast a soft haze over the space which made it seem ethereal.

Looking over his left shoulder, he regarded the young woman. She was attired as though she had an appointment with her lover for a dalliance at dusk. Her well-coifed hair shone with the announcement it was newly made. His gaze scanned down her form. She'd gathered an indigo cloth wrapped around her waist so her breasts were exposed in a manner any hotblooded man would find enchanting. Lines of beaded jewellery adorned her hair, neck, wrists, and ankles.

When she saw she had his attention, she flashed white teeth.

"I greet you, warrior." She made a show of a curtsy, bending her knees till they grazed the grass.

Makinde grunted and turned back to the stream, his moment of calm destroyed. He heard the woman approach, calling out the same greeting and praising him as a warrior. A dark cloud hovered over him, causing him to grimace. For ten years, he'd stayed in solitude and tranquillity, but recently, girls like this one had started vying for his attention, coming here. What was going on in the outside world to encourage this behaviour? Not so long ago, everyone except the very brave—or very foolish—gave him a wide berth.

"Oyinkan greets the great warrior," the girl said in her singsong voice.

Makinde shook his head. "The wars ended years ago, young lady."

His own voice was like gravel, as unused as it was. The deep sound elicited another gasp from Oyinkan.

Makinde had used the term to dissuade her from her clear intentions. Oyinkan looked like she belonged in the same age group as the younger women in his clan compound he regarded as sisters. Not that he'd seen them of late. He'd come to this hill deep in the forest for seclusion, and this needed to be respected.

Planting both hands on the ground, he hefted himself up to his full height. He stretched once more then adjusted the fraying cloth tied around his waist. He felt Oyinkan's eyes tracing his body, and when he turned to confront her, she hungrily drank in his physique.

He made to leave for his hut but stopped cold at the thought of his woman following him there. No one had yet breached that space. He'd been accosted here, by the stream, and on the footpath, but not that ghost-ridden place. It was better to dissuade her here.

"I may be young, but I am a woman of many talents." Oyinkan squared her shoulders so her bare breasts thrust forward. "Our bodies aren't made of stone, especially for a warrior like you."

"Leave," he grunted. He stalked towards her, hoping his height and girth would intimidate her enough.

Oyinkan misread his signal as an invitation and approached. To Makinde, it was like watching a hare approach a python. She stroked his left arm and leaned against him. He felt her softness, and her fragrance rushed to his head. A weaker man would have succumbed, but he had no desire for this.

"Aren't you tired of living like so?" She ran her hands up to his shoulders. "Without a woman's care..."

"Forbidden."

She blinked long lashes up at him, confusion evident on her face. Using his chin, he pointed to where her hands brushed the amulet he kept around his right bicep. He'd once torn and burned all his protection charms, but Ogele had found him and tied the one on his arm herself. *Don't drive yourself mad*, she'd said, *when you know where you can find healing*. The string of white and green beads held steadfast to his upper arm while a leather pouch hung at his neck. It was only respect for the woman who had raised him that kept them there.

"It is forbidden for anyone to touch this," he said.

At the same moment, a low growl emanated from the clearing's border. Makinde's shoulders eased as Oyinkan's air shifted from seduction to fear. She stared wide-eyed at the shadow disturbing the grass.

He recognised her fear and immediately felt sorry for it. She was in a strange place with a strange man, and now, an unseen animal moved in the bushes. He could tell her the animal was only Wuu making his entrance, perturbed by the unfamiliar presence. She had no way of knowing Wuu was a pesky creature which liked to have his belly scratched and his head rubbed.

"What are the consequences?" Oyinkan swallowed, eyes shifting left to right nervously.

"Death."

A strong wind ruffled the leaves, adding a punch to his words. Oyinkan shouted. When she'd planned her erotic scheme, this conclusion had probably not occurred to her. Her yelling made Wuu start barking with abandon, which amplified her distress. Makinde observed it all, eyes gloomy as she fled in the direction she'd come from. Wuu started chasing after her, but he called his companion back with a resounding whistle and patted his head. The dog closed his eyes and rubbed against his hand.

"If you did your job, she wouldn't have reached me," he accused, scratching behind his companion's ears.

Wuu was unapologetic. His dirty paws and coat suggested he'd been frolicking in the forested valley forming part of their home.

"Let's go." He whistled as he stood tall, and together, they made their way through the bush to his ramshackle shed.

ONIGBAOJE waited for them in front of the lean-to—one room fashioned with dry bamboo from the forest. Hastily hacked palm fronds formed a roof that blew away with the slightest rain. The floor wasn't packed mud as it would have been in any real home but comprised of dead leaves, like the rest of the woods.

Makinde slept on a bed of leaves with only Wuu to keep him warm. Sometimes, he started fires in stone circles to keep the dead away. He had no furniture or any such pretences at civilisation, so when Onigbaoje visited, he usually carried his own stool to sit on.

The older man watched his approach, his dark face jovial under the cap he wore to hide his missing ear.

His old friend grinned after they'd exchanged greetings. "I saw Aperin's daughter shouting and scrambling through the woods."

"Appeal to these women. Make them stop." Makinde leaned against a nearby tree and crossed his arms over his chest.

Onigbaoje chuckled. "Does Kuta's favourite warrior not see the need for balance? We pay homage to male as well as to female."

"I'm balanced enough." He gestured at the trees around them. There were fewer forces with as much feminine energy as the earth herself.

"Indeed." Onigbaoje harrumphed. "I know even a wild boar eats better than you. I brought dinner."

He gestured to a small basket he'd set on the ground containing wrapped leaves and shapely gourds. Makinde ignored the spread while Wuu sniffed around them. Onigbaoje shooed the dog away, but Wuu was persistent. A hunter in his youth, Onigbaoje had been conscripted to fight in a few wars himself. He'd grown to be a respected military strategist and was still demanded by rulers across the region.

Onigbaoje had no qualms playing opposite sides for a fee. No one in Kuta did, as the saying went: *All of Kuta's warriors receive their worth in precious things*. They were rented and offered their skills to kings and individuals alike. Their brutality saw them rewarded with slaves, gold and jewels, honed weapons, praise songs...all hollow compared to the price of life.

Makinde feigned disinterest, but Onigbaoje peeled back layers of the wide leaves releasing steam from the freshly prepared meal. He and Ogele were the only two who refused to let him be. They tethered him to Kuta and the wider world ignoring his desires to be alone. Yet, he couldn't deny them, the hierarchical respect embedded in him from the time he'd emerged in this world refusing to be shaken off. The aroma of grilled meats wafted toward his nostrils, and his stomach grumbled. For one who survived on fruits and roasted tubers, this was a luxury.

Onigbaoje chuckled. "If it wasn't for me, you would be skinnier than you already are."

"You have my thanks." He shrugged and sat cross-legged, waiting for Onigbaoje to unwrap the parcel he'd brought. "What news?"

"You know me well, my friend. The Oba of Jaku has passed away."

"I am aware." At Onigbaoje's frown, he added, "I overheard talk of it during my last...assignment."

About five days had passed since he'd ventured into nearby Ibere under the cover of night. In the compound one of Onigbaoje's men had scouted earlier, Makinde had allowed himself to be lulled by the flow of conversation in the waiting room of a nondescript hut. The men had discussed politics for hours unaware there was someone eavesdropping outside. He'd waited till the men got up to leave before finding the one who was his target.

"Indeed." Onigbaoje nodded, understanding. "Jaku's ruler passed on and was buried according to custom. Now his sons squabble for the throne."

Makinde's stomach sank. His skin prickled with sweat as anticipation started to beat within him.

"What does this foretell?"

"Nothing as of yet." Having unwrapped the parcels of food, Onigbaoje plucked a succulent bit of meat and threw it on the ground. Wuu went for it immediately. "We watch and see if peace reigns or if war is called for. Dig in."

Makinde didn't wait to be asked twice. The fowl was well-seasoned and delicious. There was goat, too, stewed in spices and cubes of grilled yam. The guineacorn beer Onigbaoje offered was a fresh relief from the palm wine Makinde often drank straight from the tree.

"What does this mean for me?" he asked. "His wife was from Jaku."

"I, for one, pray that peace continues," Onigbaoje replied. He didn't bother to ask who Makinde had been referring to.

"That doesn't answer my question."

"When will you stop chasing Arole? He is long dead."

"He's not," he said. "Aro...that man is out there."

The tasty meat became sand in his mouth. He broke a bone with his teeth and offered it to Wuu.

"Everyone except you is tired of war," Onigbaoje said.

For decades, few settlements in the region remained permanent due to intermittent conflict. Elders referred to the time as the era of moving villages. At the first sign of war, people packed what they could and vacated to settle elsewhere, relocating as necessary to ensure their survival. Kuta was luckier solely because it was a source of war in and of itself. Established by warriors, protected by their warrior sons, and populated with those they'd subdued. Makinde shuddered to think of it.

"For how long do you intend to live like this?" Onigbaoje asked. "Ogele is too old to continue climbing up here. Your family misses you. You leave a wife to suffer as if she is a widow."

"A wife I didn't ask for," he shot back.

"The little adventures you engage in aren't enough to appease your guilt. For years now, people from as far away as Esie speak of Ojiji, the spirit-man that moves in the night dealing justice to robbers and abusive husbands alike. If you want to make amends, you must let go of this desire for revenge. Allow the disciples of Oosa to cleanse you from within."

Makinde scratched behind his ear. He'd heard a version of the same advice from Ogele for years. "I must remain here."

The silent implication being he would remain in the forest forever. In his youthful ignorance, he'd believed he was doing the right thing as a warrior. He'd eagerly imbibed the regurgitated admonitions during training, forgetting who he was, who his mother was. Had he been more insightful, he would have seen he and his people were not champions. Realising it after the Odan-Eripa war, after the horrors Arole and his brothers in arms committed, didn't make the burden any easier for him to carry.

"You won't stop seeing the ghosts of the past if you don't return to the community," Onigbaoje said. "What you're doing is torturing yourself."

"I am at peace here," he insisted.

"Are you?"

He pushed aside the beer, having lost his appetite. Surviving on roots and fruits made him less likely to feast like he once did. He rinsed his hands with water from the nearby pond he'd created one year, digging a path from the stream so water could collect closer to his place of abode. The only downside were the mosquitos that came with standing water, but he didn't mind. The insects were company, too.

"You know Oyinkan's family?"

Too late, he winced at using the girl's personal name—Onigbaoje would think he was interested in her. And sure enough, the older man leapt.

"I do. If you wish, I could speak to her father..." he began.

Makinde shook his head. "Find something to cure Aperin's daughter. She touched my taboo and might die of mysterious circumstances."

Onigbaoje chuckled. "Not that ruse! An imaginary ailment needs no cure."

"You know what to do." He allowed a begrudging tilt of his lips to grace his face. Yet, his eyes didn't align with the forced smile. Nothing ever did anymore.

Chapter Three

E wa watched keenly as Wonu tasted the medicine. The expectant mother's face scrunched up.

"I'm sorry," she said sympathetically. The brew was bitter, yet she held the cup up to Wonu's mouth with a firm, steady hand. Sighing, Wonu opened her lips again and downed the medicine. Ewa rubbed Wonu's chest just above her breasts. "Wonu, please keep it down. You will be all right."

The woman nodded weakly and allowed Ewa to lay her back on the earthen bed. Wonu shuddered with cold even though the room was kept warm by a brazier burning with coals. For most of her pregnancy, she had reported feeling fatigue and general weakness. Everyone agreed a woman needed energy to bring forth life.

Ewa silently prayed Wonu's body would accept the healing properties of the medicine she'd just consumed. From the corner of the hut, one of Wonu's many mothers watched her administrations with rapt attention. The older woman was mother-in-law to Wonu, not that such distinctions mattered in an environment where any elder assumed the role of a parent. Wonu's mothers argued she didn't require any special care—after all, they'd stepped through the maws of childbirth many times and were skilled enough to take care of their own.

Wonu insisted Ewa provide her care, to their chagrin. Out of her stubbornness, a shaky truce was reached where Ewa checked in with her every four days and provided healing brews and balms while her in-laws observed everything. One of Wonu's sisters by marriage massaged her until she drifted to sleep, rubbing shea butter Ewa had mixed herself on her rounded shoulders.

Ewa turned towards the older woman.

"Mother, has she been taking the brews I made?"

"Of course," the mother grunted. "She's not the first person to be pregnant in this homestead."

Rather than grit her teeth at the harshness of this woman's words, Ewa gave a small smile. "What I've given her will aid with that. She just needs to drink it twice a day."

"This girl should be up and walking."

"Please ensure she takes the doses," she insisted, keeping her tone neutral. "It is crucial for her strength."

She imagined that during Wonu's pivotal hour, this woman would be the one she leaned on as tradition dictated. Kneeling on the earthen floor, Wonu would have her back pressed to her mother-in-law's front as life tore out of her. Ewa expected the woman to be kinder.

Packing her bag, she murmured her goodbyes and exited the room, squinting as she stepped out into the dazzling sunshine. As she waited for her eyes to adjust to the abrupt change from the dim interior, she fanned a hand towards her bare neck.

Over the grinding of grain and the pounding of a mortar as a meal was being prepared, she heard the chatter of women. Children complained as they dragged their feet to clean the outhouse while goats bleated and chickens clucked without a care. All compounds carried the same sounds of life.

As she started towards the footpath home, she spotted two men hunched close together in discussion. She recognised Fadahunsi instantly. It wasn't just his tall physique or the brilliant white of his tunic and trousers—it was the way her stomach flipped at the sight of him. Fadahunsi's wide smile and glossy dark skin were enough to make any woman swoon. Too bad he couldn't be for her.

Ewa pivoted. She shrugged tension off her shoulders and strode purposely towards the men.

"Good day," she greeted them both, though her eyes were on Fadahunsi.

The Ifa priest broke into his signature grin, revealing the attractive gap between his front teeth. She tried not to stare.

"Good day, our medicine woman," Fadahunsi's companion greeted. He was among the male elders of this compound—she assumed he was grandfather to Wonu's husband. Despite his age, he bowed his head at her in reverence and respect for her skill. "Fadahunsi here is telling me how much of my property I will need to sell to finance this naming."

Fadahunsi laughed, a deep chuckle that warmed her face. "We require but a few things."

"Indeed." The elder shook his head. "We will discuss further."

"Surely, it isn't my arrival that has put an end to your conversation?" Ewa asked, looking at Fadahunsi from under her lashes. Her brain told her to behave and focus on being respectable, but it was hard to in the presence of such a fine man.

"Never," Fadahunsi protested, both arms raised to signal peace.

"I wouldn't dare. We really had just concluded," the grandfather said. "Besides, I have been asked to report to the Oba's palace."

Ewa stood beside Fadahunsi as the elder retired to his suite to prepare for his summons. Alone with the priest, the space between them thrummed. Energy prickled at her skin. This kind of feeling had been alien to her until she set eyes on this man a year ago. Fadahunsi, like any Ifa acolyte of note, travelled from one town to the other learning verses, songs, and rituals of worship.

Ewa had swooned the first day she'd seen him at the temple. For the first time, her heart and body had yearned for another. Presently, she glanced up at Fadahunsi. He kept his eyes straight ahead, lost in thought. A niggling voice in her head reminded her she was a married woman. Estranged from her family, she lived at the mercy of her disappearing husband's people. It was safer to assume all eyes were on her, especially in a town as heavily masculine as Kuta. Despite her reservations towards her husband, his family loved him fiercely. It didn't occur to them that their son had abandoned the entire clan, too, and not just her.

"Let's walk," Fadahunsi said suddenly, angling his head towards the exit of the group of homes.

The footpath bordered by green shrubs and shaded trees on both sides snaked through the town. Years ago, the path they now walked would have been bush reserved for wild animals and crafty spirits. Ewa's homestead was far from Wonu's, and the compound where the priests lived and worshipped was even farther.

Her face warmed at the thought of walking leisurely beside this fine man. In another world, she would take his arm and pull him into the bushes where nature would shield them as their kisses created a sweet atmosphere.

"Ewadunni, have you lost your ears?"

The priest's voice drew her from her reverie.

Her face grew hot. She was acting like a girl who had just dipped her toes into womanhood. Such behaviour was unlike a woman who had spent close to three decades on this earth surviving war and loneliness.

"My ears are with me," she said.

"Then you would agree with what I just said?"

"I...yes...I suppose..." she began, then caught the twinkle in Fadahunsi's eyes, and they both burst out laughing. "Don't tease me."

"I was inquiring if you'll be at the next worship day. It's two days away."

"It's been seventeen days already?"

She counted the days with her fingers. Worship days circled every four days, but the seventeenth day of prayers called for some celebration. On those days, priests and priestesses of various deities gathered to worship at the temple that housed Fadahunsi where divination was made for the community.

"Of course, I'll be there," she said. A smile passed between the two. "Did you say anything else?"

"Maybe." He gave a casual shrug.

She pouted. "Don't keep me in the dark."

"There's a matter I need to confirm first. I'll know for certain in two days' time."

At that moment, a group of young women carrying pots of water approached. They stopped to greet Ewa and Fadahunsi. Ewa rubbed her fingers, eager to be alone with Fadahunsi so she could query him further.

"What would you know for certain?" she asked once they'd resumed their walk.

"Pardon?" he asked, but before she could elaborate, he continued. "You mean what I have to tell you? Let me ask you first, what occupied your mind so intensely that you missed my words earlier?"

Ewa's eyes widened. She could tell Fadahunsi everything but not that. They were good friends, and he'd become the person she went to when she needed spiritual work or advice. She blinked, quickly thinking.

"My mind..." she started. Her gaze flitted from the red earth to the clear blue sky. "My mind was...with my family."

Family.

She inhaled deeply. Which dark calabash had she pulled this falsehood from?

"Then that means our minds are in sync," Fadahunsi said.

Forgetting her embarrassment, she turned her wide-eyed gaze up at him. "I'm afraid I don't understand."

In truth, the only family she had was Ogele. It was Ogele she loved and cared for, and it had been so for years now.

"All will be revealed in due time," Fadahunsi said, giving her a small nod. "Patience, Ewadunni. Tell me, how is Wonu doing?"

Grateful for the change in topics, she replied, "She is well. Actually, I'd like you to speak with her mother-in-law..."

AS the rising thatch-roofed buildings of her homestead came into view, Ewa straightened her back and kept her eyes on the earth. Stealing soft glances at Fadahunsi among her husband's people was out of the question.

Fadahunsi could have left her at the post, but he walked with her to Ogele's front door. Everyone they encountered greeted the priest enthusiastically. The man was an asset to Kuta as a whole. Ewa was familiar with the virtues of good character and knew comparison wasn't beneficial. Every being on this earth came with their own destinies.

Yet, she couldn't help but imagine how different the reactions would have been were she walking home with Makinde. Warriors pranced about with a pomp that demanded respect, but underneath this respect was fear. Even worse, some of the men in Kuta seemed to enjoy the trepidation they inspired in others. Not Fadahunsi who smiled and extended warmth to all.

When they saw Ogele standing in front of their home, Fadahunsi called out a greeting.

"Iya Ogele," he said, falling flat on the floor in a gesture of utmost respect.

"Awo," Ogele replied, making reference to his profession. "You've brought my daughter home."

"I'm sure we find you well, Iya," Fadahunsi said.

"I'm surprised you're home at this time." After hanging her medicine bag, Ewa hugged Ogele tightly.

"Just because I have made a small heap on the farm doesn't mean I should say I'm done working," Ogele replied. "There's still so much for me to do."

Ogele was always busy with one thing or the other. If she wasn't going away to the forest on her meditative walks, she was encountering new lovers. All these adventures were fed to Ewa through stories Ogele herself told in her masterful way.

Ewa remained in the older woman's embrace and placed her head on her plump shoulder. Ogele held on to her with one hand, her carved cane propping them up on the other.

"This is what you asked for, Iya," Fadahunsi said. He brought out a leaf-wrapped package from his pocket.

"Take that for me, Ewa."

Ewa's smile twitched as Fadahunsi handed the package to her. Their fingers brushed, but it failed to elicit a thrill in her as doubt ran through her mind. *Did Fadahunsi walk with me to fulfil his errand for Iya Ogele?*

Biting the inside corner of her lips, she tried and failed to dismiss the thought. She'd been under the impression Fadahunsi wanted to spend time with her but...her fingers gripped the smooth edges of Ogele's gift. Whatever was inside felt pliable. She glanced down and noticed Ogele was wearing sandals on her feet. Beside them, a small basket sat on the ground waiting to be picked up.

"Are you travelling?" she blurted.

"Of course, my darling," Ogele replied as though they'd discussed this earlier. "I will see you when I'm back, Awo."

Fadahunsi flashed his smile at Ogele and then at Ewa. "We will meet on the seventeenth day."

She nodded absentmindedly. Ogele was no stranger to journeying. One day years ago, she'd woken up in the early hours of dawn and walked into the forest. One tree spoke to her and then another, telling her how she could use their parts for healing in exchange for her gifts of song and touch. When Ogele returned home, twenty-one years had passed, and her family had already assumed the worst. Within her was the skill of healing and many stories of foreign lands and the people inhabiting them.

However, those days of wandering were in her youth. Ewa struggled to picture the old woman pushing her way to adventure and love in the forest with her walking cane. She waited until Fadahunsi had walked away and turned to face Ogele.

"I have already made up my mind," Ogele said, pre-empting her words. She gently snatched Fadahunsi's package from Ewa's hands. "See, I even had an amulet prepared."

The words of concern that had formed on her lips died. "Then I must come with you."

Ogele shook her head. "This is a journey I must take alone."

"You can't seriously march into the forest on your own. To sleep on the bare earth, to eat dried meat, and to drink stale water…"

"Hush, child." Ogele laughed and patted her on the cheek. "There is a place I need to go."

A chill ran down her back. "What do you mean?"

"You know what I mean," Ogele replied, her light-hearted tone putting her at ease. "I have hidden very few things from you. Help me with that basket."

Ewa bent to scoop up the container. "You see, you need help with even this. Where could you be travelling to?"

"To a nearby village," Ogele said, then gave an exaggerated groan. "We have a meeting, my peers and me."

Mention of Ogele's age group made Ewa breathe easier. Ogele's position as an elder not just in the household but in Kuta at large gave her access to secret groups she knew nothing of. There were limits to what an outsider could learn, but she had seen groups aid their members financially, plan festivities, and come to the rescue when needed.

One such mysterious society sent petitions to husbands and fathers who were overly abusive and violent. Women said the entity known as Ojiji was tied to this society and dealt with such men on their behalf. Once, Ewa had seen the result herself, a screaming man bound to a tree. He'd been naked and covered in a sticky substance to attract the insects biting him. The entire village had laughed at him even as he was cut down. Ewa later heard it took a month for his swellings to reduce, and the man was forever marked by whatever had been put on him. She suspected Ogele was among such a sorority.

"Alright, Iya," she said finally.

"Am I free to leave now?" Ogele asked with a smirk.

"I wish you safe travels to and fro."

"And I will meet you in joy when I return."

Ogele extended her arms for Ewa to walk into. She held the old woman tight and took her hand as they headed for her secret path.

"I will prepare a feast for you when you come back."

"Oh," Ogele replied, distracted. "You can't even cook."

Believing Ogele's mind was already on her journey, Ewa stepped back. She stood still as Ogele pushed onward. The bush swallowed the older woman's movements, leaving her alone with a sour taste in her mouth.

MAKINDE found the hidden path easily. If he'd thought the years had dulled his memory, they hadn't. In a land comprised of interconnecting roads that more or less looked the same, Ogele's footpath proved easy for him to locate. There, where the path led to the deeper forest, was the sweet berry shrub eaten with bitter foods to lend its sweet taste to the mouth. When he saw the small tree bearing yellow plum fruits with their pale-coloured flowers, he knew he was almost home.

Home.

The idea hit him like a hammer on a finger. He paused. His panting breath brought the realisation he'd been running. Hours ago, he'd sought solace in one of the caves that marked the forest as his haven had become a stage for seductions. He'd lain on the cool sand covering the cave floor and stared up at the dark stone above him.

There'd been a moment of peace before they'd come. Scratching along the stone walls and dragging severed limbs across the ground, spectres had approached him to demand their due. The first time he'd seen them, his instinct had been to cut them down. When slicing them with his sword and axe didn't work, terror had set in. Now, his sins were familiar. He welcomed them, even as his mind objected to the torture, to the anguish on their grey faces. He would join them soon, he was sure. He just needed to find Arole. Once he fixed this, they could have him.

As his past had crowded him in the dank cave, he'd glimpsed a blurry face standing apart from the rest. It'd been her, the one tied to him and Arole. She always stood back, dark holes in place of eyes fixed on him. But he'd blinked and seen Ogele's face. The face of the woman he called mother, her large white eyes lined with kohl, her hair braided up in an elaborate style, and her lips turned down in a grimace.

He'd jerked up, dispersing the ghostly beings to smoke. His heart had quaked in his chest. Ogele shouldn't be here. This urgency had carried him to the path. He'd needed to ascertain for himself she was among the living, and there she was. Her dark skin gleamed in the afternoon sun. The silver bangles she wore on her hands clanked musically as she clasped a young woman close.

He'd come here for his mother, but his attention homed in on the woman. The sensation of hairs raising on his nape startled him. She was dressed in a long indigo fabric wrapped over her chest and reaching to her knees, far modestly than the women appearing before him in recent months. The same colour fabric covered her hair.

Her robes shielded her petite frame, but the sight of the smooth curve of her neck melding into her shoulders and her fleshy legs caused his tongue to dart out to touch his chapped lips. Awareness he'd assumed long dead blossomed to life unheeded. He shifted back when the young woman turned her wide gaze towards the forested path, worrying her lips as Ogele approached.

His mouth fell open. Those bold enchantresses must have succeeded at something. He refused to consider if Onigbaoje's words were right, that balance was essential at the end of the day.

"Did you finally come to gawk at her?"

Ogele had moved swiftly up the path and past him, catching him unawares. Her deep voice sounded close to his ear. That he didn't jump, startled, or stutter guiltily was due to his past training.

"Mother." He prepared to stretch out on the earth, but she grasped his arm with a spry strength belying her age, stopping him short.

She reached up, and memory pulled his head down so she could bury her hand into his tight coils. "I remember when you were as tall as me."

She resumed walking, and he fell in step beside her. He missed the comfort of her touch but quickly stifled it like a fowl offered for sacrifice. He was past such comforts.

One foot in the land of the dead, he reminded himself.

"You look frightening. Like a monster of some sort. You need to shave that beard and trim your hair. When last did you bathe?"

He scratched the back of his head. "Are you travelling somewhere?"

"Your wife asked the same thing," she said, rolling her eyes to the forest canopy. "But I suppose I can be frank with you. First answer this—what brought you here?"

Makinde's mouth grew dry. He struggled to find the words to explain what he'd seen. The whole of Kuta knew warriors were often tormented by past battles. Priests and priestesses held secret rituals to ease those burdens under the auspices of the deities. He shunned those rituals because he saw no need in healing or redemption. He needed to pay his dues on his own terms.

Yet, in the presence of the woman who'd raised him, who now appeared so tiny and fragile, he didn't know what to say. How could he tell her he'd seen her among ghosts? She had never been in a battlefield, for all he knew—she was a woman of many stories and might prove him wrong. He had been a snotty-nosed child when she had marched into the homestead back from the dead, according to whispers among the older ones. The woman never played by anyone's rules, and now as an adult, he appreciated how much of a challenge it must have been for her.

"You won't tell me?" she asked when he didn't respond.

He inhaled deeply.

"I saw you in the cave," he said, rubbing his stomach which now felt like lead.

"And you were scared?"

"I was."

"Makinde, son of the brave man, firm like a mountain." Ogele recited his praise name. "What do you have to be afraid of? You know the dead always remain with us."

"You're confirming..."

He stopped walking. She drew to a pause a few paces ahead, then spun and looked straight into his eyes.

"The earth is a marketplace," she said. "And I have entertained therein for a very long time. I will soon be returning home."

Tears sprung behind his eyes. He blinked rapidly but couldn't take his eyes off her.

"Do you recall when I told you about the woman with the rings around her neck?" Ogele said. "The woman by the creek?"

He nodded. The trees had beckoned her, and she had answered their call. She'd lost track of time as she communed with the forest until one day, she'd emerged at the creek where a woman had been waiting for her. Ogele took his hand in hers and coaxed him to resume their walk. Her other hand pressed the dark tip of her walking cane into the detritus.

"Be happy for me because I will be reunited with her soon," she said.

"I will also join you there." The tremor in his voice embarrassed him slightly.

Ogele tapped his calf with her cane in warning.

"Nonsense. Go and receive your cleansing. Stop allowing revenge to consume you. Ewa longs for you, and you saw how stunning she is."

Again, this dance. "It isn't revenge I long for, but justice. That life isn't mine. I didn't marry her."

They stopped at an intersection. The path split left and right, and before them, shrubs bordered the dip into the verdant valley. A bird shrieked as it sailed somewhere down below.

"Instead of dying, the earth grows bare," Ogele whispered a proverb. "Gather your wits, my son. The answer to whatever it is you seek...this isn't it."

Makinde ground his teeth and remained quiet.

"Come, my crown," Ogele said. He lowered himself so she could ruffle his head once more. The flurry of emotions erupting in him from the gesture took his breath away. "You can't follow me from here."

She pecked his forehead. The sensation of her lips on his skin remained long after she'd moved away.

"I trust you'll do the right thing."

He struggled to inhale as she walked away. He stood rooted to the spot like a tree even after her silhouette had disappeared from his line of sight.

Chapter Four

E wa sat in the temple's open foyer in the company of other devotees. The compound where the Ifa priests lived along with their families and students was more forest than homestead. Grand trees dominated the paths cutting between houses, and shrubs bearing wildflowers were abundant.

The temple was in a central location, its clearing also serving as communal space and a kitchen. Large pots of food simmered on hearths while the priests divined under the temple's awning. The message the Oracle had for the community was one of blessing.

She struggled to pay attention to the details. Her mind hadn't rested since Ogele had walked into the forest two days prior. It wasn't because she was lonely—Tope had kept her company on one night while Jomiloju and Jide had taken the other.

She suspected Ogele had lied to her. The elder kept many secrets even though she was an excellent storyteller. When Ogele spoke about her life, a stranger could be forgiven for claiming to know intimately about her. The woman was hiding something, and Ewa was desperate to find out what it was this time.

She resolved to have Fadahunsi divine for her soon. Sitting on the mat with the priest had never failed her when it came to revealing truths about the past, present, and future. Time melded in the presence of Ifa, and her faith was the steady beat of one that had yet to be failed.

After the pronouncements were read, drummers started beating their tools, creating a celebratory air. She spotted Fadahunsi weaving through the milling crowd towards her, his face beaming.

"Do you have time to talk?" he asked.

"What about?" she said, her eyebrows knitted.

"You were so eager to know what I had to say two days ago..."

"Oh." She'd been so occupied with thoughts of Ogele, she hadn't paid much concern to Fadahunsi's cryptic words. She followed him to the baobab tree tucked beside the temple. They sat on a long bench under the shade.

"What did you have to tell me?" she asked dispassionately. The sooner this conversation was over, the quicker she'd have Fadahunsi consult Ifa on her behalf.

"You once told me your family totem was Agbonrin."

His words drew her to stillness. If she wasn't sitting, she would have slid to the earth. She'd thought of Ogele and Kuta when Fadahunsi first mentioned family. But it was now clear he wasn't talking about her newfound family but the one she was born into. She heard each breath her body took loudly in her ears. Mention of the family that had abandoned her was like splashing frigid water over her head. During the chaotic period when war was visited upon Odan, everyone fled the danger and turned selfish in order to save their lives.

Fadahunsi pressed on. "Agbonrin from Odan. Those are your people, right?"

"Yes..."

She had put a lid on those memories, securing it tightly so her recollection of the time was sealed from her mind's touch. She'd done a good job, or so she believed, and with just a few words, Fadahunsi unravelled her careful reconstruction. Her chest heaved as echoes of the past stretched their spindly fingers for her. She saw the forest canopy, her second mother's sneer, the warriors with the mud-coated skin. Inhaling deeply, she screwed her eyes shut.

"I have good news," Fadahunsi was saying. Oblivious, he placed a hand on her shoulder. "A number of families have settled not too far from here. They've named the settlement Olootu."

"Olootu?" Ewa repeated.

"It is about eight-day journey from Kuta."

His hand was light on her shoulder. Ewa wondered if he could feel her trembling, not in pleasure as she'd once fancied his touch would bring, but in anguish. Her chest pounded a painful rhythm in her chest. How could he not see her distress?

"We were invited to divine on the establishment of the town, and Ifa saw blessings of wealth and prosperity."

The priest told her of his experience—the graciousness of hosts who spared nothing to ensure the priests they'd invited were well taken care of, the proposed grandness of the town. To her, it was as though the words came filtered through the fluffs of cotton she and Ogele would spin to trade once in a while.

"Imagine my surprise when I saw a woman who resembled you. Atitebi was her name. I asked and was told her mother was Lapade, married into the family of those that mustn't eat antelope flesh. She remembered you, Ewadunni. She cried when I told her you were alive."

Ewa wanted to scream, throw her head wrap to the ground, and pull her hair out. Lapade missed her? The woman who never hesitated to lash at her with her thorn-spiked tongue? Lapade had hated her even before the skirmish.

She forced herself to swallow. Ogele had taught her what to do in times like this. She shifted her toes so they dug into the dirt of the earth, a reminder she was grounded. She trailed a finger on the horizontal lines woven on her clothes, counting them until the pace of her heart calmed.

"To think I found your kin after being separated by the war," Fadahunsi said.

The priest thought he was doing her a favour by reconnecting her with her loved ones torn apart for years by violence. He didn't care to know her story before crafting his own narrative. She shot him a pitiful glance. The last embers of her infatuation were doused with water.

"They might not be my kin." She shifted, and his hand fell from her shoulder.

"But...I said Atitebi, Lapade's daughter, resembles you."

"It is possible you made a mistake."

"I understand why you may feel cautious. So many of us squash hope because we fear that our longings may be realised."

She clicked her tongue.

"I apologise," Fadahunsi said. "I didn't expect news of your family to be of such shock. If you're ready to go to Olootu, we can go together."

A scream sounded, sending a cruel tremor ran down her back. She straightened her spine.

"What is wrong, Ewadunni?" Fadahunsi asked.

"Didn't you hear a scream?" She strained her ears, but all she could pick up were the drums being played as people chattered. Was her mind playing tricks on her?

"No, I didn't."

Then his hands were on her again, this time holding both of hers as they sat side by side. Of all her fantasies with this man, this brotherly support had never featured. She wanted to pull away, but worry pierced through her being. She couldn't shake the feeling something terrible was happening.

A distant part of her remembered this reaction. In the days of constant warfare, trudging through the forest in hiding and under the pretence of some form of safety, she would feel absolute dread even when no one else remarked upon anything. Then a few hours away, their group would encounter slain bodies torn apart by enemy soldiers.

Fadahunsi gripped her hands, uttering words of calm, but really, he paid her no attention.

When she saw Tope's small form running down the path towards the temple, she leapt up. Trembling, she bounced on the balls of her feet and whipped her hands back and forth. As the distance between them shorted, she could see Tope's eyes were red, tears streaking down her face. The girl slammed into her in a fierce hug.

"Iya Ogele is dead!" she wailed, her face pressed against Ewa's midriff.

THE story reached her in bits and pieces. A group of elderly women had appeared at the homestead, bringing with them Ogele's walking stick. Their clothing and the staffs they carried denoted their ranks as important priestesses. They'd come to inform the clan that they had sent forth their mate in a private ceremony and welcomed them to commemorate Ogele's memory.

Ewa went through the motions completely numb. Was this the peer group Ogele had spoken of on the day of her departure? There was a rumour, unsaid but held strongly, whispering of elders seeing the time of their deaths ahead. Had Ogele known? If so, why had she chosen not to confide in Ewa?

She mourned as though she'd lost everything. And she had. The mother who had birthed her had passed away in her youth, and now, she was burying the one who had become a mother to her as an adult. Everywhere hurt. A dull pain hummed in every part of her body, culminating in a headache battering the back of her head.

Days blended into each other. The priestesses showed the clan to a sacred part of the forest bordered by trees wrapped in white cloth where Ogele was interred. They said she had fallen into a long-forgotten trench as she traversed the forest.

The report made no sense to Ewa. Ogele knew the forest like her own flesh—how could she have met an accident in it? She remained troubled while everyone else seemed to move from the initial shock to grief, then joy—after all, the passing of an elder was cause to celebrate a life well-lived, and Ogele had walked the earth for over six decades. Ogele was from a lineage that prided themselves on the longevity of their elders and had contributed immensely to the community not just in Kuta but elsewhere through her many journeys. She was now an ancestor worthy of being paid homage to.

Cowrie shells were tossed on the ground, revealing verses that inspired Ogele's priestess friends to chant and offerings to be made. Even with the torment squeezing Ewa's chest tight, it would have been remiss to sit while others danced for Ogele, especially for one so close to the departed elder. She had wept with everyone on that dreadful day, so she forced herself to move her feet, too.

She homed in on her loneliness even though Tope and Jomiloju stationed themselves beside her. Tope was a blessing who ensured she was well fed. Jomiloju went a step further, bathing with her. While the others slept, her eyes shifted between the rafters in the ceiling and the turned earth where they'd buried a few of Ogele's articles as tradition dictated.

When exhaustion forced her to close her eyes, she woke up with a question on her lips: *Iya Ogele has left me?* She tortured herself with thoughts of all the things Ogele would never witness, chief of which were the children she'd said

Ewa was destined to have. The usual purpose driving her to keep moving each day drained away from the soles of her feet.

Kuta returned to normal. Ogele's mates departed as mysteriously as they had arrived. Family from near and far that came to commiserate with them departed. Jomiloju went back to sleeping in her husband's chambers. Even Tope grudgingly returned to the room she shared with her siblings and mother.

The moon went through its monthly phases, then someone came with a message—Wonu was in labour. Ewa dragged herself to Wonu's side devoid of the excitement that would have coursed through her otherwise. She went through the motions aware Wonu's mothers were eyeing her this time with concern over her delicate emotional state.

After three days in labour, Wonu was safely delivered of a girl. Ewa held the screaming baby in her hands, cradling this new life twenty-one days after losing Ogele. Such was the nature of the world. The elders often said one must be willing to die in order to live.

IT WAS AFTER THE WELCOMING of Atoke, Wonu's daughter, in a ceremony announcing the child's name to the community. Ewa returned home and tripped as she entered the front room. The space was crammed with several baskets and large calabashes containing the wealth Ogele had left behind. These items had been gathered under the watchful eye of the Baale before being delivered to her.

"They are all yours now," one of the elders had said.

She couldn't bring herself to touch anything. There was a deeper sadness in her new reality. She was on her own with nothing but the items Ogele had left behind. She would trade them all to have Ogele returned.

She sat on the floor atop the magnificent fabrics falling out of the container she'd upended. She grabbed handfuls of cotton and silk. Bringing them up to her nose, she inhaled Ogele's herbal scent. Ogele always smelt of freshly plucked leaves and the fragrant flowers she mixed with coconut oil. It was at once bitter and sweet, strong and yielding.

Ewa started to cry. As her sobs grew louder, she covered her mouth with her hands and curled into a ball surrounded by Ogele's fine cloths.

She must have fallen asleep at some point. When she opened her eyes, it was night. A chilly wind blew through the cracks in the doors and windows she didn't recall shutting. A sharp scent prickled at her nostrils, and she lurched awake, startled. Despite the draft, flames danced on the row of oil lamps Ogele preferred to burn all night.

"Ewadunni."

She leapt up. This was the signal she'd been waiting for. At last, Ogele had visited her.

The elder Ogele sat on the edge of the earthen bed, hands gently folded on her lap. She had a content smile on her face. Ewa held her breath as she approached her. She didn't want to ruin this delicate moment. Kneeling before her, she reached beside the elder and ran trembling hands over the blanket folded at the edge of the bed. She gripped the thick woven cloth to prevent herself from leaping up and hugging her.

"Iya," she croaked. "Mother."

The impossibility of the situation sent her heart fluttering at the base of her throat like a butterfly trapped therein.

"Ewadunni," the woman repeated. "How are the women in your care?"

"They are fine," she lied. She hadn't visited any client since Wonu's delivery, nor had she gone out in search for roots and herbs.

"How is your husband?"

"I...I don't know." It felt wrong that the words irritated her, causing her brows to draw together so a crease formed on her forehead. She shifted this emotion aside. "How are you?"

"I am fine, but are you? You look terrible."

"I miss you."

"And I, you. Surely, you've not forgotten that I'm still here with you?"

Ewa swallowed. She'd forgotten. The assured murmurs that Ogele would come back to the earthly plane, or that she would be a highly placed ancestor, were like a finger poking into an open wound.

"Will you come with me somewhere?" she asked suddenly.

"Where to?"

"To Olootu."

It came from nowhere, this unexpected recollection of Olootu where members of the family that had unceremoniously disowned her were recreating a new life.

"What are we going to do there?"

"To start afresh," she said.

Ogele laughed, a hollow sound. "What of your husband?"

Even in death, the older woman kept mentioning the man. For this reason alone, Ewa was convinced the person she was speaking to was her Ogele and not a trickster spirit.

"I will divorce him."

Enough time had passed since their alleged wedding, and the only person to keep her in this homestead was the ghost in front of her. She had no reason to remain any longer. She allowed herself to consider the idea of reuniting with her father, her stepmother, and her sister. There might be other siblings, definitely nieces and nephews. So long had passed, surely, they wouldn't reject her twice. Fadahunsi said tears had been shed at the mention of her name. The war had ended; perhaps forgiveness was in order.

"That might not be your worst idea."

"Indeed! With your support, I can be my own woman—"

"Ensure you do things properly."

"...start my own business. What did you say, Mother?"

"In whatever you want to do, do it properly," Ogele said.

Ewa frowned. "Your words carry a deeper meaning."

"My darling Ewa, I am always with you."

When the birds chirped in the early hours of the morning, she awakened to sheets soaked in her tears and her sweat. Lying in bed, she kept her eyes closed, frantically trying to recollect her dream. It had to be a dream. So often during the war, she'd heard of people seeing loved ones who had passed away. Families would see sons and daughters who had been slaughtered miles away at the war front, not covered in blood but in their finest clothes as they came to say goodbye. But Ogele hadn't said goodbye. She struggled to recollect.

I am always with you.

She heard Ogele's voice in her ears, and her lips moved as she repeated the woman's words to herself. Her breath came easier. Death wasn't the end—how could she have forgotten? She could always communicate with Ogele as an ancestor, pouring a bit of her drink before she tasted it while calling out the woman's name and chanting her praises. Hope broke across her dour mood.

Do things properly.

Her eyes popped open with comprehension. Ogele wanted her to inform Baale and the elders of the family before leaving Kuta. Divorce was the sensible option. She wasn't going to slip away blindly at night as she'd tried to years ago. Her family had abandoned her fate to the Universe, handing her over to bloodthirsty warriors. She'd hated them for it for too long.

This loathing was now dull, overshadowed by her trepidation for the husband she'd seen a handful of times. It was probably this unbalanced blend of emotions driving her feelings now, but she accepted it. Family remained family. Her father might be in Olootu at this very moment. Was this not enough reason to go despite the murky waters between her and his wife?

The door leading to the chambers that were now hers opened tentatively. She shifted her eyes and collided with Tope's unsure gaze. She blinked, as though she were seeing Tope for the first time in a while. She wanted to gather her in a tight squeeze but slowly sat up from the bed and gave her a small smile instead.

"Good morning," Tope said.

The uncertainty in her eyes made Ewa squirm. She wondered what the girl had witnessed in her, how her grief may have irreparably changed the way Tope viewed her.

"Good morning, sweetheart," she replied, her resolve strengthening.

"We have prepared breakfast," Tope said, interlacing her fingers. "I wanted to know if you would eat."

"Of course I will."

She stood up. When she reached the spot where they stored the sticks they used to brush their teeth, she found it was empty.

"Why don't you bring some chewing sticks?"

"Y-yes!"

"And ask someone to warm bathing water for me."

"Right away!"

Ewa glanced over her right shoulder just in time to see Tope heave a sigh of relief before running out.

Chapter Five

Ewa was ready to depart the morning after that pivotal dream, but she had responsibilities. There were women and children—many of whom had been waiting for her to navigate her grief—to visit. She wasn't the only healer in town, as there were also one or two Ifa priests skilled in all types of healthcare. However, the numbers dwindled when one considered those who solely focused on the health of babies and women, and among them, Ogele had been the most renowned.

Presently, all eyes turned to her, Ogele's prodigy. She couldn't afford to let herself stumble. The shock of Ogele's death had caused her to lose sight of her community's expectations. How could she have forgotten how Asani of the Ede clan had been trying to conceive, and she had promised to deliver a concoction to help?

After months of observing her cycle, they'd been able to pinpoint the days Asani's body would be more accepting of external help. Ewa had let this window slip away while grieving. The thought of leaving town without ensuring her patients were in good hands was a betrayal of her profession. She understood why Ogele wanted her to do things properly.

She attended to the women under her care while keeping a tight grip on her newfound resolve. Anytime she returned home to an empty room in the homestead of her husband, the reminder was constant: it was time to go. Several dozen people housed here didn't feel like family.

One evening as she walked home, she found Baale Semore sitting in a high-backed chair in front of his suites at the centre of the compound. The head of the clan chewed kola leisurely, his head angled up to catch the rays of the evening sun in a posture reminiscent of Ogele. Semore had been a warrior once like most of the men in Kuta, but time had whittled him down to a slight man with a full head of grey hair. Ewa had caught him at a good time. As Baale, Semore was often either out or in conference with other members of the family resolving issues.

"Good evening, baba," she said, approaching him.

Semore took his time answering her. A slight knit of his brows hinted at his irritation at her for interrupting his quiet time. To appease him, she chose to prostrate by lying on her right side instead of kneeling down in greeting.

"Good evening," he grunted.

A moment of silence followed as she waited for him to speak, but the Baale remained quiet. Clearly, he was in no mood for talking. She would have to soldier on like a stubborn ram. She folded herself till she was sitting on her haunches and squared her shoulders.

"I have heard that my family is nearby in a newly established town, and I am here to inform you of my desire to join them."

Semore had resumed looking at the sky, but with each word from her lips, he shifted his head to her until their gazes locked. She didn't look away from the man's rheumy eyes—he had to know she was serious.

"What did you just say?" he asked softly.

She cleared her throat. "I am a married woman, yet I live like a widow," she explained. "I want to return to my father's homestead."

Semore studied her for a heartbeat then opened his mouth to respond. At the same moment, another of the male elders of the household interrupted them. Onilao strode towards them whipping a horsetail back and forth as though a legion of flies lined the path before him. He set the stool he carried next to Semore and launched into greeting.

Semore was more talkative with his fellow elder. Onilao pretended not to see Ewa as he asked benign questions about Baale's health and how his day went. Ewa didn't mind. She was ready to wait until the chance came to slip back into the conversation. All she needed was a pause.

"Good evening, Baba Onilao," she shot in.

Onilao scowled at her. It seemed the man was still upset at her. Ogele was more wealthy than she had realised. There were corals, cowries, glass beads, brass and silver jewellery, starched folds of fabric, and more articles of wealth among her belongings. It was all too much for her, so when she wasn't brewing herbs or dashing through the village, she called women of the household and shared as much of Ogele's inheritance as she pleased. She had been forced to stop when Ogele had glared at her in her dreams.

"Iya Dara mocked me for not having children of my own, yet you gave her my silver bangle," Ogele had said over a howling wind. "Do you know that bangle crossed a desert as endless as the ocean to get here?"

"Tucked in the folds of the fabric you want to give Akanke are brass anklets. You better hold on to them if you want to go to Olootu."

Ewa had awakened with a jerk. Her breath had burst ahead of her, the row of oil lamps all dead. In this manner, Akanke, Onilao's daughter, had been robbed of cloth woven from the silk cotton tree. She'd refused to acknowledge Ewa when they'd bumped into each other, and her father carried the torch in solidarity. It didn't matter to either of them that she had bought a nicely dyed indigo wrapper which was swiftly rejected.

Onilao turned to Semore. "What is it that she wants?"

"I believe she said she wants to return to her father," Semore replied.

"What? No woman who has come to this compound has left on both feet."

Biting the inside of her lip to stop from grimacing, Ewa objected. "No woman here has lived under the same circumstances I have."

"When a woman marries into the homestead, she ought to forget her own," Onilao said, eyeing her. "Have you forgotten the wretched state you were in when we accepted you as a bride? Now that you have evolved into a successful woman thanks to our family, you attempt to bite the hands that fed you."

Ewa was slowly losing her composure. She bristled at being branded ungrateful and spoiled. Onilao wasn't even the Baale. A razor-sharp retort formed in her mouth, ready to unleash, but she held back. For the sake of Ogele, she would do things properly and refrain from being labelled rude in addition to the bad character Onilao foisted on her.

"If you truly want a separation," Semore said, his genteel voice putting an end to Onilao's rant. "You shall have it."

Ewa blinked. With this declaration, the family head had more or less agreed to her request.

"I beg your pardon?"

"You don't mean it." Onilao's full cheeks quivered.

"It is only reasonable," Semore said. "But I have a question for you, my child. If we go to Ifa with a problem, do we go alone?"

She shook her head. "No. Both parties have to be present."

"There you have it," the Baale said. "All conflicts are resolved in the open."

"But, baba—" she began.

"If you want a divorce, your husband must be here to speak his mind."

Her stomach dipped. This was what she got for trying to do things properly. If she had stolen away during one of her trips to the forest, no one would have searched for her. Even children in Kuta sang of the brave warrior who lived with the animals of the bush. If Ogele had tried and failed to get the boy she'd raised to live among his people, how was Ewa expected to achieve such a feat?

She spied a triumphant grin on Onilao's face as she mumbled her thanks. She held back from stomping off like a petulant child and walked away with her head high. She refused to give Onilao the pleasure of seeing how deeply upset she was. The elders thought she couldn't do it. She made her way to her rooms gracefully and shut the front door behind her. She sank to the floor worrying her bottom lip and tying knots in the skirt of her wrapper.

When she got married, Makinde hadn't been present. The women of the household had carried out the rituals, pouring water and alcohol on her feet, making the offering and singing prayers. She had stepped into the homestead over a trail of spilled blood, a symbolic cleansing. Nausea had filled her mouth at its glaring red. Just the week before, a deeper red had stained the brown earth, marking injustice and loss. The iron tang of blood had followed her through-out the ceremony. The Iyale had held her in her lap, accepting her on behalf of Makinde. Ewa had pierced the leafy ground with her stick.

If she could marry him in that manner, why she couldn't divorce him in his absence, too? Her distress soon gave way to determination. Who gave these men the right to dictate her life in the first place? She decided she would go to the forest. And when she did, she would crush everything in her path to find the so-called husband of hers and drag him back home whether he liked it or not.

EWA swung Ogele's walking stick left and right as she marched through the forest. A dull twang resounded as it collided with a plant. The flowering bush trembled, a few of its yellow-green flowers floating to the ground like rain droplets.

"I apologise," she said. Bending at the waist, she touched an oblong leaf, rubbing her thumb on its soft hairs.

"It's me that you should be apologising to." Jomiloju appeared behind her, chest heaving. "Is there gold up there? You were running."

"I will walk slower."

When she turned to the plant again, Ewa recognised it. The smile she reserved for her sister-in-law slipped off her face. This plant healed skin sores, but its other use was in promoting virility. Ogele would invoke its leaves with power asking it to aid in bringing children into the world. She kissed her lips as she straightened.

"Ah! What did the plant do to you?" Jomiloju asked in her exuberant manner.

Ewa was in a foul mood and for once didn't bother hiding it. They'd easily covered the short trek out the town borders into the untamed forest. Then they'd stepped onto the shielded path to the right of the bamboo patch. She was a stranger in this part of the woods. Heat trapped under her wrapper caused sweat to pool on her skin, dripping down her arms and the back of her legs, which itched because insects kept biting her. It was as though she'd broken a taboo by entering a forbidden place.

Do it the right way, Ogele whispered in her ear.

"I have a solution," Jomiloju said, undoing the shawl securing Jide to her back. "Turn around, Sister Dunni."

The instant warmth and pressure of Jide's weight on her back sent some of the turbulent emotions whirling within her away. The boy gurgled, and she strained to catch a glimpse of his coily hair.

"There." Jomiloju smiled. She flexed her shoulders then stretched her arms over her head.

"Thank you," Ewa said, bouncing on the balls of her feet so Jide giggled.

"You are welcome. Now, we have to retrace our steps."

"Why must we do that?"

"This is the wrong direction."

Jomiloju twirled around and started walking away. Ewa tilted her head at the younger woman.

"Is that so?" She caught up with Jomiloju's long-legged stride.

"I was trying to draw your attention earlier, but your mind was elsewhere. Why do you so dislike my brother?"

She pursed her lips at Jomiloju who'd never met Makinde yet referred to him with intimate terms.

"Have you ever laid eyes on this 'brother' of yours?"

"I've heard marvellous stories from Togun."

"How wonderful. Everyone at home loves him," she spat. "Anytime I think of the man, I feel nothing but anger."

Jomiloju shot her a sidelong glance. "What exactly happened between you two? I know you're lovely and can't be the reason he fled to the forest."

"Is that what people are saying?" She exhaled. "If I didn't know you, aburo, I'd swear you'd been here before."

"Oh, everyone knows the way."

"Pardon?" An itch spread along the back of her neck.

"Sister Dunni, I—" Jomiloju rubbed her cheek seemingly at a loss for words, which was unlike her.

Ewa wanted to rush forward and shake her shoulders. What on Earth was she hiding? They walked a few paces.

"The women in my age group," Jomiloju began.

"The women in your age group..."

They pushed onto a path unused by humans and animals alike. Jomiloju shoved aside a low branch heavy with leaves and stood back. Ewa stepped into a clearing devoid of trees, grey stone beneath her feet. In front of them, a rocky hill blocked the way.

"See here," Jomiloju said.

Jomiloju had retained her hold on the tree. Ewa blinked, noticing a thin strip of cloth tied to the branch. The cloth might have been ochre red at one point but had been washed into a light pink, and it fluttered as she let go of the branch.

"Look at this."

Jomiloju pointed at the base of the tree where four pebbles faced west. Ewa followed the direction of her finger. Her eyes narrowed then grew large when she saw a slim trail curving up around the hill.

"What is all this?"

"As you know, the Oba conferred an award on Makinde at the New Year festivities."

"Kuta's ruler did?" Ewa frowned. She had no recollection.

Jomiloju rolled her eyes at her. "You're his wife, and you never pay attention when it concerns him."

"I have no reason to."

"Anyway, since the New Year, a number of women in my age group have been trying their luck with my brother."

"Can you speak clearly, Jomiloju?"

Sighing, Jomiloju headed for the route. Ewa scurried after her. The path was thin, and this kept Jomiloju in front while Ewa followed.

With her back to her, Jomiloju gushed. "To see if they can make him their concubine."

"Their concubine?"

A burst of laughter bubbled up her throat. Jomiloju looked back at her. Her face bore markings of guilt as though she was in the wrong for not telling her sooner. Ewa stopped laughing.

"You never heeded my advice," Jomiloju said with a pout. She resumed marching.

"My dearest Jomiloju, I don't care," she countered. "If we found that man wrapped in the embrace of a nubile woman, it wouldn't bother me an ounce."

Jomiloju was junior to her and so would be the women of her group, barely adding a few years past their twentieth year and full of bravado. Ewa remembered how she'd been at their age. Senseless war and bloodshed had quickly rid her of her delusions. The women of Jomiloju's generation hadn't had to live through unnecessary violence, and if they had, perhaps it had been as children, and their youthful memories now failed them. She supposed it was a positive blessing for them.

"Is that so? I heard Oyinkan from the Aperin family talking about him. She said he is handsome and virile. She said he licked every inch of her skin from her head to her toes."

"Perhaps Oyinkan met a forest nymph, not your brother."

they were in a space that was ancient, unsullied by human excesses. Was this how it felt to be in the sky like a bird? From this distance, the closest huts of Kuta resembled pot lids.

Jomiloju drew her attention to the sticks arranged at the base of a large stone.

"We need to find west and continue for a few paces. Then, there will be a glade, and at its centre, a tree with bright blue flowers."

Ewa undid her head wrap and lashed it to and fro as if it were a fan. She worried her lips.

"We should have come prepared."

She was thinking of water cooled in clay pots running down her throat, perhaps sweet aadun to snack on. Jomiloju misunderstood her.

"You can't turn back now," she said, grabbing her hand tight.

Jomiloju kept hold of her until the heady fragrance of flowers assailed their nostrils. Ewa's heart was in her throat as they stepped in the empty space. She rubbed her hands along the cloth she'd wrapped around herself in a makeshift dress, adjusting the knot securing it on her shoulder. Jomiloju paced around the clearing making obvious statements.

"He's not here. It's peaceful. So this is the tree."

Their breaths eased, and they drank water from the nearby stream. Ewa appreciated the sound of running water joining that of the wind rustling the leaves and the tall grass. The nearby chatter of birds added to this natural symphony. She tilted her head back and felt dappled sunlight on her face. Despite the circumstance, a smile touched her lips.

"Let's head back," she said.

This had been a waste of time and energy. Ogele knew she'd tried her best. Whenever the opportunity struck, she would slip out of Kuta like Ojiji or a spirit of the night.

Behind her, the baby sniffed. She started bouncing on her feet, anticipating his cry as he was roused from the dream world. Jide's wails tore through the stillness. She tugged at the knots holding the baby up, manoeuvring him around her till she held him in her arms. Jomiloju collected her son and cradled him. When a baby was hungry, there was no delaying feeding him. She sat cross-legged on the grass.

As Jide fed, Ewa let herself wander. She'd come to know that if she kept watching them, she would feel that pang of longing, the reminder of how alone she was.

"Hello there," she said as she walked up to the tree dominating the clearing.

It'd called to her earlier, but she'd been prepared to ignore it. Truth be told, she was no longer sure she wanted to face Makinde, after all. With the exertion it had taken to reach this part of the forest, she yearned for the comfort of her bed. With nothing else to do while Jide ate, she allowed herself to be pulled to the tree like a moth to flame.

It was unlike any she was familiar with. A thin trunk rose and curved like a bent back under the weight of tiny flowers fluffed together in dense clusters. They were bluer than the brightest indigo she had lain eyes on. The sweet fragrance emerging from the tree resembled honey simmered with water as a treat.

For Ewa, trees were roots, seeds, fruits, and barks, each with their own uses. Ogele would know what purpose this tree served. She easily saw the older woman collecting the dazzling blooms, steeping them in oils, and leaving them to bake under the sun in the small clay pots she stored her cosmetics. A pang pitched in her chest.

"You're a beautiful one," she said, reaching up to pluck a flower. "May I?"

The yelp of an animal tore through the moment.

"Watch out, sister," Jomiloju cried before a dog burst into the clearing.

"It's okay," she said. "He's too clean to be a wild. Do you see the chain on his neck?"

Her hand switched direction. Instead of reaching for the flowers, she reached for the dog's chest. The animal's demeanour was friendly, and he nuzzled up to her with relaxed ears. She lightly massaged his shoulder. Her earlier shock dissipated when he let her pet his head, grunting in delight.

"My brother must be near."

The truth of her words froze her actions. This dog must belong to Makinde.

"Where is your master?" she whispered, slowly drawing her hand down his back.

The dog's tail wagged. Either he didn't understand her or wasn't keen on betraying his owner. It seemed every living being thought favourably of that man. She pouted as she turned back to the tree.

Ewa froze midway. Eyes were observing her from the brush. A scream ripped from her mouth and sent the dog barking. She stumbled backwards. To her alarm, the dog ran towards the human-like bush with eyes. Then an imposing man emerged forward from the green.

The man was big with lean, solid muscles. A full, scraggly beard obscured his face, and knotted coils fell from his head. Scars sprinkled his skin like salt in a dish, covering every exposed part of him—which wasn't hidden with the loincloth he wore. He'd been watching them.

Ewa's hand clenched, feeling for Ogele's sturdy cane. She kept her eyes on the stranger. Beside her, Jomiloju was on her feet with Jide at her breast. This man could have followed them. Her stomach dipped. Had enemies drawn close to Kuta? She had to steel herself for them.

"There is a warrior who lives here," she warned.

It was a blessing when her fingers grazed the wood of the walking stick. She grabbed it and swung, brandishing the pointed end at the strange man.

"Kuta is home to the bravest warriors in the land. Our women are no weaklings."

She inched closer to Jomiloju, wishing she had eyes at the back of her head. Was this man alone? Were there others concealed in the shrubs? An eternity seemed to pass as the stranger watched her movements, waiting for the opportunity to set upon her.

"The only person who lives here is me."

Ewa froze.

Behind her, Jomiloju gasped.

"Elder brother," she whispered. Then she started chanting his praise names. "Makinde, son of the brave man, firm like a mountain. Powerful, ferocious one."

The cane fell from Ewa's hands with a thud.

"Son of Latilu who slaughtered a leopard because his wife shivered with cold," Jomiloju went on. "Bravery is your birthright. Wherever Makinde rests knows peace."

She shot an irritated look at Jomiloju. When had the woman found the time to memorise all this? Besides, this man couldn't be Makinde. The Makinde of her memory was larger than this, radiating dread where this one appeared dejected. The man she recalled had shouted and danced as his names were called while this one's shoulders bowed as his eyes welled with tears. Panegyrics were said to tap into the deepest connections in one's soul—they calmed the angry, and they sated the lost. Makinde's watery eyes confirmed his identity.

"Thank you," the strange man who was apparently Makinde said. "It has been so long since I heard that." He exhaled and then fixed his accursed eyes on Ewa.

Turning away, she sputtered, "Who are you?"

"Makinde, son of Latilu. As she said."

Even though she refused to regard him, she shuddered at the weight of his haunted eyes on her. It was a relief when he addressed Jomiloju.

"You are with a child. Is your husband aware that you are here?"

"My husband is Togun," Jomiloju spoke freely. "Your younger brother. This is Jide, your son."

The children of one's brothers were considered theirs, and Jomiloju carelessly proffered her son to Makinde. Ewa recoiled as he approached. Swallowing her fear, she maintained her position between Jomiloju and Makinde, blocking his access to Jide.

Jomiloju shifted to the side, still pushing Jide forward. Ewa was prepared to spirit Jide away from Makinde's tainted hands now reaching for the child. She uttered a soft prayer when he stopped short of touching him. Makinde bowed his head to Jide.

"What are you thinking, aburo?" she said, grabbing the boy from Jomiloju.

"Jide should know his relatives."

"This is the height of irresponsibility! To you let any stranger carry your child—"

"Why are you here?" Makinde said.

"Divorce me," she snapped.

MAKINDE blinked. There could only be one woman demanding that he dissolve their union. The voice of the woman he hadn't married echoed in his head.

Divorce me.

His family had married Ewa for him without prior notice, and the wedding ceremonies had been carried out in absentia. He lifted a hand to scratch the back of his head. He didn't miss the way she shifted suspiciously at each movement he made. It was to be expected. Distress had radiated off her the first time he'd seen her. She'd been a young woman pushed into his apartment soon after he'd returned from his very last campaign. Haunted by what had happened in Odan and what Arole had done, he'd been in a haze of anger and pain.

Ewa's disquietude on that day was fresh in his mind. He recalled the manner in which she had pressed her elbows into her sides, shrinking her body while keeping her gaze averted from him. She'd recognized him for the monster he was.

The years had given her the courage to confront him. Now, she held his gaze squarely and lifting her chin even though her posture was rigid. She stood bravely between him and his junior's wife, her stance one of protection. She was ready to fight. The distrust in her wide, feline eyes was for him. She was at once fearful and disgusted, another reminder of the past he couldn't escape.

Despite this, sensations he believed he'd driven out of his body swirled to life in her presence. When he'd spied on her from the borders of Ogele's wild garden, his mouth had tingled at the flare of her hips. This close, she was even more alluring. The sheen of her red-brown skin demanded his attention. Her small breasts heaved, and the swell of her hips couldn't be hidden by the wrappers she'd swathed around herself.

Makinde took all of her in. He wasn't the tallest or sturdiest warrior, but Ewa barely reached his chest. Heat flared in his centre, a sensation so strange due to its infrequency. Looking at her now, he wondered if he should have waited. A floral coconut scent teased him, and with it a fantasy of sinking into her softness to completely lose himself in her. It'd been too long since he'd reached for a woman in a sweet atmosphere—a weaker man would have gone mad. Not him. There were other things to torture him. The shivers running through his body were an aberration.

"Did you hear me?"

He grunted. A man was allowed to dream, even one as burdened with wrongs as he was. Fantasy was fleeting while reality waited, and this woman with her heart-shaped face and full lips wasn't part of it.

"I said—"

"Very well."

Her mouth fell open. His fingers tingled with a vision of touching the side of her face then running his hand up to push her head wrap back. What hairstyle did she favour? He pictured a crested style decorated with feathers and beads.

"Oh. Alright." Her stance softened. She cleared her throat and turned to Jomiloju.

"Sister Dunni, are you sure?"

"Of course I am," she snapped, then her tone softened. "Let's go home."

A dream again, of Ewa speaking to him in that balmy tone. For someone he had hardly exchanged words with, the woman was furious with him, and he couldn't blame her.

The women went through the motions. The baby who was his nephew was strapped onto his wife's back. As she adjusted the white shawl securing the baby, Ewa tossed a demand over her shoulder.

"You will be informing the Baale of our separation."

He'd never been talkative, but as they moved away, he became invisible. He'd longed to be forgotten and erased from communal memory, so why was there a pang in his chest now she no longer looked at him?

"It must be done before nightfall tomorrow," she said. "The sooner we can complete this journey that never began, the better we will all be."

She clicked her tongue before setting off. His brother's wife sent an apologetic look in his direction before scurrying away. Wuu whined as they left. Makinde crossed his arms over the span of his chest and nudged his dog with his foot.

"Run along," he said.

Alone in the clearing, he rubbed at his chest. Something underneath thrummed, but he had since expelled his heart. There was no reason for him to feel the murmur of hope, of what would have been. There were warriors like him who married and lived otherwise happy lives. He wasn't to be one of them. He didn't deserve it.

Bursting into a sprint, he leapt into the nearby stream. Let the crisp waters wash away the strangeness that had stolen his soul.

EWA'S legs had transformed to guineacorn pudding. She paused to rub at her knees. Closing her eyes, she breathed in deeply, opened her mouth, and exhaled loudly. The tumult within her wasn't solely due to the physical effort of their hike. Going down was easier than coming up, and as the evening approached, cool air caressed exposed skin. But she was uncomfortable.

"Sister Dunni," Jomiloju said, rushing her words. "Isn't he wildly handsome? There is a rough quality to him. And that voice! So deep! I understand why those girls came all the way here."

Ewa held her tongue. It was better than launching into a spiel about young women and their fanciful lies. Didn't Jomiloju see how haunted his eyes were? As they walked home, the question of how strange women recognized the man when she'd failed to crossed her mind. It slowly dawned on her—the long line of Makinde's nose and the face squared as though chiselled by a sculptor were features shared with Jomiloju's husband. There were also his long eyelashes. This Makinde looked nothing like the warrior she'd seen.

Shouldn't a man who had been living rough in the wild for years look worse for wear? Makinde's skin lacked the lustre of shea butter, not that she'd been observing, but the hair hanging around his face in thick locks appeared clean. The full beard on his face didn't take away from his beauty. His shoulders were so broad and inviting, the skin on his torso smooth save for a tuft of hair in the centre of his chest and a dark trail around his belly button inviting downwards. The worn loincloth did a poor job concealing his girth.

Ewa groaned. What had possessed her? She had to stop before she started doubting her initial memory of him. She had seen Makinde; she'd even been in the same room with him for a few seconds that had felt like eternity. He'd been part of the campaign that'd ripped through her birthplace, shattering it so Odan no longer existed, its families forced to start anew elsewhere.

"Do you think he'll come down?" Jomiloju asked. Before Ewa had the chance respond, she went on. "Maybe that's why the family head asked you? Of course! It would take his wife to bring him down the hill."

"Jomiloju," she said, caution in her tone. For someone she usually referred to as 'sister' or other terms of endearment, Jomiloju hushed upon hearing her name. "The elders say good looks are empty beside character. He couldn't even bother coming for his mother's funeral."

"We can't ascertain that. He might have arranged with Iya's group."

Ewa threw her hands up in exasperation. For the life of her, she couldn't figure out why Jomiloju was so defensive of this man. Today was the first time she'd exchanged words with Makinde. Everyone adored the man who'd spurned them for the wilderness. Was there something in the food Kuta consumed?

A traitorous thought crossed her mind. Perhaps this loyalty made Jomiloju the better daughter-in-law. She rubbed at her forehead now slick with sweat. On her back, Jide gurgled, probably sensing her discomfort. She had to seek calm, but there were too many emotions wrestling inside her so she was at a loss for where to start. She was angry, upset at the inconvenience of venturing there, unsure whether the man would honour her request to come home, and there was also the heat in her belly, simmering like slow burning coal from the sight of him. She needed a lover instantly—her body was betraying her.

"My Togun will be so thrilled," Jomiloju said.

This reminded her. "How do you know his praise names?"

"I learned it from the older women," Jomiloju replied airily, likely assuming she knew them, as well.

That was what women did when they married into a homestead. They learned the family history they would pass on to their children; they took on the family trade and worked several skills to earn wealth. Ewa had taken to Ogele in favour of harvesting, processing, and trading foodstuff like the rest. The other women in the compound ground grains into flours, fermented them to beers, cooked a variety of dishes, and sent younger children like Tope to hawk the prepared food at nearby markets. Ogele was the outlier in a number of ways; she never married and bore no children. Most importantly, it was she who had ventured into the forest and come back with the knowledge of healing. Ewa supposed this made her an outlier, too.

Chapter Six

"I cannot believe my eyes." Onigbaoje clapped his hands, astounded. "You're actually doing this? We should have sent your wife up sooner."

"She isn't my wife," Makinde said. "Besides, she wants divorce."

"Who are her people again?"

He shrugged. He'd gathered all his belongings, their meagreness a testament to the kind of life he lived—all he had was his weapons for hunting. Onigbaoje had brought the clothes he currently wore, a pair of loose-fitting trousers tight around the ankles and secured around the waist. He eschewed the tunic of matching material and instead wrapped a shawl over his newly bare head. Onigbaoje had shaved Makinde's hair himself while mumbling about being more presentable.

"I thank my Creator for keeping me alive to witness Makinde's return to civilisation." Onigbaoje was undeterred.

Makinde adjusted the shawl so it covered his chest and shoulders. He held the large swatch of cloth close—it granted him the anonymity he desired. He brought his fingers to his mouth and whistled for his dog. "I am merely relocating. Too many people have found this place, and I blame you."

More than once, the idea Onigbaoje was the one leading young women searching for suitors to him had crossed his mind. He cast a narrowed glance at the old warrior who grinned shamelessly.

"What man stays ten years without a woman's tenderness?" Onigbaoje asked.

"I do," he said defiantly. He picked up a machete—another item among the number Onigbaoje had brought—and started breaking down the shabby construction housing him.

He had been searching for something since his final conversation with Ogele. What this something was however remained a mystery. Days after she'd walked away, her mates had found him and led him to her grave. He'd sat below the tree marking the spot and grieved. He'd seen her in his mind's eye crossing over to her true home. It brought him a measure of peace that his mother wouldn't linger any longer than necessary.

He'd returned to his hovel with a renewed perspective. This part of the forest that had been his home for years was now tainted; it no longer offered seclusion. He had to relocate, but he couldn't transpose himself too far from Kuta, not if he expected Onigbaoje to visit with updates. Additionally, years and habit had informed him of the power of the tree with blue flowers. There had to be another one like it in the forest surrounding Kuta, yet he had searched for days without luck. No other tree carried flowers that felt like wool to the touch or brought him peace of mind if only for a few seconds.

"Shall we get moving?" Onigbaoje asked.

Makinde ignored him. The man was too excitable, and he regretted having him here. Going to meet Baale was the least he could offer to the woman who had been chained to him due to no fault of hers. Two days after Ewa's surprise visit, he'd seen her face when he closed his eyes. She was like rainfall after a drought, a reprieve from the spectres lurking around demanding vengeance.

Ewa deserved better. Seeing evidence one of his younger brothers had married and was even a father, he was certain she desired the same. Only a few women were like Ogele who'd been content with raising the children of others. Ewa had every reason to hate him.

Once evidence of his habitat had been destroyed, they moved with Wuu dashing around their heels. Bile filled Makinde's mouth with each step down the path. Even with Onigbaoje beside him, his head spun. He was thankful for the weight of the shawl which he drew tighter over his face.

"Why do you insist on resembling a thief?"

"You have yet to understand me after all these years?" He spat into the bushes.

"On the contrary, I know you better than you know yourself. Do you remember you were a boy of merely seventeen years old when we fought together at Ire?"

"I can't forget."

The warm blood gushing over his hands as he drove his sword into a charging soldier, the crack of bone as his arrow sailed into a supine neck, the smell of iron all around him. He ground his teeth.

They were close to the town when a group of farmers passed by. Makinde's fingers gripped the edges of the shawl tighter. The farmers prostrated in greeting. One of them lifted a grisly face and mouthed words at him. He inhaled a shaky breath. Up on his hill, they only came at night, but among people, the dead walked freely.

"Onigbaoje," he grunted.

Onigbaoje was so engrossed in his tales of war that he failed to notice Makinde had stopped walking. The old man stopped chattering and turned. Makinde jerked his head to the bushes off the path.

Onigbaoje frowned. "What?"

"We walk here," he said, diving off the path before his friend could reply. He whistled for Wuu to come along.

"You should be returning to a hero's welcome." Onigbaoje beat at the bushes as he joined him.

"I'm not a hero."

He trudged on, bringing to mind the welcome ten years ago. The adrenaline had still been pumping in his veins as he'd performed a mock battle to the delight of his extended family.

That wasn't him.

Onigbaoje grumbled his discomfort but didn't leave him behind. Makinde's feet guided them towards the hidden path Ogele had formed herself leading to their homestead. Before long, they pushed aside the brush appearing at the back of the compound. A sole bungalow stood at the edge of the riotous garden.

He was relieved Ewa wasn't home. Elsewhere in the compound, pestles were lifted and smashed into mortars. The sound was accompanied by laughter as women pounded food. Other people shouted in conversation, and a baby wailed.

"Was this truly necessary?" Onigbaoje asked, dragging a hand down his fine silk tunic while the other adjusted his embroidered hat.

Makinde scoffed. He patted Onigbaoje's shoulder before marching ahead. He stuck to the shadows behind the scattered buildings until he reached Baale Semore's chambers located at the centre of the homestead.

"We're here."

He slid into the building. It was a grand one with murals and carved pillars. The entrance opened to a central courtyard holding an earthen shrine dedicated to the ancestors.

Makinde let the shawl fall as he approached the sanctified space. It was habit driven into him from youth rather than piety that pushed him to prostrate and knock his head on the earth in greeting to the departed.

When he lifted up, a sprinkle of red dust coloured his forehead. He looked around at the encircling rooms, their darkened entrances gaping like open mouths. He used to practice in this courtyard, engaging in mock battles with his brothers under the watchful eye of an elder and the ancestors. This was where the older men told stories of the wars of the past, of their fathers and their father's fathers. He would curl in the corner next to the wooden post embedded with images of women carrying pots and cooking. One year, the entire family had gathered in the same courtyard after an elder had died. He'd only been seven years old and had slipped away in the middle of the ceremonies because he'd been hungry. The entire family was supposed to be mourning a loss, but he'd found his birth mother in their hut hastily throwing items into a sack. She'd jumped when he'd called out to her, clasping both hands over her mouth.

"Good day," Onigbaoje shouted, his tenor jarring him from the past. "Is anyone home?"

The place was quiet. He looked down and noticed his dog was missing.

JOMILOJU worked her shoulders and arms as she moved a stone back and forth over the granite grate, grinding herbs into powder. Sitting on a spread mat in the shaded porch in front of the rooms Jomiloju shared with her family, Ewa felt like an elder. She'd entered the forest with Jomiloju at dawn, and upon their return, had set her to work. The ones needing to be brewed were sitting in pots back at Ogele's quarters. The women had relocated because Jomiloju wanted to try making something new. From her position, Ewa watched her actions while playing with Jide.

"It's done," Jomiloju announced.

Ewa went over to expect her work carrying Jide on her hip.

"It should be finer than this," she said, looking down at the brown powder on the grate. "Keep at it."

"Sister Dunni!"

"Wasn't this your idea?"

Jomiloju scrunched her lips up and rolled her eyes but continued the motion. The sound of stone against stone and dried herbs being broken down rose once more. What she was in the process of making was technically not medicine.

When mixed with honey and consumed, the powder became an aphrodisiac. It enhanced love play, heightening a woman's pleasure beyond her imagination. Ewa had shown her the leaves to stop bleeding, to aid in conceiving, to cure pains in children and let them grow well, but the first thing Jomiloju wanted to learn how to make on her own was medicine designed for sexual intimacy.

"I will scream the homestead down tonight," Jomiloju said, putting more work into her grinding. "There will be a stream flowing right in front of our room tomorrow."

Ewa laughed. "Don't let the elders hear you saying that."

Tradition dictated women shun sex while breastfeeding, but Jomiloju was done waiting. As for Ewa, the only pleasure she found was by herself. Under the springs where water played with her body and her fingers did the rest. To know even more pleasure existed out there was torturous. Once she was free of Kuta, she would find a lover who would make her bawl in pleasure even without the aid of aphrodisiacs.

She accepted the round seed Jide handed her as play. It was coated in his saliva. She waved it in front of his eyes then made it disappear. It was only hidden under her bottom, but Jide's little body tilted as he laughed. She chortled as she held him straight. Elsewhere in the compound, children screamed excitably. She dismissed it until a familiar dog dashed past her left chased by a group of boys. The dog reappeared around the sharp corner of the hut to her right, beads jangling around its neck.

Ewa seized Jide, holding him against her shoulder as the dog hid behind her, whining. Three boys arrived panting shortly after.

"Stop." She looked back to confirm this dog belonged to Makinde. The mash of green beads, black seeds, and metal trinkets chained around its neck confirmed it. "Don't you boys have anything better to do than to harass this poor animal?"

"Since when did you own a dog?" one of the boys asked.

"I know its owner." She put one hand on the dog, the other holding Jide close.

Jomiloju had stopped working. "Isn't this the same dog?"

"It is."

"You rascals," Jomiloju started. "Brother Makinde better not get news of you maltreating his pet."

At the mention of Makinde's name, the boys grew wide-eyed before running off. They would announce this news to the entire clan. Ewa petted the yowling dog. So the man had finally come after taking his precious time?

"He really came back," Jomiloju said. Her voice turned lyrical as she sang, "Our warrior has returned."

Ewa stood up again. Unlike Jomiloju, she knew Makinde was too crafty to come out of hiding for no reason.

"The powder should be ready now," she said. "Hold on to Jide."

"Finally! Ah, are you on your way to meet him? Shouldn't we beautify you first?"

"I'll see you later."

She refused to give room for Jomiloju to grow even more exuberant. Ewa passed son to mother before making her way to Semore's apartments. She wove past the kitchen to get the dog a treat. The bone dangled from his mouth as they continued on.

Semore wasn't in front of his huts as he had been the last time she'd come here. She announced herself before entering into the building. The dog rushed ahead of her, and she heard Onilao shout. She gave a half-suppressed chuckle and pressed her lips close as she approached the four men seated in a circle at the centre of the open courtyard. Unsurprisingly, they'd started discussions without her. She silently thanked the dog for alerting her of this travesty.

"Good day, elders," she greeted. She avoided looking at Makinde and the finely-dressed man sitting on the stool beside him who grinned widely at her. She focused her attention on Semore.

"Eh, Ewadunni, shouldn't you be busy?" Onilao said.

"All conflicts are resolved in the open," she replied. "I am here to bear witness."

She stood demurely, hands clasped at her front. Her future was here and not outside. She tasted the promise of possibility on the tip of her tongue. These men wouldn't allow her to be absent for it.

"As she should." Makinde stood up from his chair. "Sit. Please."

She was forced to regard him now. The sunlight hit his skin, making it glisten as though he were carved of bronze. He had cut his hair, and it only made his chiselled features stand out more. It was hard for her to tear her gaze away, but she did as directed, sitting next to the men so as to avoid any unnecessary dialogue with Makinde.

Ewa fiddled with the folds of her wrapper, her ears as hot as roasted yams. She could feel three pairs of eyes studying her closely. She wanted to be here and would have preferred to stand. She cursed Makinde silently as she smoothed her robe. She focused on Semore, the Baale's kind face helping her breathe easier.

"The elders have discussed my request?" she asked.

"My child," Semore began. "I suppose we should thank you for bringing our son back home."

At this, Makinde cleared his throat. "We will be leaving shortly."

"Nonsense! Preparations have—" Onilao started.

"Forgive me, fathers, for interrupting," Makinde said, inclining his head slightly. "I accept Ewadunni's request to be separated."

Goosebumps erupted up Ewa's arms at the mention of her name. His low tone tickled her insides as though he had leaned close to whisper next to her ear. How did he know her name?

She missed what one of the elders said in reply. The only elder she didn't recognise was speaking—he was the one who had been smiling at her with curiosity when she entered. He appeared familiar. She might have seen him in town somewhere, but she failed to recall where.

"Where will she be going to?" he asked. "Where is her family?"

"She claims her people are in Olootu," Semore responded.

This time, the man addressed her directly. "Olootu? I have never heard of this Olootu."

"It is a newly established town my family has settled in," she explained. "We are Agbonrin from Odan, dispersed after the war."

A sudden tautness cut through the air at the mention of Odan.

"Have you been there before?"

Ewa wondered where this train of conversation was heading to as she replied, "No."

Onilao was also clearly impatient. "If she wants to go to this Olootu, who are we to stop her?"

She resisted kissing her teeth. This was the same man who had sent her up the hills. A few days before, Onilao had been against her leaving the clan. She shook her head then froze with the realization someone was watching her. The hairs on the back of her neck rose. She looked up to meet Makinde's haunted gaze skittering away.

"I am thinking of her safety," the strange elder said.

Her brows furrowed. Where had she seen this man before?

"That isn't a problem," she interjected, keeping her tone even. "The priest Fadahunsi will escort me to Olootu."

It was a matter she was yet to discuss this with her friend, confident Fadahunsi would agree to accompany her.

A rumble went through the small audience. The old men shuddered and shook their heads—her suggestion didn't please them.

"A stranger?" Semore asked.

"I said it, didn't I? Baale! She wants her family to believe we are stingy not to have sent her with one of our own," Onilao added.

"Isn't it better for the husband to escort her?" the third elder suggested.

Ewa's stomach flipped. She glanced at Makinde, but he was glaring at the elder with his mouth slightly agape. She turned to Semore. She had no intention of travelling for days with this strange man the clan kept forcing on her. By his grumble, Makinde wasn't inclined to the idea either.

"Think about it," the man was saying. "Her relatives can and should see that this family took good care of her."

Ewa wanted to fade away into the building as the discussion carried on without her. Once more, she thought about slipping away unawares without all this spectacle. She was certain Makinde felt the same. After a few minutes, the elders had reached their conclusion.

Makinde would escort Ewa to Olootu.

Chapter Seven

E wa's belongings fit into five raffia-woven baskets of varying sizes—the largest of which she could fit into if she curled herself into a ball. Her personal belongings barely fit in one basket, but what she had inherited from Ogele filled the rest to bursting.

She rolled the woven fabrics of cotton and silk into logs before sliding them into round wooden boxes where they would be safe from the elements. The jewellery was kept in brass containers. She coiled the beaded necklaces along short twigs so they wouldn't get tangled. Combs, neck rests, blankets, and even a carved stool gathered in containers with everything neatly stacked to prevent them from shifting or breaking. Two grass mats were rolled and placed against the wall, and one basket held nothing but clay pots secured with string.

All of these would come later. After she'd settled in Olootu and built her own modest accommodation, she would hire porters to transport her belongings. In the meantime, Jomiloju would be in charge of watching over everything.

Ewa glided to the corner of the room where Ogele's belongings were buried. There was an indentation where she had worked the mud to dust and collected dirt in a square white sheet to carry along with her.

"I'm leaving, Mother," she said, kneeling down on the floor. "I did as you asked. Watch over me as I leave Kuta."

She wasn't one to begin a journey without making sure the deities went ahead of and with her. She had started her propitiations the day before under Fadahunsi's guidance. By the time he'd led her through the rituals, she'd been thrumming with positive energy. Her feet had tingled as she'd returned home, her head light with the mystic messages, warnings, and advice that had been divulged to her. She'd seen beautiful things when she slept and had awakened with a smile on her face. This was the right decision. Wonu, Asani, and her other clients would be all right.

She stepped outside Ogele's home and pulled the door shut behind her.

"Is it that you don't trust us in this homestead?" Jomiloju asked. Her lips pursed as Ewa placed a lock on the door that had always been open in Ogele's lifetime.

"You know I do." She placed the slim key into her friend's hand. "Help me look after Iya Ogele's belongings. You know many of our relatives weren't happy when I stopped sharing her wealth."

Jomiloju tucked the key in the folds of her wrapper with one hand while nudging Jide on her hip with the other. "We are your relatives now, are we? After you made the decision to leave us. I will miss you, Sister Dunni. Our baby will, too."

Ewa gathered both of them in a tight hug. She rubbed noses with Jide, tickling his chubby stomach, and was rewarded with a dimpled chortle.

"You must come visit me."

"Olootu is a week away."

"Maybe I'll be closer."

Jomiloju's eyes grew wide. "You intend to go elsewhere? Did my brother suggest a relocation?"

"Not that." She tutted.

She'd said too much. With what had happened in the past, it would have been unnatural for her to be free of doubts with regard to reuniting with her family. On the one hand, she couldn't shake the feeling she was making the right decision. But behind this certainty was the idea she was making a grave error. This other side whispered that the tears Fadahunsi spoke of her people shedding weren't from their longing to see her. At least, she was leaving Kuta—this was progress no matter how one regarded it.

"Are you certain you're carrying enough?" Jomiloju pointed with her chin to the bags hanging from Ewa's shoulder—one of felt alligator hide from Ogele's inheritance and another of cloth.

A medium-sized raffia basket held a few changes of clothes, a blanket, and dried meat wrapped in board leaves. She also carried the tools of her trade along with folded sachets of herbal powders and insect-repelling leaves.

"I have medicine for constipation here." She laughed. "It's more than enough."

"You're overly joyous. I've never seen you like this." Jomiloju's pout deepened.

Despite her disapproval of Ewa's departure, Jomiloju offered to carry the basket before they headed out. Fadahunsi was waiting for them on the road leading out of town. Ewa took in his winning smile and his sage aura noticing how his presence no longer moved her as it once did. Regardless, she would miss him. The trio trekked to Kuta's outskirts as the sun made its early ascent up the sky. Makinde had agreed to meet them at the moat. They arrived ahead of time and found various trees to lean against as they waited.

"Did we get here early?" Fadahunsi asked, his gaze travelling up and down the lonely path.

"He might be hiding behind a tree," Ewa replied.

"You should have seen how he emerged from the bush," Jomiloju said.

"Jomiloju screamed." She chuckled.

"That is because he was like an otherworldly creature. My mouth fell to the ground."

Fadahunsi patted the pockets of his trousers. "That reminds me. This is what you asked for."

Ewa took the leather-bound amulet the priest gave her and slipped it in one of her bags.

"I thank you," she said. "For everything. I told Jomiloju to visit me when I have settled. I extend the same invitation—"

Jomiloju jumped with a shriek. Ewa looked back to see Makinde emerge from the surrounding forest as though he belonged there. If the family had thought his reappearance meant he'd come back to them, they were sorely disappointed. He refused to spend a night in the homestead despite Semore's attempts to keep him there. The man slipped away in the middle of an impromptu feast put together in his honour.

Such an impudent man had no business looking so tasteful dressed in a simple pair of trousers paired with a tunic. The cut of his tunic accentuated his shoulders, making them appear so wide, one's fingers ached to hold onto them.

Ewa blinked the treacherous thought away. She pulled Jomiloju into another tight embrace and turned to Fadahunsi to hug him, too. He stiffened and tapped her back twice. She let go and turned to Jomiloju who was now shedding tears.

"What is the meaning of this, aburo?" she said, rubbing her friend's wet cheeks. "We're seeing again."

"I love you so much, Sister Dunni." Jomiloju sniffled.

"I love you, too."

Ewa held Jomiloju tight and rubbed her shoulders. She lowered her voice as she said, "You don't want to keep your precious brother waiting."

Jomiloju nodded in the crook of Ewa's neck. Her eyes were red when they broke apart. Ewa lowered her head for Jomiloju to balance her basket up there. Standing tall, she flexed her shoulders, grateful the load wasn't heavy. As they set off, she kept looking back to see Jomiloju waving at her with Jide on her hip, Fadahunsi standing solemnly to the side.

THE elders said one shouldn't take three years to prepare for action. It seemed Ewa took such advice to heart. She stomped ahead of Makinde on the road with Kuta behind them. The load atop her head made her posture regal. Her neck appeared longer, her back ramrod straight.

It was more sensual for the fact she appeared unaware of the effect her beauty had on men. Ewa didn't need to perform as the young seductresses did. Watching her walk ahead of him, his lips quirked imagining how soft her bottom would feel in his hands. He struggled to tear his eyes away from the flare of her ample hips. He clenched his hands into fists—touching her was forbidden. He had trained for years to gain ultimate control of his body. For one woman to unravel what had been drilled into his bones was impossible.

He had meant to resume his search for the blue tree soon after meeting with the elders, but Onigbaoje had forced his hand. He had pulled the older man aside afterward, incensed at the turnaround.

"I didn't come here to travel to Olootu," he'd said, fuming.

"And what would you do if harm were to befall her during her journey?" Onigbaoje had asked. "Think about it, my friend. Here, she was protected by Kuta warriors. Do you suppose a priest can keep her safe on the road?"

Makinde's stomach had hardened. The mere suggestion of seeing Ewa's face among the ghoulish throng had made his head spin. And it would haunt him because whether he'd selected it or not, she was his responsibility.

He questioned what his old friend's intentions were. As comrades, Onigbaoje must have felt some kind of responsibility towards him. However, the man didn't know where to stop. He'd strong-armed Makinde into staying with him and his family, doing all in his power to ensure he didn't return to the forest. The pallid visages he saw transposed on the faces of living people had been the surest sign he didn't belong in a homestead surrounded by friends and family.

But Onigbaoje didn't care if the forest was the only place to bring a measure of peace to him. Makinde could scream and run, he could throw stones at spectres sure they wouldn't make contact with flesh, and he could slip into civilisation unnoticed. He didn't sleep in the few nights he'd spent with his old friend.

He wasn't one to follow duty—after all, he'd ignored his responsibilities to sequester himself in the wilderness for years. He certainly had no business journeying with Ewa. He had managed to convince himself this was an opportunity. Instead of depending on Onigbaoje, he would start probing for information himself. He'd cowered for too long, leaving Onigbaoje to gather intelligence when his friend clearly had his own motives.

So here he was trailing behind Ewa, distracted by the curves of her body. Wuu had made his preference clear and weaved around her. Her mirth had vanished since they'd left her friends. He had seen the priest now, a slight man with skin unblemished like that of a toddler, who appeared too feeble to lift an axe to fight. He tightened a hand on the satchel hanging across his back, recalling how desperately Ewa had clutched the man. From what he had gathered, she was a healer. A priest and a healer were natural companions like thunder and lightning.

He clenched his teeth as his mind trailed a dangerous path, considering if Ewa was engaged in an affair. The rational side of him knew he had no right to blame her, reminding him it was his own choice to live away from everyone else. Still, a bitter taste remained in his mouth.

His ruminations consumed him in entirety. He didn't realise Ewa had stopped walking, and he bumped into her from behind. Her hands reached up to steady her basket while his hands shot out to hold her. He gripped her waist, securing her flush against him.

Her closeness burned. He couldn't resist pressing his fingers into yielding flesh and was rewarded with her quick intake of breath. The sound conjured up images of them conjoined in sweetness, but the spell was hastily broken as she pulled away.

"Even children don't walk with their eyes closed." She moved the basket to her hip and eyed him mercilessly.

Makinde raised his hands in a conciliatory manner, but she was unyielding. She jerked her head left. He saw the carved pillar emerging from the earth indicating the town's entrance—an indication to travellers that they were close to Kuta.

"We have reached the border," she announced.

"I can see that," he replied slowly. He remained unsure of how to speak to this woman.

She stared at him as though they had a prior agreement.

"If we keep going ahead—" he started, running a hand over his head and missing the thickness and length of his hair. "Then turn eastwards—"

"You can cease the pretence." She cut him short.

No one ever spoke to him like this. Any other warrior would be incensed, but Makinde was fascinated. He lost himself watching her lips move, trying to understand what drove this woman's motives, and missed her next words.

"Meaning?"

If a look could kill a man, he would have been reduced to ashes. He took one step back, trying to show her he meant no harm. His gestures were useless.

"I don't need you to follow me to Olootu," she said, tapping her foot urgently. "As far as your clan is concerned, we are separated. Frankly, we were never a married couple to begin with. The farce doesn't have to continue."

"It isn't safe."

"While you were hiding in the forest, women and children have been plying this route for trade. The wars have ended."

Her chest heaved as she glared at him, and he instantly wanted to apologise though he was unsure of what. He wouldn't even know where to start. He took another step back and asked calmly.

"Do you know the way?"

"I do," she replied, her tone daring him to question how she did.

"Alright."

Ewa looked at him through squinted eyes. Then she turned, adjusted the strap of her bags, and marched forward. When she was a few paces ahead, she glanced behind to ensure he wasn't following her. She had no reason to bother—the only being behind her was Wuu the betrayer. At the sight of the dog, she laughed.

"Aren't you a disloyal one?"

The wind carried her words to him as she bade the animal to return back to his master. Makinde had never once wished he could trade places with his dog outside this moment. He remained rooted to the spot until Ewa vanished in the horizon and Wuu came running back, tongue hanging out of his grinning mouth.

IF Ewa concentrated, she would make fire. She straightened her back, took in a deep breath, and for good measure, touched the twigs piled in front of her.

"I call on my ancestors to intervene," she said.

She struck the stones. Sparks jumped, but the kindling remained uninspired. Her shoulders slumped. Around her, darkness crept as the sun bid the Earth goodbye. She was seated on an old blanket and spread next to her were her water gourd and evening meal—triangles of agidi wrapped in leaves.

When it came to meals, she didn't lack. She'd had the foresight to pack a number of useful things. Tope had ground melon seeds and locust beans, fermenting and spicing the mixture before toasting it. But turning the seasoning into stew required fire. Her stomach groaned at the prospect of eating the cold blocks of starchy meal alone.

She swept away the sticks with her hand for their lack of cooperation. Others easily accomplished such feats. She thought of little Tope always in the kitchen—the girl could light a fire. Every day, Tope ferried hot coals on a wire mesh for Ewa to brew medicines. Practice made perfect, and although Ewa was never relegated to kitchen chores, it made no sense to her how she failed at such a simple task.

Shadows stretched towards her. She brought her knees up to her chest and drew her arms over them. The forest transformed at night, wild predators who avoided humans during the day emerging to cavort in the absence of light.

She tilted her chin up and brought a hand to where she'd tucked the amulet Fadahunsi had prepared for her within the folds of her clothes. It should protect her from the wilderness. But even among people, she kept lamps burning while she slept. How was she going to rest in the dark forest?

She shivered and considered the dismissive words of Onilao as he rebuked her for her incompetence. It must have been the influence of the night that encouraged her to wonder if there was some truth to the elder's word. Even before she'd manoeuvred her way to Kuta, Lapade had complained, "You are worthless. Are you even a woman? Why, you are so weak!"

Ewa heard her stepmother's voice, high-pitched and ringing in her ear. She'd forgotten those words until this moment. It appeared this shift in her destiny was resuscitating long-buried memories in a latent part of her mind. Her grandmother never made her do household chores. As she grew older, her father had tried to get her to learn a trade, but she'd preferred to play with her friends. In her early days at Kuta, after she'd burnt yam fritters and prepared lumpy amala, the women had been astounded until Ogele had remarked it wasn't Ewa's destiny to cook. In time, they'd both discovered the only things she easily prepared were medicines.

Resting her chin on her folded knees, she sighed. It wasn't even a day since she'd left Kuta—regret was out of the option. She refused to admit how travelling alone was a terrible idea. Not that she wanted to be with that brooding giant of a man. Even now, she felt the imprint of his hands on her waist. It'd been as though he'd touched her bare skin. Her body had reacted instantly, sending shivers to the juncture of her thighs.

Her face heated at the memory. The man was a wizard. Her mind flitted to Jomiloju's stories of Makinde's sexual escapades. What if they were true? This meant all the time she was dousing her desire alone, he was slaking his away with the help of nubile temptresses. Her lips pinched together.

As the last of the day bled into night, she ate her bland meal. She downed the contents of her water container before realising too late she should have been more frugal. There had to be a stream around here, but tracing it was a mystery. In her bag was a square of cloth upon which she'd made Fadahunsi trace a map for her with charcoal. She failed to recall if he had indicated any streams.

It was too dark to check now. A heavy silence surrounded her. Ewa found herself longing for the chatter, pounding, laughter, bawling, even the goats bleating. She hadn't seen another soul since she'd parted with Makinde. If she had thought she was lonely before, this was agony. How had Makinde lived for years without even talking to another human being? She shook her head—she needed to stop thinking about him.

A twig snapped, the sound chilling her to the bone. Her pulse raced as she strained to see ahead of her. It was pitch black, but she thought she saw eyes staring back at her.

"Mother," she whimpered.

Slowly, she eased herself onto her back and screwed her eyes shut. Lips pursed, she held her breath hoping the animal would think her dead and leave her be. But what if the animal was a big one? Her heartbeat thrashed in her ears. She prayed to her Creator and ancestors.

Something large tumbled to the ground. She held from flinching when she felt a balmy breath on her face. A cold snout pressed against her cheek, nudging her.

"You can open your eyes."

Makinde's deep voice paralysed her like a scorpion's sting. If only the earth could split open and take her whole. Her fear rearranged itself into discomfiture. There was a clash of stones, and then warmth blazed to life beside her.

It was better to pretend to be asleep, she decided. A wet tongue lapped at the side of her face. She cranked an eye open to see Makinde's dog hovering over her. Behind him, Makinde crouched in front of the fire. His eyes met hers. She swallowed.

"It's you." She lifted up, propping her hand on the blanket. "What are you doing here?"

He opened his mouth as if to reply but sealed it, choosing silence. She flushed. In the light, she spotted the cleaned remains of a grass cutter standing on a stick. The oblong beaded pack he carried was on the ground next to it.

"I asked you to leave."

He looked at her, and she thought she saw concern in his eyes. Her heart was pounding, and this time, it wasn't due to alarm. She shouldn't have been so relieved to see this man.

"Your friend refused to listen," he replied.

"Who?"

"The one beside you."

The dog gazed at her expectantly, and she couldn't stop the smile spreading across her face.

"Do you call him by a name?" she asked, settling more comfortably so as to pet the animal.

Makinde cleared his throat. "Wuu."

"Wuu," she repeated. The sound brought to mind a longing bark. She gave a light chuckle. "Wuu can stay."

"I suppose I will have to take this game with me." Makinde tilted his head at the roasting meat.

Ewa bit her bottom lip. She wasn't supposed to be smiling at this man. Come to think of it, he wasn't supposed to be making comments like this.

"I will escort you to Olootu," he said, his tone final.

She wasn't going to argue with that. Just the day before, the deities had offered advice to her: patience, good character, to not repay kindness with evil. Makinde had brought food and warmth. Despite her small dinner, her stomach made gentle noises at the prospect of meat.

"It's only few days' trek." Looking down at Wuu who'd placed his head on her lap, she added softly, "Thank you."

Makinde grunted. Her eye twitched at this. He was a man of few words. She'd noticed this by now. She supposed a grunt in response to one's thanks was good enough for a man who hadn't lived with polite company in years. Before that, he'd been with warriors. She had seen men communicate with whistles and clicks sounding like bird song.

As dinner roasted, the air shifted. Suddenly, the forest didn't appear peculiar anymore, and silence didn't have to be oppressive or tense.

"This, too, will do," she whispered, keeping her gaze on Wuu.

Chapter Eight

The forest was still as though carved by a sculptor. Ewa started at the mask looming above her. All she saw was a white slash of teeth grinning against a camwood-red face. She blinked, and the illusion disappeared. What hovered over her wasn't a wood carving but a man. Another man squatted at her feet, his hands clenching a long spear impaled into the earth.

"You're as beautiful as they said."

She woke up with a start. She laid on her back with her arms folded over her chest, the image of stillness if one discounted her ragged breaths. Fingers of foreboding rubbed the length of her body, leaving her cold. She blinked up at the dawn sky lightening the canopy. Beside her, the dying embers of the fire crackled.

What had she seen in her sleep?

Even with the brightness of the open flame, she'd initially doubted her ability to sleep in Makinde's presence. Then the fatigue of the walk had dragged her eyes closed, and she'd slept so deeply, she'd dreamt. Now, the dream was fading away, leaving only a gravelly voice sounding in her mind.

She sat upright and looked over to the right where Makinde stared in deep contemplation of nothing with Wuu curled at his feet. This was the same spot he'd settled in when he'd appeared abruptly. It seemed he hadn't moved an inch since last night. She wondered if he had witnessed her in the clutches of a nightmare. She dismissed the thought—he hardly paid any attention to her.

"You've awakened."

She cleared her throat and inclined her head without saying a word. Makinde shifted so his back was to her, implicitly understanding she needed privacy. Her brows furrowed at this non-verbal communication. It must be Ogele's influence, she thought as she shrugged off her coverlet.

There was no need to overthink this—many others like her and Ogele didn't speak to anyone in the morning until they'd spoken to themselves in prayer. Growing up with Ogele, Makinde must have witnessed her communing with her Creator first thing in the morning.

Ewa walked away from the circle that had been their place of rest for the night. She held an unused chewing stick, a cotton washcloth, and the last of the water she carried. Finding a tree with a trunk large enough to shield her, she set her things down. Her fingers trailed the trunk as she made her way down to the ground. Legs curled to her side, she began her morning prayers.

"I pay homage to the One whose reign encompasses the world. To the rising sun and to dusk, to Mother Earth..."

She offered praises to the deities and the ancestors, as well as to her parents and Ogele. By the time she focused on her inner self, the disquiet that had followed her from the land of sleep had been firmly dislodged. She spoke to herself, affirming her reasons for embarking on this trip, reminding herself her faith wouldn't lead her to places that weren't good for her wellbeing.

Ewa prayed like she did every morning, uttering her requests to the Universe. As she concluded her prayers, warmth filled her. The most eager sun rays pierced the leaves ahead to dance on her skin.

"Whatever I might have said is accepted."

With those words, she started cleaning up. She stuck the stick in her mouth and ran it up and down her teeth. Behind her was the warrior she belonged to only in name. A strange mix of emotions welled in her belly at the thought of spending the entire day with him. She didn't trust him yet couldn't be unappreciative of his attention. The sooner she reached Olootu, the quicker she would be rid of him.

With this resolve, she dampened the towel and ran it over her skin. She then adjusted her clothing and returned to the clearing where she found him standing tall. It was as though he'd read her mind about continuing the journey with haste and agreed with her.

Her brows quirked at the sight of both her bags hanging over his shoulder. Yesterday, she would have argued, but today, she said nothing as she folded up the coverlet along with the faded blanket she'd slept on and stuffed them in her basket. As she moved, the only words exchanged were in the language of birds and Wuu who barked at them. Olootu was only seven days away— she hoped they could get there in five.

A MAJOR GRIPE LAPADE had with Ewa was in how it took her too long to admit her alleged wrongdoings. She was often blamed for broken water pots and unfinished errands assigned to her younger sister. Defending herself led to ugly spats with her stepmother. Rather than humble her, these experiences had strengthened her with confidence that only served to anger Lapade further.

Ewa was known to be stubborn to some in Odan, but this trait was beloved to Ogele. The old mother would be overjoyed if she saw them now, walking side by side on a path that had started inclining as it transported them from the light forest into a denser wilderness. For all she knew, the woman was laughing in the afterlife at the sight. Ogele frequently praised Makinde's kindness, "He is a good boy called to defend his family. That was something anyone in Kuta would proud of."

To Ewa, those were the sentimental words of a mother. She knew what she'd seen and what she'd felt upon Makinde's return to the homestead. Surely, a man making a fire and carrying her bags weren't enough to overturn her convictions of him? This awareness didn't prevent her from stealing glances at him. His dashing profile was proof Obatala must have been in a particularly creative mood when he moulded him. A man ought not to have such smooth skin. With his long hair gone, every feature was brought into focus: the whites of his eyes appeared brighter, his nose perfectly broad. The curve of his bottom lip made her remember all the gibberish Jomiloju said her friends had told her. Except when she imagined those lips on her body, the talk didn't seem nonsensical any more.

When she felt her basket sliding down the crown of her head, she had seen enough. She adjusted her load and mentally chided herself. She refused to be lost in this false sense of serenity. Words didn't fill a basket, no matter how beautiful they sounded. If this man was so kind, he wouldn't have abandoned her for years on end. A decent man would have set her free if he wasn't interested.

She straightened her spine and increased her pace, putting some distance between herself and Makinde. It was necessary lest she moved on from fantasising about his lips on her collarbone to his large hands cupping her breasts while his manhood pressed hot at her back. She heaved a frustrated sigh. Her face was as hot as a blacksmith's furnace.

Wuu ran up to her, jarring her back to reality and providing the perfect distraction. The dog had kept ahead of them, surveying the road before returning to walk at their pace. He sniffed at her knees and then dashed to Makinde. Ewa sucked her tongue. This was only the second day of journeying, and she needed to muster self-restraint.

Wuu started barking enthusiastically.

Makinde called out. "Wait, please."

Ewa paused. It was the second sentence he'd said to her all day.

"Is all well?"

They were in unsettled territory. Fadahunsi's directions indicated they should traverse this path into the denser woods before emerging by a steep hill. A short distance north of the hill was Ibukun where she could rest and prepare before continuing on to Olootu. They'd walked a considerable distance, the sun close to its zenith. However, there was still more ground to cover. Any delay meant more time in his company, and she didn't want this.

Makinde stood off the side of the path, his face level with a tiny bird perched on the bare branch of a naked tree. The bird was unperturbed by Wuu's snarls, and from where she waited, she saw it was unperturbed by Makinde, as well, remaining bold as the warrior approached it.

She clamped her lips into a thin line as he seemed to communicate with the bird. All animals boasted some spiritual significance, but birds especially so. This one with its feathers streaked brown and white opened its dark beak and chirruped as it flapped its wings. The high-pitched sound added to the cacophony of the forest.

The bird flew away singing, and Ewa breathed easier till it returned to beat its wings at Makinde's face. She counted as the bird repeated the motion five times. By then, Wuu's interest had ceased. She had mockingly referred to the man as a forest spirit once, and it seemed her words carried weight. She'd heard tales of hunters communicating with animals of the forest. Makinde must have earned the skill considering how he lived. As the bird flitted away once more, he stepped behind it.

"Where to?" she demanded. She hadn't moved from her spot.

He blinked at her as though he'd forgotten she was there. He cleared his throat. "This bird...It shouldn't take long. Follow me."

The man communicated better with living creatures than with humans. Sounds and gestures were all he and the bird needed as she followed them deeper into the trees. She was witnessing a spectacle in which a man communed with a bird. Stories like this would be entertainment for the children she would have, but as they trudged on, she grew impatient.

She bit back a grumble and kept after Makinde who tracked the bird as it hopped from tree to tree, chirruping as it went. After what felt like an hour, she heard a telltale buzzing before they reached their destination. The bird flew by and circled a large tree with a crack in its middle. Bees hovered around the gaping hole.

"Stay back."

He didn't have to warn her. She had been stung once while foraging with Iya Ogele, and that painful experience had instilled enough caution.

"Why were we led here?" she asked.

Makinde eyed the tree for a moment before suddenly spinning. He crossed the short distance between them in three steps, stopping so close to her, she shuffled back.

"When birds call like this—" he said, setting the bags he carried on the ground, "—they want honey."

Her gaze darted to the buzzing tree. "Won't you get stung?"

His reply was a grunt. He whipped out a short spear from his beaded bag, pressed it on the ground, and then pulled his tunic over his head.

Her eyes widened as he worked his trousers down. She turned away, but the damage had already been done. She had seen near-naked men before—there was no reason for her insides to turn hot and pulpy like roasted pears at the sight of the wide expanse of Makinde's shoulders.

The forest's detritus was more interesting when she bowed her head, her downcast eyes offering a full view of the corded muscles of his calves. Her head swam. She was possessed by a strange malady. There was no other explanation for her reaction to the man she hated.

As he rubbed a grassy mixture on his skin, she retreated farther away. She found a fallen tree solid enough to sit on and set her things aside. She was now far enough to evade any angry bees but still felt pulled to observe Makinde.

The man was strange, she decided. And it wasn't solely due to his communication with birds and dogs—maybe even bees. His form was ethereal as he began the task of gently extracting honey combs with the tip of his spear. Before her eyes, he transformed from a bloodthirsty warrior to a forest nymph. The sun breaking through the tall trees highlighted his features, bringing metal to her mind once more. She grew transfixed at the motion of the spear's end probing the beehive with care, honey oozing down the length of the tool reaching his hands.

She shook her head and covered her face with her palms. It was no use. She fought and failed to tear her gaze away from him. Her chest was heaving as he placed honeycombs onto the earth. The bird that had led them there immediately attacked the bounty, pecking at the combs while chirruping.

When he was done, he looked around for her. Her breath caught when his focus landed on her. Makinde stalked towards her, and she found herself rising in anticipation. The sun behind him made him glow as though he was carved of fire. Then he was in her space, his hands lifting up to her face. She couldn't breathe, but it didn't matter. She gripped the edges of her wrapper and waited.

A spongy stickiness touched her lips, and she gasped so he could press a piece of honeycomb into her mouth. The decadent sweetness of the treat flooded her tastebuds, eliciting a moan. Wanting more, she flicked her tongue to lick his thumb.

The salt of his skin elevated the cloying taste in her mouth and set her entire body aflame. Her mind filled with the need to spread honey across his skin just to trace her tongue over his wiry muscles, paying special attention to the indentation of the scars on his torso. The vision was so powerful, she had to close her eyes.

She felt the coolness of the air as he moved away. Her mouth was dry when she lifted her lids to see him feeding his dog. She took her bottom lip into her mouth and adjusted the folds of her wrapper. She wanted to pinch herself.

"Do you have an empty container?" he asked casually.

"Yes," she replied, her voice as low as a breath.

As she searched her basket for an extra water gourd, she wiped the sweat building at the base of her neck and on her forehead with her free hand. She found a stoppered gourd about the size of an extended hand with its own small lid.

Her knees shook as she approached Makinde with the container. Why did it feel like the honey he'd fed her was slowly transforming her insides into goo? She suddenly wanted to know what would happen if she fed him honey. Would he be as affected as she was? Would he lick her fingers, too? Her emotions worked her up into a state of utter confusion as Makinde filled the jar and secured it with twine he fashioned from a dried vine hanging off a tree.

"Shall we?" he asked as he returned her gourd.

"Let's pause for today. I need water."

She had to be away from him. She snatched the honey and started walking blindly, but he stopped her. His hand on her shoulder seared. Sparks danced on her skin as she leapt away.

"Forgive me," he said. "I will find the water."

Ewa nodded and gathered her water container as he shrugged on his clothes. When he was done, she thrust it blindly at him. She then retreated to the log, staying rooted to the spot while he built a fire and then disappeared into the woods with a tilt of his chin. Wuu stayed behind with her.

Alone, she released a breath and forced her shoulders relax. She wrapped her arms around her middle to stop herself from trembling. Her insides felt like they were erupting. She beckoned the dog close.

"Has your master woven a spell on me?" she asked.

Wuu whined in a reply she failed to understand.

EWA overflowed with questions she couldn't demand answers to. Makinde had learned as much after spending barely a day with her. She was strong-willed but not impractical. Otherwise, she would have chased him away when he'd come up to her the previous night.

She had been shrouded in darkness, tiny in the face of the dangers looming in the wild—from animals to men. He also knew she naturally objected to anything he said. This was why he had fed her. Or so he'd told himself. He hadn't been eager to feel the softness of her lips, to relish in the feel of her tongue lapping at his finger. The wet slickness had sent signals to his manhood. Blood had rushed south from his head, leaving him spinning. His own tongue had darted out to lick his lips at the memory. Honey sweetened the affairs of life, as the elders said. He savoured the feel of her for a moment longer then reminded himself he was here on duty. There was nothing to explore other than the scenery as he escorted her home.

He had to do right by the woman whose life he'd unwittingly ruined with his self-serving actions. That was all. It was what Ogele wanted. After Ewa had walked away outside Kuta, he'd considered heeding her demands for a brief second. Then he'd felt a cold wind around the back of his neck which could only be Ogele's disapproval from the beyond, wordlessly admonishing him for even thinking of letting Ewa out of his sight.

Over the next few days, he would steel himself. There wouldn't be any possibility of getting distracted in the way she moved. In a day, he'd memorised the gracefulness of her step, especially with a basket on her head. There was the line of her arm holding up the load, the soft fuzz of hair under her armpit, the way her posture made her wrapper pull downward exposing more of the swell of her breasts. He swallowed. *Be firm*, he reminded himself and hoped he wouldn't lose his mind.

Just as years in the forest had taught him what to expect from honey-birds, he easily found a water source. Crystal-clear water gurgled over mossy stones, forging an eastward path in search of a larger body of water. The elders often told stories of powerful human beings transformed to natural forces. He imagined such water sources were gifts from the deities themselves. He lowered himself to his knees to fill Ewa's container. At the moment he realised he'd forgotten to bring along his own casket, he saw an arm stretch from thin air on the other side of the spring.

It appeared as though someone lay on the ground, covered by the rocks and grass, but he knew better. There'd been a time when closing his eyes brought up images of the wars he had lived through. Somewhere along the lines, he no longer had to shut his eyes to see the crimes he'd committed for rulers, wealth, and fame. All traces of the amorous atmosphere Ewa had created in him vanished as an unworldly chill landed heavily on his back. His ears tingled as the wind whispered in them.

You're still alive.

He gritted his teeth in resolve. His hands clenched around the gourd now overflowing with water.

"Soon."

It took all his strength to straighten up with his legs now heavy weights. The forest chirped with life, uncaring of his plight. He was sober as he returned to where Ewa waited. A sonorous voice cut through the haze of pain, and regret surrounding him as he drew closer. The lyrics were familiar, a fantastical tale about a dead man speaking.

"All you landlords, close the door."

Makinde almost heard Ogele singing along with her. Such stories were how she consoled him after his mother had fled. As he drew closer, the aroma of seasoned sauce reached him. Ewa had set a pot on the fire. He waited until she'd drawn the song to a close before announcing his arrival.

"Iya Ogele often sang this."

She started at the sound of his voice. When she glanced up at him, he thought her eyes spoke of desires he was forbidden from entertaining.

The expression was gone too soon. She accepted the gourd he proffered with a steely demeanour and muttered her thanks. She went about the meal preparations as if he wasn't there. He leaned against the nearest tree, observing her. The pot contained leftovers from last night's dinner bubbling in palm oil. She brought a square of cloth from one of her bags and emptied its contents, a handful of black tumbled stones. She dumped them into the water gourd. Ogele used stones like these to purify water.

"How dare you mention her name so casually?"

"Pardon?"

"You weren't around when she lived, and you weren't around when she passed away. What right do you have to call her mother?" Ewa's attention was on the fire as she accused him. "You didn't bid her farewell. The woman raised you, and you were absent when we sent her forth."

"I did," he stated.

He crossed his arms over the expanse of his chest. When Ewa wasn't silent, she donned an invisible armour and released sharp words like throwing knives.

"Are you a spirit? Do you move in the shadows like Ojiji? How did you send forth Iya and no one witnessed you do it? All the years you were away, she missed you dearly. You didn't come to see her once."

"I saw her before she departed." He didn't want to sound defensive. He wasn't the best son, but Ewa had no idea how precious Ogele was to him.

"Nonsense. I've been to where you secreted yourself. Iya Ogele was too old to make that trek."

"She was." He had said too much.

Ewa drew her lips together. "Were you at Odan?"

The blood running through him grew as cold as spring water collected at the crack of dawn. He met her accusatory gaze. Odan was where she'd spent the early years of her life, and she had to know the answer yet she'd asked. There was another question left unasked hanging in the air which she chose not to give words to.

Makinde let his arms fall to the side as his chin dipped, avoiding her gaze.

"Yes," he said, his voice a low timbre.

Ewa looked to the side, her eyes watery. She remained silent for the rest of the day. A younger Makinde might have struggled to explain he was at Odan but not like those other warriors with their insatiable lust for blood and violence fed over the course of thirteen brutal days. He was nothing like the ruler whose selfish actions ignited the flame and the other one who had blown the fire until it blazed high and long enough to consume the neighbouring states. He had failed to control things in his unit then, but there was no use in crying over a broken pot. No one understood, and he didn't expect them to. He'd made his choices and his failures. He could have chosen to visit the temple; he could have paid for the lives he'd taken in the secretive rituals.

But he needed to remember. The hauntings he saw weren't spiritual retribution.

They were a clarion call to fix things the only way he knew how, with his weapons spilling blood.

Chapter Nine

This part of the forest was shadier. Thick trees grew closer like siblings, making the day appear like evening. Ewa's mind was closed to the verdant beauty around her. She didn't stop to appreciate the branches heavy with leaves and flowers or hear the cacophony of the forest animals in conversation.

Even Wuu failed to bring a smile to her lips. Her mind was cast to the past, deep into the waters where she'd flung memories too painful to remember. Since leaving Kuta, they came to her in dreams that frightened her awake, only to disappear from her consciousness as she rose to greet the day. She had no business being attracted to Makinde when he was part of the reason her hometown had been wiped off the Earth.

Losing focus was unadvisable. She was walking an unfamiliar path with the warrior trailing behind her. Regardless, she pictured Odan. It had been a sizeable town surrounded by a deep ditch, like Kuta was. To the south and west was lightly-wooded forest broken by patches of farmland.

Palm trees dotted the hills behind her parents' home. Her father grew the grain her mother fermented into different kinds of alcohol. She followed her mother to Eripa—the neighbouring town less than half a day's trek from their home—to sell the drinks. She would steal sips when her mother wasn't looking. Those had been the days she knew true happiness. The merriment vanished on the day her mother died in the clutches of bringing a younger sibling into the world. Barely a year later, her father introduced Lapade to her as her new mother.

"We should find shelter," Makinde said, his cool voice a monotone slashing through her contemplation.

She twisted her lips in a grimace and kept walking. She intended to ignore him like he did her. However, she was unused to meeting statements directed at her with a wall of silence. With each passing breath, the back of her neck itched as though he were staring at this spot.

"There remains a lot of ground to cover if we want to make it to Olootu in time."

"It is going to rain," he replied.

Ewa stopped walking. The soles of her feet felt prickly in her sandals and were begging for rest. With some difficulty considering the basket she carried on her head, she tilted her head right and was rewarded by the brilliant blue sky. The heat of the day clung her clothes and to her body.

"I believe we're fine," she said, already resuming her trek.

She was scared to imagine the results of lingering in Makinde's company. The honeycomb incident was proof enough. She might forget the man had been among the party responsible for serious crimes. *When elephants fight, the grass suffers.* This had been the case of Odan and Eripa, towns ripped apart due to their leaders. Every single family in Odan had felt the blows of their ruler's crime.

The mere fact lust coiled in her belly at the sight of him was an abomination. It would be an insult to her people for her to entertain the fancies his physique tempted her into.

She quickened her pace and kept at it till a drop of water fell from the sky, landing on her back. She flinched as it travelled down her wrapper. Another drop splashed on her upright arm. Damn it. She started a slow run. Wuu whined excitedly as a pleasant drizzle sprayed over them. It was now impossible to ignore the promised deluge. She angled her face away from Makinde as she retreated under the generous arms of a dominant tree.

She pressed her back against its rough trunk just as Makinde stalked in her direction. He took position to her left, not next to the tree but close enough to benefit from its shade. Ewa transferred her basket to the ground. She knew this tree, its upside-down leaves—thinner at the stem, widening to a soft curved tip—marking it as one of two ingredients used in a medicine to heal wounds.

"Thank you for the shelter," she whispered.

Storm clouds dimmed the day into dusk. Strong wind shook the forest around them, whipping dirt against her face. Blinking the dust away, she said a prayer to the forces of nature.

"Winds of the Heavens, bring blessings to me."

When thunder sounded, she praised it as king. Wuu curled behind Makinde, uncharacteristically frightened of the downpour. Minutes passed, then lightning cracked to reveal figures emerging in the distance.

Ewa counted three bodies shrouded by rain and mist dashing from the opposite direction they'd come from.

Makinde took a stance in front of her as if he meant to protect her. She bit her tongue to keep from tossing a barbed word his way. She wished he would stop pretending to be good-hearted.

Tense, his hand was on the satchel on his back. He was poised to easily remove the same spear he'd used to fetch honey and launch it in defence. She briefly wondered what other weapons must be wrapped in that bag.

The child reached them first. She refused to come under the shelter of the tree and laughed wildly at her parents lagging behind. The rain soaked the length of cloth she held over her head. Ewa grinned when the girl stuck her tongue out at them. When the adults appeared, the woman waddled awkwardly supported by her man, her stomach round like a full moon.

"Greetings!" Ewa called. She beckoned them to the relative dryness of their natural shelter.

"It is raining so heavily, isn't it?" the man said, panting. He guided his heavily pregnant wife away from the rain.

"With how bright the sun was earlier, who could have foretold a storm?" she replied.

Makinde grunted, slinking away from them with his dog in tow. Ewa had real company now—she wouldn't miss him. It was just as well he was as mute as a statue. She moved aside so the woman placed her back against the tree and slid to the leaf-strewn ground.

"Gbala, come out of the rain," the mother called weakly to the daughter who splashed in the mud.

"Listen to your mother. You've played enough."

Gbala obeyed. She offered her greetings to Ewa who beamed in response. Then Ewa stuck out her tongue at Gbala, causing the girl to burst into peals of laughter.

"We have met under fortuitous circumstances," the woman said when she'd caught her breath. "I am Tundun, and this is my husband, Ore."

"I am Ewadunni."

The family were traveling light, and their clothing appeared threadbare, but the affection within the unit was easy to remark upon. Ore was tenderly wiping down their daughter with the edge of his sopping shirt while Tundun made Gbala blow her nose into the edge of her wrapper. Ewa opened her basket in search for a blanket. The girl was bound to catch a cold with the way she played in the rain.

"And what of your husband?" Tundun asked.

Her hands froze as she touched the thickly spun indigo fabric. "Makinde. Please accept this blanket for Ore. Is it wise for you be travelling at this time?"

She was jumping from one sentence to another, but she was only desperate to distract the couple. Makinde had left, but she wished he'd disappeared earlier. It hurt to accept Tundun referring to him as her husband, but the woman was a stranger and so didn't warrant the lengthy truth.

Tundun rubbed her belly, and as she cast a pleasant gaze on Ore, her lips broadened into a grin. Ore made an impatient sound while smiling in return. Passing the blanket to Ore, Ewa realised she was on the outside of a secret between the two.

"Thank you, Ewadunni." Ore wrapped Gbala snugly and held her close as though she were a baby. "Maybe you can help me admonish her."

"What for?"

Ore shook his head in an exaggerated manner. "I said we should leave weeks ago, but my wife insisted on selling all the produce first."

"How else would I ensure you earned enough to give me the best care?" Tundun replied.

They laughed in unison, even Gbala joining the chorus with silent giggles. They made their companionship appear so easy. Ewa had seen many couples joke like this, teasing each other over minuscule things. Her parents had been similar. Whenever her mother bought a new bolt of cloth, she would wear it and parade in front of her father like a peacock. They would share meaningful glances she now knew signified love, an emotion that was a stranger to her.

She cleared her throat. "You're coming from the farm?"

"Yes," Tundun said. "And now, we're heading home to welcome our second child."

"I can't wait to see everyone," Gbala interjected from Ore's arms. She took over, talking about brothers and sisters in the homestead and the delicious soup her father's mother made.

"Is it better than my own soup?" Tundun teased.

"I will eat mama's soup and grandma's, too," Gbala replied without care.

PERCHED behind where he saw but wouldn't be seen, Makinde was buffeted by rain and wind. Wuu shivered at his feet. The first rains of the season were temperamental. If Ewa had listened to him earlier, he might have found a cave where they could have set a fire for warmth. He would have constructed a shelter to protect them from the storm.

But she'd stubbornly refused, and now, he stood in the rain. Ewa was of course more courteous than him, offering conversation and her own blanket with ease. Her attention was a stark contrast to the face she showed him.

He closed his eyes and listened to the banter just to focus on her voice. His head rocked back. For the umpteenth time in just a few days, he thought of what he couldn't give her. Whatever destiny led her path to cross with his cursed one, he should have done things properly years ago. As beautiful as Ewa was, she would have found a suitor immediately. Fate could have twisted things so she was the one with a farmer husband who rubbed her extended belly and made her throw her head back in teasing laughter.

Rather than placate him, though, these thoughts caused his chest to burn. He clenched his teeth. He had to stop fantasising about Ewa and redirect this energy to Arole, the brother-in-arms who had betrayed him at Odan, shocking him with his appalling behaviour. All these years, he'd bidden his time, waiting for revenge and then redemption.

But now, his head ached with inconceivable notions as the tinkle of Ewa's laughter mingled with the rain. Would it be too late to return to her after he'd dealt with Arole? Would she even have him?

The rain battering over his head told him the answer. They were heading to Olootu to finalise their separation.

AS the shower drew to an end, Ewa breathed the clean-scented air into her lungs and exhaled with a sigh, refreshed. She'd talked with Tundun to the point where they'd transformed from strangers who had met on the road to old friends.

As evening settled, the men managed to get a fire going. As the women warmed by it, the men wandered off to gather fruits. Ewa set an earthen pot to simmer with the watery stew made from Tope's spices. She shredded the meat Makinde had hunted two days ago and added it to the broth. Ore had produced small tubers of yam now roasting on the charcoal. Gourds of water holding the last of the rainwater sat near the flames. Ewa had put purifying stones in each container, even the ones belonging to the farming couple.

As dinner cooked, she couldn't resist examining Tundun. She felt her pulse and then held the woman's belly, prodding and probing. She put her ear to Tundun's stomach.

"You really should have been home by now," she said.

"Is anything amiss?" Tundun asked.

At her concerned expression, she reined in her censure.

"Nothing is amiss."

She grasped Tundun's thin hand. Too used to community, she viewed giving birth outside the watchful eye of older women with trepidation. Oftentimes, elders were a pain to deal with, but it was no reason to discount the important roles they played. The mothers held the woman in labour—they washed her with leaves and prayed for her well-being; they counted down to the child's arrival; they ensured she was well-fed. The list was endless.

"We needed the money, Sister."

Ewa nodded in understanding. She hadn't lived among a prosperous clan for too long as to grow insensitive to the plight of others. She rifled through her belongings, and when she found what she was looking for, placed the clay jar into Tundun's hands. Tundun shifted the lid of the pot to examine its contents, gnarled roots that sent a sharp fragrance through the air.

"Try to boil and drink this twice a day. It will strengthen you for the journey ahead."

"You are truly a healer. Who travels with herbs among their belongings? Thank you, Ewadunni."

Ewa beamed in reply then turned to check on their dinner.

"Your man says very little." Tundun observed casually.

"He is reserved," she replied, glad her back was to the woman.

"How were you married?"

"My family arranged it."

"Oh! Did you love him?"

"I didn't."

"What a pity. You make a handsome couple."

How many lies must she tell this woman? If Tundun kept asking questions, she feared she might carelessly reveal the ugly truth. A small cough from Gbala, who had been laying with her head on Tundun's lap, drew Ewa's attention.

"She must be cold," Tundun said, rubbing circles on her daughter's back underneath the blanket. "See why you shouldn't be playing in the rain."

Ewa left the fire to face them. They were all huddled around it for warmth so she didn't have to move far. She placed the back of her hand on Gbala's forehead. It was only slightly warm and not feverish. As she drew her hand away, she noticed circular scabs on the girl's head. She'd missed them before with the way Ore had wrapped her up from the rain. She studied the scabs.

"How long has Gbala had those rashes?"

Tundun lifted Gbala's arm to show more patches of ir-ritated skin, causing the girl to wince. "It has been about a week. But she's a hearty child so we weren't worried."

She kept an arsenal of dried medicines in her bag because Ogele had taught her to always be prepared. Ewa carried a mixture of shea butter and leaves that brought down fevers, but she racked her brain to figure out if she had something for Gbala's scabs.

"I should have an ointment to warm her up. When you reach your home, consider calling on a healer."

"Thank you. May you be blessed richly. May your chil-dren take care of you in your old age."

Ewa gave a tight smile in reply. She searched for the fever-reducing balm while inwardly chiding herself. Tundun had prayed for her as any grateful client would. She should be happier at pronouncements of this nature—her freedom was already hers. She would find a loving husband who would take care of her and her children.

"Sister Ewadunni," Tundun said. "You mentioned you were coming from Kuta. Is that your hometown?"

"I'm from Odan," she replied. She resumed her pretence of watching over dinner.

"Ei! The same Odan from that war?"

She averted her gaze. What was taking the men so long? She needed Ore to come and distract to his wife.

"I am so sorry. What those warriors did was barbaric. We give thanks such dark days are behind us."

Ewa needed to introduce another topic. She racked her brain for ideas but was unsuccessful.

The detritus rustled as Ore stepped into the ring of light.

"I hope you aren't discussing war," he said. "It's bad luck."

She noticed Makinde behind him, his lips pressed to thinness, suggesting he'd heard Tundun's words, too. She wanted to ask him what his role had been at Odan once again. Perhaps in front of an audience, he would be forced to give a reply. She was certain he'd been there—the warriors that had set upon her and her family had known the name Makinde.

Never one to cause a scene, though, she pursed her lips and lifted the pot from the fire.

"We all pray that war no longer visits the land," Tundun said.

Ore shuddered. "With the way the sons of Jaku are squabbling for the throne, I hope your prayer is answered."

Gbala coughed again.

"Baba," she said stretching her hands out so Ore could carry her.

From the corner of her eye, Ewa noted Makinde's demeanour had shifted. He was a quiet man who kept to himself, but mention of war made a muscle in his jaw tic. His eyes narrowed as though he saw something they couldn't. *What did Odan mean to him? What did Jaku?*

"It is time to eat."

Food was the best conclusion to the tumultuous discussion. As soon as they finished eating, she would tell a story. She decided on the one with the tortoise.

The fire divided both families. She and Makinde were terribly unsuited for each other, eating in silence when across from them. Ore and Tundun lavished attention on each other. Ore broke clumps of yam with his fingers, dipping it in the sauce before feeding Gbala. Tundun lifted one of their water containers for her husband to sip from.

It was all too much for Ewa. She lost her taste for the food and for storytelling.

Chapter Ten

The following day, Ewa rose with dawn. The delicate coughs of the little girl had kept her on the shores of sleep, barely delving into the deeper rest she needed. The morning was colder due to the rain of the previous day, and she shivered. She'd offered one of her two blankets to Gbala, and as a consequence, had slept rougher than usual.

The trio curled beside each other, fast asleep with Gbala cocooned between Ore and Tundun. She envied them for the warmth they enjoyed. To her right, Makinde sat with his back pressed against a tree. His eyes were shut, and his chest rose evenly with his breathing, but she doubted he was asleep. There was an alertness in his posture bringing to mind a stalking predator lying in wait for the perfect opportunity to strike its prey.

Giving him a wide berth, she tiptoed away from the camp and rushed through her morning salutations, whispering them as she wove through the woods while early birds called greetings to each other. The low leaves brushing her bare shoulders were heavy with dew. With the soft light of the rising sun, she searched for the ẹru plant. Its five-pointed leaves relieved sores when made into a paste—they would cure the scabs on Gbala's head.

By the time she returned, everyone was awake. Tundun shook out the blanket she had lent them.

"Good morning, Sister," she said. "You're back."

"Good morning." Her eyes searched for Gbala who was walking away with Ore. "How is Gbala?"

"She is well but insisted her father take her to ease herself." With the blanket folded, Tundun extended it to her. "Thank you for your kindness."

"Are you resuming your journey right away?"

"We ought to. The sooner we arrive home, the better it will be for all of us."

"Wait for the while it takes me to make this leaf paste." She showed Tundun the leaves clutched in her right hand.

"What are they for?"

"To heal the sores on Gbala's body. Help me boil some water."

Makinde was fixed like a solitary star around the hubbub of their activity as the women worked. Ore fed Gbala dark purple berries. Wuu rested his head on his crossed front paws, sleepy.

"You didn't greet your man this morning?" Tundun asked in a low whisper. They were crouched in wait as the leaves boiled.

Ewa pursed her lips. Tundun was a kind soul, but her constant prodding was irksome.

"If you're arguing, just cleave to him."

"We aren't quarrelling."

Tundun seemed to think herself an authority on marital relations. She carried on despite Ewa's objection. "If he's the one that upset you, smile at him, and he will forget everything. He regards you as if you are a precious egg."

"He is only eager to resume the journey. Do you happen to have any palm oil?"

"I believe so."

"Get it ready. We will need it for the paste."

Ewa managed to evade more intrusions as they made quick work of the paste. Afterward, she gathered her belongings and bid her new friends farewell. Tundun and Gbala embraced her tightly while Ore bowed his head with thanks. As the family walked down the path she and Makinde had come up from, she kept her eyes on Gbala's frail shoulders and Tundun's rolling gait. She prayed they made it to their destination in good health.

"We should continue," Makinde said.

"So you speak." She turned to see him carrying her basket and bags for her.

The polite thing to do was to thank him for his help—after all, her head was now free of the load of her belongings—but she sniffed and began walking. She felt him follow her without a word. They would rest in Ibukun before heading on to Olootu, and she entertained the thought of dismissing him there. She could find a group of traders travelling in the direction of Olootu and join them. She had enough of being in this man's company. Meeting with Tundun and her family had reminded her of the normalcy she craved. Makinde existed outside of that sphere.

Not an hour after setting off, she heard shouting behind her. She spun and saw Ore barrelling towards them.

"Help!"

Her heart immediately leapt to her throat. Fear stole her tongue as Ore skidded to a stop and doubled over, panting.

"What is the matter?" Makinde asked, unreasonably calm.

Ewa blinked up at him then at Ore. The absence of his wife and daughter sent her mind racing to the worst scenarios. First, that they were under attack, and then that Tundun had gone into a premature labour.

"It's Gbala," the farmer managed to spit out. "Please save my daughter. We thought she was fine, but she still has a fever. She's too weak to continue the journey."

Ore's eyes bore into Ewa, his hands clasped before him in supplication. She dipped her chin. She knew the remedy for sores on a child's head, and she knew how to reduce a fever. She had given Tundun those medicines. Whatever afflicted Gbala now would only reveal itself through observation.

Her head spun at the short window of time. Before she could see Gbala, go out in search for the required medicine, and then prepare it, the day would have wasted. Forcing herself to breathe, she straightened her back.

"Take me to her."

They backtracked on the dirt road. She jogged beside Ore, grateful not to be saddled with her belongings. She schooled her features to prevent showing panic. She ought to have known. The child had been coughing through the night. Ogele would have been able to tell what afflicted the child by merely looking at her. After all these years of studying, Ewa was still lacking. If only she was in Kuta where there was an assortment of medicines readily available with

Jomiloju primed to help. Herbs were more powerful when picked at dawn or at dusk, and the high sun mocked her.

Her throat constricted, and it had nothing to do with how running set her lungs on fire. She pushed on in fear the child may be dead by the time they reached her. She could already see it in her mind, Tundun wailing over her daughter's body. She muttered a prayer to condemn the image.

"How can I lose a child with another on the way?" The words rushed out of Ore's mouth between gasps for air.

"Don't speak like that!"

Ewa needed to think. Doing this without seeing the child was risky, but time wasn't on her side. She racked her brain in search for possible illnesses based on Gbala's symptoms. Gbala coughed and had a high temperature. There were rashes on her body. Half a dozen possibilities popped into her mind. If only she could split herself in two, sending one part to the forest while the other reached Gbala. Her attention was so focused inwards, she didn't notice the tangle of vines in front of her until she slipped.

The reddish earth reached for her, and she extended her arms to break her fall. Pain shot through her wrists and her left hip as she collided with the ground. At the same time, her insides protested from the physical exertion she'd just put her body through. Her chest heaved violently with each breath, and tears stung her eyes. No one had passed away under her care, and already, she felt responsible for poor Gbala.

"What I have won't be enough," she said, her voice cracking. "I need to...need to find the herbs."

A large hand wrapped around her upper arm and pulled her up to her feet. Her eyes clashed with Makinde's intent gaze. He leaned over her, and for a second, she thought she saw anger in those deep brown pools. The way the space between his brows creased told a different story—he was worried.

Makinde scanned her face, the corner of his lips tensed. Her heart was racing, and she couldn't bear his attention. She looked at Ore.

"There isn't time enough for me—"

"Use me," he cut her short.

In any other situation, her head would have snapped in his direction. But Makinde still propped her upright, and his face hovered so closely above hers. His firm fingers found her chin and turned her face to his. It was bewildering how even in this moment, desire started rising in the midst of fear. She put her other hand to her belly. This wasn't the place.

"Tell me what you need," he said.

"Can you...?"

"I can."

Not many knew how to identify useful herbs. It'd taken her years to tell apart the ìrà tree from the idí tree, as both had wide oval leaves. His tone was assured, reminding her this was the boy Ogele had raised.

There was no time. She steadied herself, pulling away and breaking their contact. She called out the names of cleansing herbs, those she didn't have. She retrieved her medicine bag from him but left the rest of her materials in his care.

"I'll find you," he said before disappearing into the woods.

Ewa hoped he remembered it all. She inclined her head at Ore before they resumed running.

IN his youth, Makinde had walked to the woods with Ogele when he wasn't combat training. His fellow comrades—boys his age—teased him mercilessly for it. "The boy whose mother ran away, always begging for a mother!" they mocked. Then he and Arole would leap on the bullies. Ogele used to eye the bruises and wounds from their scuttles and shake her head.

"You know why your mother ran away?" she'd asked. Not expecting an answer from him, she'd continued. "No human that has been enslaved, no matter how splendid the house they are kept in, won't long for freedom."

One of the reasons he cleaved to Ogele was her brutal honesty. If not for her, he would have remained ignorant about his mother's true backstory—of a woman captured in war and kept as booty by his own father. He would also have been lost in the forest, not knowing how to approach trees the way a healer might.

His own bloodied hands were inadequate; regardless, he resolved to do his best for Ewa. He collected the herbs she needed and tracked them back to where they'd camped the previous night. He stood by her side, ready to complete any task she required. She was strung up with tension, and for the first time, didn't resist his assistance. He noted she only started breathing properly when Gbala was no longer in pain.

Two sleepless nights passed by with Ewa attending to both child and mother.

Asking her to walk with him to the stream he'd found was pushing his luck, and he didn't waste time questioning why he of all people concerned himself with her wellbeing. She needed rest and time away from the farmer and his family. While he was yet to exchange more than a few sentences with Ore and Tundun, he knew they were kind. Yet, their concern for their daughter overrode any they'd for Ewa's comfort. They would have Ewa working from dawn till dusk with her not minding one bit. He had expected some resistance, but her positive response was welcome.

Now, he led the way to the stream. There was no path here, and she followed him so closely, her breath caressed his back. The vines overhead draped along his shoulders, but if he closed his eyes, it could have been Ewa running her fingers down his skin, tracing the scar below his shoulder blade.

"She must have been sick for a while," she said, yawning. "They will need to find a priest when they get back home."

To be completely cured of the pox, one must be admitted to the temple of Obaluaye. Gbala had yet to be inoculated, as young as she was. Makinde ran a hand over his head. He was unused to small talk. Everything he'd discussed for ten years either concerned Arole, his activities as Ojiji, or to justify his choices.

His silence snatched Ewa's words as they moved. Soon, the battering sound of water flowing over rocks grew louder. He stopped abruptly at the edge of the short cliff overlooking the stream. She bumped into him from behind. Her hands brushed his back, and he stopped breathing. Her fingers imprinted on him, her brief touch surpassing anything he had imagined.

"Forgive me."

She withdrew, and the sweep of her fingers against his skin zapped him like lightning. He longed to feel her hands on every inch of him.

But the moment was gone.

In front of him, the ground dipped almost directly into a shallow river so clear, the stones at its bottom were visible. He lowered down first and turned, arms raised to aid her. His throat bobbed at the anticipated contact. She would hold on to him, her body pressed flush against his before sliding down into the water.

Ewa surveyed the distance from the cusp of the trees. Makinde opened his mouth to encourage her—she didn't need to fear when he was there. To his surprise, she bent at the knees and leapt. She landed with a splash. Cool water hit his side as she squealed in delight.

"So you do smile?"

He hadn't realised how his facial expressions had morphed into a lie of happiness. At her words, he schooled his face. She paid him no mind. The water reached her knees, and she dipped her hands in, cupping some of the clear liquid to her lips. The sunlight reflecting on the water created crystals of light that sparkled around her form.

He tore his eyes away and began filling the gourds, then placed the full containers high on the ground. Inevitably, his focus found her once more. There were questions stamped on her face. Perhaps she wanted to ask him how he always found water, or how he'd found the herbs she needed earlier.

She elected to keep her lips sealed, seeming distracted by a silver form darting in the stream.

Her face lit up as she said, "Let's fish."

He wasn't eager to return just yet. Especially now they knew Gbala was out of death's cusp.

"I will sharpen sticks."

They easily crossed to the other side of the shallow stream. Ewa found a large rock with a smooth surface to sit on while he disappeared to get what they needed. He scanned the detritus for solid branches. He disliked hacking at trees, and besides, he didn't have the tools for that with him. The knife at his waist was only suitable for sharpening the ends of the branches and fashioning them into spears.

He tapped his fingers against his thighs, concerned by Ewa waiting alone by the riverside. He snatched up sticks lying on the forest floor until he had four in his hand. With quick steps, he hastened back. He burst out of the woods, but as he neared the stream, his stride eased. She was stretched out on her back, her sleeping face upturned to the sky. She'd curled on the stone as though she was a spirit just crawled out of the water to rest under the sun.

Small beads of water flaked her skin, the flawless fawn reminiscent of an antelope. She'd loosened her wrapper and carelessly tossed it across her chest, revealing the mounds of her brown breasts. Each breath threatened to send her cloth gliding lower, promising him a glimpse of her nipples. His mouth watered. The manhood he'd trained to sleep because revenge needed no distractions awakened with a roar begging to dip in Ewa's pool.

With great difficulty, he turned his back to her and retreated to the cover of the trees. He sat on the ground with a thud and began sharpening the sticks. The woman was tired. He had asked her here to rest, and she clearly needed it.

He lost himself to the repetition of dragging his knife across wood, the sound of the stream and chattering monkeys keeping him company. He'd finished while she remained in deep sleep. As the day progressed, he was loath to disturb her rest. He made his way back to her and stood, taking in her shuttered lids below thick curved brows, her plump lips and bridge-less nose, her pointed chin.

This was enough. This must do, he promised himself. Whatever lust propelled him towards Ewa wouldn't go past this point. He would drink in the sight of her and then deliver her to Olootu. Afterwards, he would tear down the country in search of Arole. And then after that? He didn't know.

Stretching out his right hand, he gently rubbed Ewa's shoulder. Her brows creased, then she blinked up at him. Under the influence of sleep, her regard was gentle. There was the ghost of a smile on her lips that turned into a gasp as she shot upright.

"It's getting late," he said. "If we still want to fish..."

He let the sentence hang in his usual manner.

"Yes, yes." She righted her wrapper, knotting it around her neck and securing the shorter length of fabric right under her breasts.

As she slid from the stone bed, he tossed his tunic over his head and bent over to roll up his trousers.

"The tools?"

"Here."

He dashed to get the makeshift spears, handing one to her. She took the lead, hiking her wrapper up to her knees, exposing toned legs.

"You stand there," she said, pointing behind her. "I'll guide the fish I miss to you."

Makinde cocked a brow but did as told. Ewa stood ahead while he assumed position a few paces behind and to her left. His throat itched, so he cleared it with two grunts. He reminded himself of the promise he'd made barely a minute ago.

"Where did you learn this?" he asked.

"You have no faith in my technique?"

She leaned forward, still as a tree as she peered into the stream. When she jabbed the spear into the waters and lifted a fish in the air, it was clear she was skilled. She left the first catch at the shore and returned.

"Growing up, my friends and I spent days fishing. We would smoke our catch and sell them."

"That's quite...entrepreneurial." He lunged at gliding fish, eager to show her he, too, was good at this.

She threw her head back in laughter at the sight of his empty spear.

"You startled it."

His accusation caused her to laugh harder. She appeared less burdened today, and he basked in it. He saw himself getting used to the sound of her joy. He also wanted to keep talking to her, the melody of her voice almost comparable to the times he sat in meditation with nature.

"I was the opposite," she said.

"The opposite?"

"I'm not business-minded. All the money we made from selling, we used to buy palm wine, distilled alcohol, and grain beer. We danced till dawn at the night markets."

This broke his attention. He stared at her, at her tight head wrap she never removed and sombre-coloured wrappers. Ogele had once described Ewa as proper during one of her attempts to lure him from the forest. Ewa could do no wrong. She was the epitome of womanhood, resilient but flexible, and always respectful to others. With the blue skies above them and water trickling between their legs, he tried to picture her in her youth rebelling against societal expectations. How did they get here, together, because the elders had deemed it so?

Ewa triumphantly brandished another fish.

"Have I grown another head?" she asked as she wadded to the shore.

"No." He scratched his ear. "Were you punished for visiting the night markets?"

"All the time. My father's wife couldn't stand me."

"Your father's wife? And your mother that birthed you?"

He didn't miss the way her face darkened. "She joined the ancestors when I was about Gbala's age. Baba swore he would never remarry. The family ensured he did."

"I am sorry."

He hadn't lost a mother to the cycle of life and death—however, he'd only been a few years older than Ewa had been when he'd walked in on his mother's escape. In the rooms with her satchel bursting with valuables, Asake hadn't expected to see him. He remembered her rubbing his hair and pushing a plate of fried plantains in his hands because he complained of hunger. He had bit into the stone-cold plantains as she'd slipped away. Her behaviour had been strange, but he hadn't thought much of it until uproar had erupted later that night. "Where is Asake? Bring her to me!"

"You broke it."

Ewa's voice tore him away from his reflections.

He held the split spear in his hands. The stick's roughened edges bit into his palm, but he didn't feel any discomfort. He retrieved another stick from the river's edge. They resumed fishing. Mercifully, she didn't demand to know why he'd reacted this way for seemingly no reason. He was relieved to add to the growing number of fish she caught.

"Were you a good son?" she asked suddenly. "Iya Ogele must have doted on you."

"I have always done as needed," he responded, staring at the flowing water.

From the corner of his eye, he noticed her pause. She straightened, placed a hand on the curve of her hip, and regarded him. She had to know the question she'd asked so light-heartedly pricked something in him. This was why he favoured silences. He longed for laughter and ease, perhaps more so than he would ever admit, yet, walking there inevitably opened the door to tension and painful memories.

Silence reigned as they gathered more fish than was necessary for their party of five. He was in charge of cleaning them while she shaped them into rolls, pinning tail to mouth with a stick. It didn't escape him how efficiently they worked together. Was this what Ogele meant?

He thought back to the evening when he'd run from the cave. He entertained the possibility of Ogele's dream, holding it in his mouth like he was savouring a delectable soup. He couldn't keep it down. He'd agreed to separate with Ewa—she wasn't his and would never be.

He turned his mind to his future, him and Wuu in the wilderness searching for his comrade turned tormentor. It was all he had thought of for years, and yet, in this moment, there was a dryness in his mouth as he replayed his convictions.

"We will leave early tomorrow morning," Ore said.

They'd eaten a dinner of roasted fish and the tubers the farmer travelled with. Gbala was slowly regaining her appetite and ate only a little. The fire at the centre of the circle they formed cast orange glows on all their faces.

"I understand," Ewa replied. It made no sense to tarry longer considering how heavy Tundun was. If only they had magical shoes to transport them to the nearest town with Obaluaye priests.

"You said you're going to Olootu?" Ore asked. At her nod, he carried on. "Our farm is within a day's journey from there."

"Our journey ends at Olootu." She wondered the direction Ore's words were going to, and it was only after she'd spoken that she realised her choice of pronoun. Her fingers flew to her lips. She'd said "our" as opposed to "my."

A flush spreading across her cheeks, she cut a glance at Makinde. Judging by his cool regard of the fire, he hadn't noticed her blunder. She kept forgetting the man was a statue. Indeed, he'd carried her bags and built a fire, and he'd fetched herbs for her and had invited her to spend time at the river, but that wasn't enough to have weakened her resolve. She straightened her spine.

"If you go there, you will find plantain and palm trees," Ore said. "I apologise that I won't be there to hand them to you personally."

And thus began the dance healers and clients did after care was provided. Ewa feigned ignorance. "I don't understand."

"It is our thanks to you," Tundun interjected. "And you know it. I left some shea nuts behind that you can sell, too."

"We don't give thanks to those closest to us," she insisted.

Ore, Tundun, and Gbala had become like family to her—accepting the gifts they mentioned would mean cutting down on the profits they could make from selling their produce. She shifted on the blanket she and Tundun sat on.

"And we don't let our people go hungry," Ore replied. "Go to our farm. Select whatever you like. You must not refuse our gratitude."

Ewa could not impose on this kind couple. She didn't pay any attention while Ore rattled on, sharing the directions to their farm. Unsurprisingly, her thoughts turned to Makinde. She saw the slight smile on his face and the way he'd woken her up with a shoulder rub. Olootu was close now, and her heart had no business flipping with such abandon. She ought to be thrilled at the prospect of mending the past, but something inside her refused to care.

"You have made up," Tundun said, leaning towards her conspiratorially.

"Pardon?"

She quickly turned away from regarding Makinde. Perhaps she'd sent more gazes at him since they'd returned from the river, but she thought she'd done so with subtlety. She winced. If Tundun had noticed, Makinde must have, too.

"Don't be shy with me. It wasn't right that you two were arguing. No man can hold his anger at a woman as beautiful as you."

"T-thank you."

"That's the spirit. I know when we leave, you two won't be able to keep your hands off each other."

"Tundun! That is enough."

Tundun giggled and then inhaled. "Ewadunni, thank you. Thank you."

"I already told you, you don't need to thank me. When you give birth to this child in your womb, send for me. I will come and celebrate with you."

"Promise me." Tundun grasped her hand.

"I promise."

Chapter Eleven

E wa emerged from a river of blood. As she tore open her sleep-sealed eyes, Makinde's war cries shrilled in her ears. In her dream, she watched in horror as he swung the wide blade of his sword cutting through men, women, and children alike.

Clammy hands grasped at her blanket. The woods appeared darker than usual, and the lack of warmth at her side told her she was alone. She lurched upright ready to run. In the dim blue of dawn, Ore secured Gbala on his back, and Tundun lifted their belongings on her head.

She squeezed her eyes shut then opened them slowly. She inhaled—those days of fleeing, hiding in the forest while war raged on, were behind her.

"Almighty, protect me," she whispered.

"You're up?" Tundun said. "We didn't mean to disturb you."

"I wanted to wish you a safe journey." She stood up. She'd sacrificed her morning routine for this family. There was no space to draw into herself and examine what her dreams were telling her. She hugged Tundun and ran her palm in circles across Gbala's back.

"Be well, you hear? My dear Gbala, soon, you will be jumping in the rain."

"Will you play with me then?" Gbala burrowed her head between Ore's shoulder blades.

"Of course!"

"We will take her to the temple as soon as we get home," Tundun said, drawing Ewa into another tight embrace.

Ewa walked with them to the dirt road where more hugs where exchanged. She waved at their backs till they took a turn and vanished. With her jaw set and chin held high, she returned to the camp.

Makinde wasn't there, and neither was Wuu. Good. She crumbled on her blanket. The images her mind had shown her as she slept served a purpose—they reminded her of who her travel companion was. She'd been losing grip of her senses, free-falling into what could only be her own doom. With all she knew, how could she? Was it so easy to lose oneself in a dashing man? Was this the reason young ladies made treacherous trips into the forest in search of a recluse?

Makinde barely spoke to her but was slowly undoing her with little things. That smile he'd flashed at her yesterday... She tightened her hands into fists. She dare not. Makinde was taboo to her. She would wrap a veil of coldness around her shoulders as they resume their journey.

With renewed determination, she folded her blankets and waited. When he appeared with their refilled water containers, she pretended not to notice the warmth in his gaze. A curtain fell over his eyes. He moved without saying a word.

Her face crumpled when she recalled the flirtatious manner in which she'd acted the day before. At the stream while fishing, she'd shown him a part of her he'd no business glimpsing. She had only acted this way because she'd been exhausted and relieved Gbala's life was safe. That had to be the reason.

In a few days since they'd left Kuta, her feelings towards this man couldn't have changed so abruptly. She'd hated him and all he represented for years. What was a few days in the face of a decade? She wasn't a slip of a girl to be confused by a man who could change like a chameleon. Cutting his hair and shaving his beard didn't change who Makinde was—a warrior. One whose praise names boasted of ferocity.

She would push them forward today till the road grew more busy than lonely. Let it be today that the dirt road would widen and passers-by call out greetings to them. Ibukun was near.

THE town of Ibukun was a bustling one that cut through a large swath of the forest. Long ago, four hunters from different towns had made this area their meeting ground because it was abundant in game and natural resources. Eventually, the friends decided to settle on the land, bringing their families along with them.

Ibukun kept expanding, more trees sawed down to clear land for building houses, more wells dug, and more people trooping in hoping to strike their luck in the town regarded as blessed. There were no walls or fortifications around Ibukun, indicating its openness to all and sundry. The many homes comprising it scattered around woods like a fistful of rice flung at the earth, but at the heart of the town was the palace with its attached market and mansions.

When Ewa had expressed interest in pausing at Ibukun, Fadahunsi had informed her she would have to present herself before the paramount ruler.

She stood in a queue leading into the palace now with Makinde silent beside her. Wuu had run off on his own, already exploring the place as he was inclined to. It was just as well—she doubted a dog would have been allowed into the palace. As it was, she'd had to leave all her belongings at the entrance with a guard who'd promised they would remain safe.

The palace was beautiful and vast. Fresh white paint coating its outer walls hinted it was well-maintained. They'd been led past a main gate and through one of many courtyards by Jobayo—an overly familiar attendant about the same age as they were. Jobayo was stout and burly with a small pebble nose. He boasted the palace had several courtyards, each with a different theme, then quizzed them on their origins before leaving them.

The queue snaked from somewhere deep inside past a low parapet and down four steps to the airy waiting room. Several other visitors joined behind Ewa and chatted in low whispers about the building's grandness. She entertained herself by staring at the veranda posts where life-like figures rode horses, held hunting weapons, or pounded into mortars. She tried to decipher the stories captured in the brass doors of the palace which held snake and chameleon motifs.

The line moved slowly as the Oba granted visitors permission to stay in his town. Fadahunsi had explained this was a method of record-keeping used by Ibukun to ensure the town remained safe. Only a few were turned away, dragged out of the palace by stern-faced guards. She wondered if there was an Oracle next to the ruler who informed him of the true nature of his guests. What would such an Oracle say about her? Would it read Makinde's sins and chase them from the town?

As the distance between evening and night grew shorter, they were finally admitted into the principal courtyard. Murals told the story of Ibukun's foundation on each wall. Silk curtains billowed gently in the evening breeze as Jobayo positioned them at the far end of a veranda.

"Greetings to the Oba," Jobayo said.

"Greetings to the Oba," Ewa repeated. She lowered herself flat to the ground like Jobayo did. From the corner of her eye, she glimpsed Makinde's jerky prostration.

A large impluvium separated them from Ibukun's ruler. The Oba sat on a low throne in a niche extending from the eastern wall. His face was hidden by the beads cascading from his crown. Attendants flanked him on either side, waving large raffia fans. The Oba lifted his hand in greeting.

"We have here Makinde, a noted warrior from Kuta, and his wife, Ewadunni," Jobayo introduced them. "They are on their way to Olootu and wish to spend a night in our illustrious town."

Ewa flinched. Being described as Makinde's wife had the same effect as being stung by a bee. She counted down to the moment Ibukun's Oracle would appear to grant them permission. She imagined the deity was in the sparkling waters of the impluvium. She didn't notice the Oba leaning forward on his throne.

"Makinde, son of Latilu? The one who, when his name is called, sends entire towns fleeing?"

The Oba's tone was measured and curious. His words sounded like a praise name to Ewa, but there was no means to confirm it. Unlike Jomiloju, she hadn't thrown herself into learning Makinde's family history. She peeked at him, and her mouth fell open. He stood feet apart and arms crossed, not bothering to lower his eyes in front of a ruler.

"Answer. Quickly. Are you Latilu's son?" Jobayo fussed when Makinde remained silent.

Ewa clenched her fists. This man didn't know how to behave and would get them thrown out of town with his discourteousness.

"I am," Makinde said, breaking the tension.

She remained concerned. It was difficult to breathe easily when there was a possibility this Oba might have a bone to pick with Makinde. The thought had crossed her mind earlier, but if that was the case, dragging them out of the palace might not be enough. It was always an eye for an eye with warriors. The Oba could decide to have them slaughtered. Sweat broke across her upper lip.

"Makinde, son of Latilu," the Oba said.

The vastness of the court seemed to amplify his voice. She held her breath with the certainty that negativity would soon be visited upon them and it would all be Makinde's fault.

"You saved the life and honour of one of my wives. She came to this palace with tales of your kind bravery. All our children know you by name. Jobayo, ensure they are well taken care of."

The Oba lifted his hand again, signalling the end of the session. Ewa was stunned at first. There was no magic revelation save for the vast knowledge stored in the Oba's person. It was due to this that many regarded rulers as deities themselves. Relief flooded her as she prostrated in thanks. Jobayo ushered them out to the main courtyard facing the entrance they'd come through.

"You're this accomplished yet introduced yourselves so humbly," he complained.

"Discretion is a better part of warfare," Ewa said, adopting the manner of speaking elders preferred and using a proverb. It fell on her to defuse the situation because by now, she knew Makinde wouldn't entertain Jobayo's small talk. Their lodging was in the man's hands—she had to ensure they were on his good side.

"You are skilled with words." Jobayo's compliment was aimed at her, but he eyed Makinde with open curiosity. "Follow me."

Once they'd retrieved their belongings, they filed past a bustling marketplace with traders selling prepared foods and household necessities. A few of them had set out oil lamps with licking flames anticipating the nighttime.

"Multitudes of people come to trade in our town," Jobayo said. "Almost all our lodgings are fully occupied, but trust me, I have a nice one for you."

Just round the corner from the palace was a long, sprawling house with its front doors swung open. Jobayo wove through courtyards and corridors buzzing with activity. Women laughed as they chatted, men counted their wares, and somewhere, a woman hushed a wailing child.

"These are all visitors just like you," he explained.

They walked through two courtyards before he stopped at a corner room. He opened the door with a flourish and beckoned them in. Ewa ducked her head and surveyed the rectangle room. Triangles were cut out from the mud wall forming windows that cast lines of light on the clean floor. The room was sparsely decorated with straw mats and two headrests. A lone slab of raised earth extended from a wall, the room's only bed. There was a threadbare leather poof that, although looking imported, had seen better days. She wondered how many heads, feet, and bottoms had rested on it. There had to be finer accommodations in Ibukun. Nonetheless, the room was clean and smelt like lamp oil.

"I will leave you now," Jobayo said. "But I will return with bedding. Do you need anything else?"

"Lamps, please." Noticing Makinde who waited on the other side of the threshold, she asked, "Is there just one room?"

"Count yourself lucky that there is even one room. Don't tell me you need space for the dog I saw hanging around you earlier? Everywhere is at maximum capacity with the market day. Some traders will sleep in their market stalls."

Jobayo etched a bow before disappearing to retrieve the items he'd mentioned. No sooner had he gone than Ewa heard the quiet rumble of Makinde's throat.

"I should take my leave," he said.

Inside the room just by the door were her basket and bags. She scoffed gently. Of course, Makinde was ready to take his dog and vanish at the most convenient moment for him.

"Where will you stay?" There was a pang somewhere between her heart and her belly she tried to ignore because she didn't understand it.

"Somewhere out there." He waved his hands haphazardly.

She knew he meant the forest; he was really a nymph.

She rubbed circles around her middle. Was this knot within her disappointment at how quickly he was letting her go? Even as she pushed him away, she stupidly wanted him to remain by her side.

"That is all right. Do ensure you bathe so I don't have to travel with a smelly companion."

Instead of being offended, he offered her a small smile. Her breath caught at how the lift of his lips turned his face boyish. This was the second smile she'd drawn out of him in just as many days. She wondered how he would look if he allowed himself to fully display happiness. Her heart sank as he showed her his back, ready to leave. She swallowed through her constricted throat.

"What will you eat?"

She wanted to pinch her arm. She should have let him go without a word. It was as though the sensible Ewa who had made the decision to firmly ignore Makinde until he was no longer of convenience to her had melted away like shea butter left under the sun. This new Ewa who struggled to hold Makinde back was witless. The hostel was filled to the brim with people, and she wouldn't lack for company.

But when he turned to face her, his hand still on the overlapping wooden door, her treacherous heart beat easier.

The lift of his brow told her she'd made a mistake. A man like him could never go hungry in a forest.

"Aren't you tired of hunting and scavenging? We can eat pounded yam here. I saw a vendor. Besides, Jobayo might want to speak with you. What will I tell him if he doesn't find you here?"

She bit her lip and squeezed her wrapper tight with her fingers. What was wrong with her? Before she could open her mouth and beg him to forget her words, he spoke up.

"I will return shortly."

EWA failed to notice she was holding her breath until she was alone in the room. She released a huff from parted lips and landed on the poof chair when her knees proved too weak to support her. The leather groaned as her body made contact with it. She had made a grave error...so why did she feel like throwing her head back and laughing?

She was restless and unable to sit still. She left the room and explored the hostel's five courtyards. Then, she found the bathroom at the back of the building with directions from another guest. The bathing area was a hut with an open roof and large clay pots installed outside. Some were propped on mud stoves with wood burning underneath their bases to keep the water warm while others held fragrant herbs.

She peeked into a bubbling pot and imagined her insides must resemble this with all the emotions clashing through her. Olootu was a stone's throw from Ibukun. Soon, she would have to bid goodbye to Makinde, never to see him again.

She pinched her bottom lip. After fighting for this separation, why did this thought make her heart lurch? Wanting to distract her convoluted mind, she occupied herself with trying to decipher which herbs were mixed with the water. There were dried calabashes of varying widths stacked close to the stalls. She grabbed a small bowl from the many set near the bath house and started scooping. By scent and feel, she deciphered the leaves were to cleanse the skin and not the water.

She entered the bathing space after filling one of the larger calabashes with warm floral water. She unwound her wrappers and placed them on a hook. The moon glowing above her head illuminated her naked skin and made her feel wanton. It had to be external forces encouraging her to imagine Makinde tracing the soapy loofah down her back.

Ewa bit the inside of her mouth picturing him cupping her breasts from behind, then lowering one hand to touch her centre. She dumped water over her face and went out to fetch more. She washed several times before she was satisfied. She finished with a cold splash of water that made her gasp.

When she emerged, her skin had shed the grime of the journey and carried a soft floral scent reminiscent of Ogele's unique fragrance. She returned to the room. In her absence, Jobayo had lit fires in the wall sconces and deposited four thick blankets on the mat. Oil lamps were set on the floor along the walls. The space appeared warm and inviting.

As she massaged coconut oil onto her damp skin, she longed for her adopted mother. She hadn't paid attention to the cosmetic remedies Ogele favoured because she'd thought herself more concerned with saving lives. She had no one to beautify herself for, and this remained the case even as her actions betrayed otherwise. She selected a clean white wrapper wondering what kind of advice Ogele would give if she saw her now. Since their departure from Kuta, Ogele had stopped visiting her dreams.

She folded the length of cloth over one shoulder, tucking the ends under a dark blue upper wrap in her usual two-cloth style then went out of her way to place a long, beaded necklace on her neck and coral earrings in her earlobes—gifts that had once belonged to Ogele. She slipped bracelets on her wrists and wished she had camwood to redden her feet. It didn't occur to her to question what or who she was preparing for.

An ancient part of her knew.

Chapter Twelve

The forest beckoned to him, yet Makinde hovered in front of the hostel. For the umpteenth time, he took a step forward then withdrew. His indecisiveness only made Ewa wait longer. Her icy demeanour had thawed as they'd progressed to Ibukun, and now they were here, it was evident in her words and the way she carried herself that she didn't want him to leave.

Deep down, he longed to shed his worries and hold on to her. Such longing was dangerous. The destiny he'd selected for himself didn't give space to matters of the heart, and he would rather die than hurt her. For the best for them both, he should have found Wuu and faded into the forest until dawn. Despite knowing this, he hesitated.

"Great warrior! Makinde of Kuta!"

The palace attendant assigned to them rushed forward from the night with a young lad bearing a blazing torch hurrying alongside. Makinde scowled at the him. The man had neither the tact nor comportment one would expect of his station. He resisted the urge to ask him to keep quiet about this warrior business. Already, people milling about the hostel aimed interested glances at him.

Jobayo wheezed as he reached him.

"Our Oba sends his greetings. I have delivered items to your wife, but our ever-generous ruler has sent more."

Jobayo thrust his arms out, offering a box of delicate carved wood to Makinde who made no effort to collect the gift. Undeterred, the attendant continued.

"The Olori herself sweats in her kitchen preparing dinner for you. And tomorrow, I have been ordered to dispatch one of our finest horses from the royal stables to hasten your journey."

This was all too much. He struggled to recall any queen he'd saved. Warriors were in the business of feuding, not rescuing.

"Thank you." He inclined his head. He'd spent years in the wilderness but not too long as to forget one couldn't reject offers from royalty especially while under their protection.

"I will transmit your gratitude directly to the Oba."

Jobayo thrust the box at Makinde's chest. The minute he caught the gift, Jobayo started his retreat.

"Your meal will arrive shortly," he said over his shoulder as he rushed elsewhere. Then he stopped abruptly and turned. "Your dog is with us. We have been ordered to care for him tonight."

Makinde turned the box over, running his fingers over the polished surface and smooth indentations. Just who was this Olori? He tested the weight of the gift in his hands. The box was a light rectangle, slightly larger than the board used in playing mancala. It would be unseemly to demand an audience with her so there was no other option than to wait.

Also, he had more important things on his mind, foremost the wife he'd never known. He inhaled deeply, filling his stomach with air, and with an exhale, marched into the hostel. The first courtyard was empty of activity, but the lamp posts held fire, and he heard merriment from within.

He crossed the space to the larger courtyard which appeared to have been transformed into some kind of tavern with nightfall. People sat on stools and mats shouting as they ate and drank. The bitter scent of insect-repelling herbs tainted the air. Drums were beating in a corner, and a lone cowrie-covered gourd rattled along with the rhythm. A few energetic couples danced, the synchronised movements of their hips and waists suggestive of more carnal motions.

Makinde tore his gaze away, massaging the back of his neck as he headed towards the room allocated by Jobayo. He found Ewa leaning against the wall in front of the room, head tilted as she conversed with a strange woman.

He drew to a pause. Ewa appeared as though she belonged in the Oba's harem. Her skin glowed silky smooth. The beads trailing down her front emphasised the length of her neck. She was a natural beauty, but in this moment, she appeared like a star to him. He watched her so keenly, he noticed as she slowly became aware of his presence.

She first straightened. She let her hands drop to her side, and her attention departed from the woman she'd been talking to. She scanned the room, and once she caught sight of him, her eyes sparkled. He imagined how he appeared to her. His hair was combed out in a soft short fuzz. He wore a new change of clothes—a brilliant green tunic paired with light brown trousers and was freshly bathed. A barber in the nearby market had shaved off the new growth on his face.

Did she find him pleasing? He prayed so. In the dancing illumination of the oil lamps, the pulse at the base of her throat jumped. He took it as an affirmation. If a finger had pushed at his back, he would have fallen headlong into her arms. An energy stronger than any he knew propelled him towards her. Her shoulders pressed against the wall, thrusting her chest out in invitation, like she was ready for him to take her.

"Makinde of Kuta?"

Jobayo's young assistant approached carrying a large tray on his head. Makinde cleared his throat. His name had been bandied about in the excess in this town.

"Yes."

"Your meal has arrived."

"I'll get the chairs for you," the woman who'd been talking to Ewa said before slinking away.

Ewa pushed away from the wall. As she approached him, for an unknown reason, he took a half-hearted step back. She appeared not to notice as she thanked the boy.

"Don't tell me you prepared all this yourself?" she teased.

The boy glanced away shyly. "It was the Olori. She is grateful to the warrior Makinde."

"Is that so? Would you thank her for me?"

"I am too small to speak to a wife of the Oba."

Ewa chuckled as she collected the tray. She passed it to Makinde and then brought out a string of cowries from nowhere which she slipped into the boy's hands. The chairs came along with a low table. She settled down and directed him to lower the tray. As soon as he did, she began lifting lids from clay plates.

"Won't you sit down?" she asked, her attention on the food.

He pursed his lips and lowered onto one of the low-backed chairs. The smell of spices wafted to his nose, causing his stomach to groan in anticipation. There was mashed beans, cocoyams pounded with plantains, sautéed greens, seasoned roasted plantains, and a meat stew. A small bowl held kola nuts while another contained dark berries and orange-red plums. It was a grander feast than he had seen in years.

"This wife of the Oba must really have a soft spot for you."

He sat upright. Had he heard a twinge in Ewa's voice?

"I fail to remember who she is."

"Hm."

They ate from the same tray as real lovers would. It took only a few bites for his hunger to be satisfied. Afterwards, he was consumed by another more primal longing. Watching Ewa eat and inhaling the intoxicating scent of her perfume was enough for him but not for the hostel's guests.

A man in the audience stood up. He wore a long, flowing tunic and many beads around his neck and both wrists. He gestured towards the drummers, and the music slowed to an abrupt end. A patron shouted in complaint.

"I greet the house," the man in the tunic said. His deep voice carried through the building. "I said, I greet the occupants of this house."

When the house responded to his liking, the man continued. "We can all agree that the moon is full tonight."

"Yes!" the room chorused.

Makinde glanced up at the moonlit sky, wondering where the man was headed with this opening.

"I say it is time for a story."

"Who will tell us one?" a woman hidden in a corner shouted.

"I, of course! I will be your storyteller for tonight."

"What kind of story will you tell?"

The storyteller made a show of spinning round and observing the crowd. "I see we are all adults here. I will tell the story of the Iyalaje of Mekun market."

Those in the crowd familiar with the story hooted and jeered. Makinde's skin flushed with heat. What was in the air to infuse lust in each and every person? He turned back to the food.

"Alo! Alo!" the storyteller began.

"Alo!"

"There was once a man desperate for a wife. He cried over here and cried over there. He threw himself at the feet of maidens on the way to the stream. 'Marry me,' he pleaded."

The crowd laughed as the storyteller mimed actions with his words, running across the improvised stage. Ewa tittered.

"Meanwhile at Mekun, a beautiful woman managed the affairs of the marketplace. Everyone desired her, and in her footsteps, the energy of love lingered on the earth."

"They say she was busty with a generous behind," someone in the crowd yelled.

"No, she was slender and had large round eyes," another countered.

Ewa leaned to him. "She was tall and had gorgeous skin. Iya Ogele told it better."

Ogele wasn't one to shy from telling the raunchy story of a man who used honey while making love to a wealthy woman in order to enchant her. Makinde's thumb tingled at the memory of Ewa's tongue against that patch of skin. When the storyteller reached the part where the bachelor dipped his manhood into honey, Ewa clamped her lips shut and covered them with a hand. As the storyteller dragged the tale with the audience, each adding more detail than was necessary, she shifted in discomfort.

"You never sleep" It wasn't a question.

"I can't." The implication of his words hung in the air. A gust of air wove through the courtyard. Among the dozens gathered, only he felt the cold enough to shudder.

"Iya Ogele taught me a brew for that."

He shrugged. He regretted it immediately as her shoulders deflated at his rejection.

"Is all well?" she asked.

Nothing escaped her attention. The food he'd just eaten turned his mouth sour. He reached for a plum even though he knew it wouldn't help. His eyes darted back and forth across the open space. The blood in his veins turned cold as he recognised a face in the crowd. It was her. Her hair wrapped in thread, her eyes shedding black tears just like the bleeding wound in her chest.

"I am well," he snapped without meaning to. He breathed and repeated more gently. "I am well."

The spectre's lips began to move in wordless injunctions. He shot up, and the wooden chair fell to the floor. Ignoring Ewa's calls, he wove past the crowd to the exit. Everyone stared at him as though he'd lost his mind, and they were right.

"Murderer," someone whispered to his right.

"Makinde, the slayer of Kuta."

He cupped his hands over his ears. With hurried steps, he burst into the night where more ghosts of his past lay in wait.

EWA rushed out of the building taking care not to distract the guests held in rapt attention to the storyteller's words. She burst past the front doors to pitch darkness. Insects chirped in the night as she waited for her eyes to adjust.

"Makinde."

She thought she saw movement to her right and didn't question it. She ran all while calling his name. Ahead of her, the lamp posts in front of a grand house illuminated his retreat.

"Makinde! Please, wait."

If he hadn't stopped walking, she would have missed him. The muscles under his skin jumped when she touched his arm. She felt the tension coiled within him like an irate snake preparing to strike. The flickering glow of the lamps cast his handsome face in shadows. Her breath caught. His eyes were fixed on a spot over her shoulder. When she looked that way, she found nothing but darkness.

"Are you content?" he asked.

When she and Jomiloju had met him in his forest hide-out, she'd noticed the haunted veil over his eyes. That expression had quadrupled. Even in the dimness, the torture contained in his features sliced through her.

"Why would you say that?"

"You wanted to know why I don't sleep."

Her left hand raised to lightly touch his face. He didn't withdraw.

"Why do you insist on punishing yourself?" she asked softly.

Being a warrior was a cursed profession. Men returned from the battlefield bearing more scars than the ones mapped on their skin. A memory rose like fruit bobbing on water's surface of a warrior returned from war who had to be pulled off his sister when she'd crept up on him unawares. She'd simply meant to surprise him. The priests had said the warrior carried the ghosts of war and that he needed to seek forgiveness and cleansing.

Ewa had always assumed he was an unfeeling killer. Could the ghosts of war be the reason Makinde never slept? Why he secluded himself? As far as she knew, he avoided even the cleansing administered by priests. But one couldn't take a life without paying for it one way or another. Rituals helped but weren't sufficient when the individual had given up on their own soul. A spiritually fortified person could still fall due to the bite of an ant.

"You are from Odan," he said. "What happened..."

She was aware of what happened—she'd witnessed the violence that tore her birthplace apart with her own eyes and barely managed to escape. For years, she'd feared men in general and warriors in particular even as she sought refuge in Kuta, a stronghold of warriors. Yet, in Makinde's presence, with her hands on his warm skin, she faltered.

"You aren't like that." As the words left her mouth, she felt her heart squeeze in conviction. "Here in a strange town, a stranger speaks of you to her children. She cooked for you. Look at me, Makinde."

His jaw tensed underneath her hand. His chest heaved with the effort to breathe.

"You have to stop running. Come with me."

Lacing her fingers through his, she led them back to the hostel. A new story was being told in the courtyard. Hearing raised voices from the front door, she chose to evade the audience and enter through a side door near the bath house. Worried of letting Makinde out of her sight lest he disappear again, she dragged him to their room where she found the required leaves and then to the kitchen out back.

He followed her quietly. Despite the late hour, some women still cooked. She borrowed a miniature pot, water, and smouldering coals. They squatted in wait for the liquid to steam. Now she'd laid her hands on him, she needed to keep in contact with him. She ran her fingers over his short hair and down the side of his face. He nudged his nose into her palm like Wuu would. She wondered what secrets he kept buried but wouldn't ask. She had secrets of her own.

"I apologise for the trouble." He pressed his lips into her palm.

She drew in a shaky breath. "The least I can do is make you a brew."

She grabbed the small pot by the rim in folded layers of her outer wrapper. Finding a cup, she strained the mixture into it. When they returned to their room, she gently shoved him on the raised bed and sat next to him.

"It's still hot." She blew on the cup.

He was silent. His body appeared defeated, his expression glum and chin pointing down.

"Tell me a story."

He lifted his head. "A story?"

"Your favourite one from Iya Ogele."

It took so long for him to reply, she thought he'd rejected her suggestion.

"I enjoyed the way she told the story of the great dancer of the Obatala family."

She was familiar with this tale about the most junior sibling who bested his elders by dancing a complicated sequence of two hundred and one steps perfectly. Makinde narrated the story, his voice growing more animated as he progressed. When he reached the song, she forgot to blow on the tea.

"You can sing," she said.

"I can do many things. I used to..." The spark on his face dimmed.

"Makinde."

"You've called my name so many times today."

"It is only because I need you to listen, really listen to me."

She passed him the cup. His hands stilled as he brought it to his lips.

"It isn't poison," she teased.

"I know you wouldn't. I...If I accept this now..."

She hushed him, then placed a palm under the cup and lifted it to his lips while he held it. His throat bobbed as he downed the brew.

Later, she watched him stretch out on the bed. It would only be a few minutes before he slept. She doubted any other person in the world had had as many countless nights as this man. Makinde needed more than one night of sleep.

MAKINDE'S eyelids fluttered open. The oil lamps in the room burned, but he didn't see any shadows hovering above him. A strange sensation enveloped him. It took several moments for him to recognise the feeling as well-rested. The lack of light outside the triangular windows suggested dawn was yet to come.

He propped himself up on his elbows. To his left, Ewa lay curled on a mat on the floor, her head resting on arms folded on the bed. Her head was close to the headrest he'd used as he slumbered. Their breaths must have intermingled as they slept, and the image, though simple, set his pulse racing.

She had given him sleep after years without it. With her delicate hands, she'd chased away the spectres. He wouldn't let her to care for him again—once was more than enough.

He slipped off the bed and crouched next to her. Witnessing her fast asleep was a blessing, and with extreme tenderness, he took her in his arms and moved her to the bed. He drank his full of her before turning towards the door when he was pulled to a stop. He peered down at her hand clutching the edge of his trousers.

"Don't go."

"I must."

She tightened her grip on his clothes and rubbed at her eyelids with her free hand as they opened in awareness.

"Where are you going to?" she demanded drowsily.

"You need to sleep comfortably."

"You, too."

Just tonight. Tonight would be the exception. He eased beside her on the earthen bed. Although she had made it comfortable with blankets and he had slept peacefully on it, he was restless. Her nose brushed his chest; their toes touched. This was closer than they'd ever been before.

"Did you sleep well?" she asked, her voice muffled.

He lay stiffly. There was no chance of him getting any more rest like this, surrounded by her scent of flowers and coconut oil. If he moved his hands forward, he would touch her velvety skin. The long unused staff at the juncture of his legs stirred to life. He screwed his eyelids shut in mortification. He jerked as her fingers gripped the embroidered front of his tunic.

"Makinde."

Having Ewa repeat his name in her careful manner with that falling inflection of hers was better than hearing his praise names chanted. He stopped breathing as she hoisted herself up so their faces were on equal ground. She brushed her nose against his, her whispered breath igniting the skin on his face.

Time slowed as her lips brushed his. He groaned as she undid him. She tasted like honey. He took hold of the back of her neck and deepened the contact. She sighed against him and ran her fingers across his cheeks and ears.

He ought to have walked away without looking back. They were never a couple, and then, they were divorced. He had no business tasting her like this. But she threw her arms around his shoulders and held him tight. He buried his head in the crook of her neck, grasping her as if she were his anchor. She clutched at his fingers and lifted his hand to her breast. Her nipples strained through the fabric, eager for his touch. The velvet feel of her skin spurred him to seek more.

He eased her onto her back. His hands faltered as he undid the knot securing her wrapper. She tugged her clothes loose. He was drenched in sweat, mouth watering at her curvaceous body spread for him in the glow of the lamps. His heart thumped a frantic rhythm as he lowered his head and lapped at a pert nipple.

Ewa jolted as though struck by lightning. Her feet kicked against the bed, and her hands grabbed his head in place. She gasped loudly with each flick of his tongue. Her cries were going to alert their neighbours, but he didn't care. His hands dipped down the curve of her waist.

"May I?" he asked, hands hovering above her waist beads.

"Yes!"

She eagerly granted him permission. He played with the fat beads, dragging them along the taut skin of her belly and eliciting shivers. He used her waist beads to massage her lower belly while teasing her nipple with his teeth. Kissing a trail lower, he dragged his tongue along the black hexagonal lines tattooed on her stomach.

She pressed her nails into his skin, murmuring affirming sounds. When he touched her most vulnerable part, his fingers came back coated with her nectar. He pressed into her wetness, drawing tight circles while his thumb caressed her nub, pushing her towards the end. Ewa screamed and squirmed as desire consumed her. She clawed at his back, lifting her hips for more.

For once, the only thing demanding his attention was the woman clinging to him. It was his years of abstinence and discipline that allowed him to stop it there. While his member strained to feel her, he made himself remember why they were in Ibukun. They were to be separating, not joining together. As her breathing returned to normal, he embraced her and held her close till she fell asleep.

Chapter Thirteen

Elongated triangles of light cast lines across Ewa. She squeezed her eyelids against the beams of the morning sun and slowly stretched her arms above her head. The bed was empty. However, signs Makinde had slept on it were stamped on her body.

Her skin recalled his intimate touch, the ghost of his tongue tickling her belly, a damp souvenir of his visit slathered on the insides of her thighs. They all distracted her from her morning invocations. She drew the blanket over her head hoping the darkness would aid her focus. The heat underneath the heavy throw brought to mind Makinde's breath hot in the crook of her neck. She jolted upright.

"Humble reverence, humble respects," she said, cutting her prayers short. "I pay my respects to all!"

Wrapping a cloth over her naked body, she crossed the room to an empty courtyard. It occurred to her she might have overslept. At this hour, those resuming their journeys must have left, and those trading would have set up stalls in the marketplace. Makinde had most likely gone ahead to prepare for their journey. She briefly wondered where Wuu had spent the night.

In the bath house, other women washed themselves. She greeted them as she entered, interrupting them in the middle of a conversation. They replied noncommittally, eager to return to the topic. She lathered her loofah with black soap and began scrubbing her skin without the leisure of the previous night.

"But what would make a woman scream like that in the middle of the night?" one of the three asked.

"I wonder what kind of love play that is," her plump companion replied.

They were talking about her. Ewa clamped both lips between her teeth and turned her head to the wall away from them. When she played with herself at the springs in Kuta, she often shouted herself hoarse with no one to hear her but the animals and trees. Makinde had made her feel just as good, and she hadn't been able to keep quiet. Her cheeks heated at the sudden image of him making love to her under the steady stream of water.

"Whoever that woman is, we need to locate her lover," the third woman spoke up. "I will make him my concubine."

"Tolagbe!"

"Why are you pretending like you don't want to be shouting out in pleasure, too, friend?"

"Are you suggesting that we interrogate every woman in this place?"

"Why not?"

The women filed out the bathroom still discussing their plans. Ewa shook her head and wrinkled her nose behind their backs. They couldn't possess what was hers. It would serve them better to hunt for sex elsewhere.

When she was done bathing, she returned to the room. She would need a wrapper not of a pristine white for the road. She turned to the basket holding her belongings and noticed a strange box that wasn't there last night. Her face lit with the realisation the box could have only been left by Makinde.

She pushed back the top and gasped at the stunning bolts of fabric carefully rolled inside. She ran her fingers across the spun silk. One had alternating blue and crimson strips while the other appeared to be delicately embroidered with cream thread.

A bubble of joy burst from her lips, and she covered her mouth to shield her smile. The only person who had gifted her things had been Ogele and before her, her mother. She put the box away and covered her body with a brown wrapper more suited to journeying. She gathered the blankets Jobayo had loaned and folded them.

"May I enter," a smoky voice called from the other side of the door just as she smoothed out the creases from the blankets.

"Yes."

Before she could get to the door, it opened from the outside, and a woman stepped in. Her posture was elegant, the red-purple wrappers she'd tied highlighting the palm oil colour of her skin. Coral earrings grazed the top of her rounded shoulders, and a multiple-tiered necklace of the valuable beads covered her neck. Her hair was plaited and gathered in the centre of her head.

The woman surveyed the small room as she entered it. She was stunning. Everything about her outfit and the way she carried herself spoke of privilege. Ewa guessed the woman before her was the Olori who spoke of Makinde's adventures, the one who'd sent food to them the previous night.

"Good morning, Olori," she said, lowering herself.

"Rise," the Oba's wife said. "How did you know?"

Ewa smiled in reply. "Thank you for your hospitality. We are truly grateful."

Behind the Olori, an attendant rushed in to set a beautifully carved stool on the floor. As the woman settled down, Ewa lowered herself to the straw mat. She couldn't stay in one place, curling her leg in one direction then the other. Finally, she sat cross-legged with her hands clasped in front of her stomach.

"The warrior Makinde isn't here," the Olori said. "I was out on my morning stroll and hoped to catch a glimpse of him."

"We leave Ibukun today. He is currently preparing for our onward journey."

"So I heard. Are you from Kuta, too?"

"I am from O...the town that used to be Odan."

The Olori clapped her hands. "I knew it. Such otherworldly beauty can only be from our region. I am Usiade, of the blacksmith's compound."

Tilting her head, Ewa regarded Usiade. She imagined there were blacksmiths in Odan but had never had any reason to visit their quarters. How had a woman from humble beginnings arrived here? War had ripped Odan and sent its citizens scurrying away in every direction, but it had never occurred to her some of those people would have ended up among royalty.

"I am overjoyed! The warrior is married to a sister of mine," Usiade said. "I can rest assured that he is well taken care of."

Where prior, Ewa would have cringed at those words, her head dipped as a smile spread across her face. Usiade noticed.

"Ah. I can see that he's taking care of you, too."

She had to steer the conversation onto safer ground. "I can't cook delicious foods like the ones you made for us."

"There's more to love than cooking. Sister from my hometown, please thank your husband for me. I'd hoped to do it myself, but as I can't..."

"I will extend your message," Ewa said, rising up as Usiade did. "Before you leave, can you please tell me how he saved you?"

The corners of Usiade's lips dipped, and she shook her head.

"It was thanks to your husband that I was able to leave Odan with my life and dignity. You're around my age. You must remember how filled with bloodlust those warriors were."

Ewa's memory was scant, but the things she saw in her dreams, the utter terror she felt for years after arriving in Kuta, were enough souvenir of the horrors she'd witnessed. However, Usiade's words failed to provide clarity. Makinde wasn't from Odan and must have been fighting for the other side. She struggled to form a response to prod Usiade to reveal more—there was so much she was ignorant of. Luckily, she didn't need to.

"When he saw what the warriors were doing, your husband didn't tolerate it," Usiade said.

A crease appeared between Ewa's brows. Usiade spoke of Makinde clashing with his mates, his fellow warriors. Usiade confirmed the careless words Ewa had said with utter conviction the previous night: Makinde was different.

"Not at all. He ensured a safe passage for me and several other maidens. Forgive me for assuming, but isn't that how you met?"

Ewa dragged sweaty palms down her thighs. "Not entirely. I fled to Kuta from Odan, and we met there."

Usiade nodded, seemingly satisfied with her cryptic response.

"If you are ever in Ibukun in the future, notify me. Stay for longer than one night. We will throw a feast for you at the palace."

"I am grateful."

"We're sisters. You don't need to thank me."

After wishing her safe travels, Usiade departed. Ewa raised her right hand to her heart. She'd been wrong about Makinde. It was easier to admit this now, to home in on the positive feelings she had for him. After an eternity of amplifying her fear, anger, and disgust, she was ready to know him. She resolved to speak with him before they arrived at Olootu.

JOBAYO found her in her room shortly after Usiade had left.

"Greetings, Ewadunni!" he crooned. "Your warrior has been waiting for you. Lift these up."

He directed the attendant hanging by his side like a shadow to bear her belongings.

"I passed the Olori's entourage on my way here," Jobayo said. He let the sentence hang, obviously wanting to know more.

"She is from my hometown," Ewa replied. She felt a kinship with Usiade and wasn't going to help Jobayo foster rumours about her for palace gossip. "Where is my husband?"

"He is at the stables. Our king has offered him a gorgeous steed. I am sure you are pleased with our other gifts."

"Yes. Thank you."

She emerged from the room behind Jobayo when she noticed she'd referred to Makinde as her husband. She froze.

"My husband." Her tongue tangled over the syllables.

"Pardon?" Jobayo swung around. He was a brisk walker and was already in the corridor leading to the front yard. "I trust you aren't frightened of horses."

She grinned. "Not at all."

Jobayo and his attendant walked her to the stables. The smell of dung clashed with hay, and the horses neighed in the enclosed space. Makinde waited at a tree opposite it. Beside him was a long-legged horse in a pale white with a yellow tail. The horse had already been fitted with a saddle and guards. As he noticed their approach, she saw his face shift from the tense frown he usually favoured to an expression that was kind and full of care.

It was for her. Her footsteps quickened. Wuu lifted his head and bounded towards her, his tail wagging. She knelt down to hug the dog.

"Good morning," she greeted Makinde, looking at him from below her lashes.

"Good morning, Ewadunni."

His resonant voice sent a shiver down her spine. Her name on his lips felt like a caress. *This could be home*, she thought. With the way her heart soared at being in his presence, she wouldn't mind.

"I missed you this morning," she said quietly. Jobayo and his attendant were loading her belongings on the patient horse.

Makinde grunted and looked away. She chuckled at what she read as shyness. She was the one who ought to be shy after their passionate encounter. She lightly touched his forearm right below a protective charm he wore. A teasing note was on the tip of her tongue, but he moved away before she could voice it.

"Everything is prepared," Jobayo announced.

Ewa approached them fitfully. Makinde held the horse's reins while rubbing its flank, his lack of interest confirming he was closing himself off.

"Thank you, kind Jobayo," she said, passing coils of cowrie shells to him.

"You're the one I should thank." Jobayo shuffled his feet in a quick dance as he accepted the money. "We will escort you to the town's borders."

When Makinde lifted her on the leather seat, the flutter within her chest at his touch was muted. Dark clouds covered the nascent joy that had enveloped her earlier. Regardless, a sharp pain speared her chest. She recognised what Makinde was doing as she'd done the same herself. She chewed her inner cheek in dread.

He guided the horse to the outskirts of Ibukun where Jobayo bade them farewell. Now they were alone, they could speak freely. She had scarcely opened her mouth when he mounted the horse behind her. His strong arms encircled her, and he urged the horse into a trot. She gasped at the quick motion, leaning back against him. The sound of Wuu barking as he dashed to keep up with them melded with the wind in her ears.

"Be careful!" she said. "Why the rush?"

The answer came to her without him saying a word. The horse cut down the trekking time. If they'd secured one at Kuta, she would have reached Olootu without encountering Ore, Tundun, and Gbala. Makinde was eager to be rid of her.

A bitter taste flooded her mouth. She held on for her life as the forest peeled away to cultivated farmlands. Then they travelled on a level road through light woods. She had no time to appreciate the range of stony hills in the west covered with verdant clusters of trees. By the time they reached a winding stream, she was at her limit. The sun's position indicated it was noon.

"Stop. I need rest."

Makinde jerked the horse back. The constant galloping motion made her head spin, and the abrupt stop didn't help matters. Above all, his stony silence was most disturbing. He disembarked first then helped her down. As her feet touched the ground, her knees buckled. She thought she would faint, but he grasped her waist. The way he gazed down at her with worry raised her confusion.

"Did you eat?" he asked.

With all the excitement of the morning, she'd forgotten to. Once assured she could stand on her own, he turned to the items heaped on the horse's back. With how fast they'd moved, she was surprised her basket hadn't dislodged itself. Wuu lapped at the stream. Shielding her eyes with her hand, she traced the river's path. According to Fadahunsi, Olootu was somewhere along these shores.

"Here." Makinde had returned bearing wraps of yam fritters and smoked meat.

She glared at him.

"I'm not in the mood to eat." She stared at the dog who now rested on the earth.

"You need—"

"What is the matter? Why are you cold to me?"

She hated the way her voice quivered. Anger jumped through her when he refused to look at her as he replied.

"I don't want you to misunderstand."

"Misunderstand what?"

He sighed. "What happened last night was a mistake."

A sharp ringing resounded in her ears. Her lungs constricted, making it harder to breathe. If she had a plate, she could crack it upside his head. She was so mad, and to her horror, her vision grew watery.

She stormed off in the direction of the river, where she waded in until she felt water around her calves. The elders said that death was preferable to disgrace. She now understood the wisdom behind this proverb. Pining for something that was never real had turned her into a fool. She had no business caring for a man who was like a furnace that turned everything entering it into ash.

The flowing water offered comfort. With the lap of each wave, the anger that set her body shaking was washed away. Ewa unclenched her fists as calm set in. There was a new bitterness lodged in her heart. When she was certain she wouldn't shed tears, she returned to the horse.

"Get me to Olootu today," she said.

"The food."

"Today."

EWA had understood the message. Makinde was solely here in order to fulfil the promise he'd made to Baale Semore. So when the horse grew fatigued before they reached Olootu, she proceeded on her own. She waited until she was alone, after having sent him to get her water because the one in the river was unfit for drinking.

He didn't ask about her purifying stones, and she offered no explanation. He bowed to her unreasonable demands. Earlier, the fact he'd never asked any questions of her had fascinated her. He wasn't dismissive in the way she'd seen men sometimes act to their wives. It wounded her how she'd shown him her love and opened up to him only to be rejected. Her womanly pride jeered at her. She should have been the one to reject him. She cringed at the memory of chasing after him, of kissing him.

She walked in the pitch-black night with nothing but the stars to guide her. She remained close to the riverbank, her arms sore from holding her luggage. She first cursed Makinde then herself, but as she moved, her thoughts shifted. It occurred to her he viewed himself the way she had all these years—as an unfeeling, wicked instrument of war. He couldn't escape himself, not like she was trying to. He had no Olootu to look forward to. He was more than his praise names, and the fact he regarded himself unkindly brought a pang to her chest.

She was relieved when she saw the first flickering light indicating lodgings ahead. She quickened her pace, and in her hurry, slid along the muddy bank. One foot landed in the water as she struggled to maintain her balance. She gripped her basket, but her bags slipped down her shoulders.

If destiny had led her to a different path, she would have arrived in Olootu bedecked in fine silks, beads, and brass with Makinde at her side. Instead, the reality saw her approaching a humble bungalow at night, her feet caked in mud and water dripping from her clothes and bags.

"Is anyone home?" she called. The burning lamps outside the building indicated it was occupied. From the front porch, she counted more lights in the inner courtyard.

"Who is it?" a hoarse voice from within the building replied.

The tone was cautious, and she was unsurprised when a tall, muscled woman emerged brandishing a notched arrow. She carefully dropped her basket on the ground so the woman saw her pale palms.

"I am a traveller from Kuta. Ewadunni is my name. Is this Olootu?"

The woman eyed her unconvinced. "Why are you searching for Olootu?"

"I am here to reunite with my family after many years of separation."

"And which family is that?"

"I am the daughter of Ojugbe. Fadahunsi, an Ifa priest currently in Kuta, told me I could find them here."

"Ojugbe?"

"She must mean Lapade's husband," a new voice chimed in.

The tall woman lowered her weapon just as a round face emerged from the house carrying an oil lamp.

"Lapade is my father's wife," Ewa said.

The newcomer squinted in the poor light. "She looks just like Atitebi! Can't you see it, Amoke?"

"Now that you mention it..." Amoke narrowed her eyes at Ewa.

"I apologise for disturbing your evening."

"Not at all." The friendlier woman waved the hand not holding the light. "We should be the ones apologising for this harsh welcome to Olootu. Please come in."

The woman introduced herself as Tifase. She made Ewa sit down on a long bench and then brought drinking water. Tifase offered food and a warm bath. Ewa gracefully declined both. Amoke hovered over Tifase protectively, holding onto the bow.

"I must locate my family," Ewa said.

"But we have just prepared dinner," Tifase objected.

Amoke interjected. "The woman travelled from afar. We shouldn't keep her waiting."

Ewa had no energy to engage in the back and forth required in social settings. Her feet were sore, and her heart heavy from the journey here. Somewhere nearby, her father probably ate dinner. In her memory, Ojugbe was a skinny man of average height with a brilliant smile. He had a thick bush of black coils probably white by now. She was less enthusiastic about reuniting with Lapade, the churlish woman her father had married after the death of her mother. They'd never gotten along.

"Why don't we have Ojo take her there?" Amoke suggested.

Tifase shouted the name, and a young boy of about ten years old emerged from one of the rooms in the house. Ewa stood up and said her thanks. Meanwhile, Tifase instructed the boy on where to take her. Amoke lit a torch to guide them on the brief walk to Ojugbe's home.

"When you're settled, come and visit us," Tifase said. She playfully pushed Amoke's shoulder. "We need to show you how hospitable Olootu is."

By now, it was difficult to ignore the adoring glances Tifase shared with Amoke. Ewa was tired of seeing happy couples. She was grateful for the night. Ojo carried her load as he led the way while she held the torch aloft. The fire warmed her face, but she felt cold. Fate seemed to be mocking her. Why was everyone loved apart from her? Tears sprang into her eyes.

"Heavenly spirits, support me." She whispered a prayer to keep her buoyed. "Heavenly spirits, make this successful for me."

What 'this' referred to, she was uncertain. Ojo took a central route past squat houses overlooking the river. The town smelled new, of turned earth, freshly cut wood, and red plaster used to paint exteriors. Some of the buildings they passed were under construction, without roofs or doors and in one case missing an entire southern wall. There was a vacant market comprised of hastily put together bamboo stalls. On the other side of the river opposite the market, torches blazed on tall posts, and music resounded. The water amplified the sounds of the drums, flute, and rattles which came accompanied by guffaws.

"Is that a tavern?" she asked Ojo.

"Yes. My mothers forbid me from going there, even though the river is shallow enough to walk to the other side."

Ewa laughed softly. "Listen to your mothers."

"I do. Are you tired? We're almost there."

At last, Ojo pointed at a pair of sturdy compact bungalows with front doors facing one another. He marched through one of the doors without announcing himself. Rather than lower her head to enter the house, Ewa froze. She studied the other building. It stood quiet and gloomy, but voices sailed freely from the house in front of her. It sounded as though many people were gathered.

"Little Ojo, what brings you here at this time?"

She couldn't make out Ojo's response. There was an empty feeling in her stomach that she tried to stroke away. It was too late to accept Tifase's offer of food.

"A good-looking lady, you said? But where is she—"

A wrinkled woman appeared at the veranda. Ojo was ahead of her and pointed at Ewa triumphantly. Lapade's mouth fell open, her eyes growing as wide. The years hadn't been kind to her. Lapade favoured her left side as she recoiled, suggesting a foot injury. Perhaps it was the dim light that made her skin appear dull and grey.

"I told you," Ojo said.

Lapade drew her lips together and jutted out her chin. Her eyes glinted like metal, and when she spoke to Ojo, it was without her earlier levity.

"Go home now, Ojo."

"You have to admit I was right," Ojo shot back.

"Now."

That singular word sent shivers down the back of Ewa's legs. Her mind flashed back to Odan, back when it was peaceful and the only skirmish brewing was in Ojugbe's home because his new wife and his daughter didn't see eye to eye. Ojugbe wasn't supposed to remarry, but he had, and Lapade couldn't bear Ewa's presence.

"Bear with her. She limits herself with the idea that your father will never love her the way he did your mother. Bear with her, my precious."

Eleven-year-old Ewa had curled on her grandmother's lap. She'd bawled, the skin on her cheeks and back reddened from contact with Lapade's palm. Her father's mother had been her sanctuary, but that had been temporary. After her grandmother died, she was left to face Lapade on her own. This tone in Lapade's voice had frightened her back in the day, and now, a lifetime away, she clutched her wrappers. Ojo skittered away before she thought to hold him back and give him money to buy something for himself.

"Who are you?" Lapade demanded once they were alone.

Bracing herself, Ewa walked forward. Lapade blocked the entrance.

"Iya." Ewa's voice broke at the word—this woman had never been a mother to her. She cleared her throat. "It is me, Ewadunni."

"We don't know any one of that name."

Ewa swallowed. She was certain this was her stepmother.

"I am Ewadunni, Ojugbe's daughter."

"I don't know how you know my husband's name, but that rotten man joined the ancestors years ago."

Ewa drew a sharp breath. The tears she'd been struggling to keep in all day threatened to spill from her eyes. She blinked hard. When she opened her eyes, Lapade was shooing a lady standing behind her. Before the woman could retreat, Ewa recognised her half-sister's.

"Atitebi," she said.

At the mention of her name, Atitebi froze. She turned to Ewa, and the resemblance was clear. They both had their father's round eyes and pointed chin, but Atitebi had walnut skin and appeared taller than Ewa.

Lapade leaned against the threshold, shoving Atitebi behind her. Eventually, the shadow of Atitebi's form vanished. Was this the sister who had shed tears of joy when Fadahunsi had told her Ewa was alive and well in Kuta?

"The Ewadunni I know died in the forest as we were fleeing." Lapade placed a hand on her hip.

Ewa clenched her teeth. "I didn't die. You left me there."

"What are you accusing me of?"

"Look, I have already forgotten the past. Where is my father buried so I can pay my respects?"

"Not here. Ojugbe has reunited with his cursed wife and their loose daughter in the afterlife."

Her stepmother had always had a vile tongue. Ewa's insides twisted in anger.

"How dare you."

"How dare you?" Lapade shot back. "You come to a stranger's house at night demanding entry like a snake from the bush. Who are you? Why are you here?"

Fadahunsi hadn't seen tears of joy but had witnessed the guilt these women felt. Ewa had to remain dead for them to keep on living. She threw her head back and batted her lids at the starry night sky. She refused to cry or bicker with Lapade.

Bear with her, Grandmother had said. Those words had held little meaning to Ewa when she had been a slip of a girl. Their recollection now let her know there was nothing for her here. She cursed her mind and its shaky memories. Ogele often said it was normal for people who witnessed wars to encounter empty blocks of their past. Ewa only wished her recollection hadn't failed her before leaving Kuta.

"I forgive you," she said, shifting her gaze from the sky to Lapade. She dropped her knees to the earth in respect to the woman who'd never shown her any. "My mother forgives you, and my father forgives you, too."

Ignoring Lapade's gobsmacked expression, she ran her right hand down her left forearm then repeated the motion, switching hands. "I wash away all negativity between us today with Mother Earth as my witness. We may try to kill lies, but they only grow stronger."

"Are...are you...are you placing a curse on me?"

"You aren't my enemy, Lapade. But you will remember this day."

Lapade screamed. Ewa dusted at her knees as she rose. A fat tear rolled down her cheek as she turned away. Her throat felt engorged as though she'd swallowed hot coal. Quick steps led her farther away from her family. The sky had stars and clouds; even the stream had fish. She had no one. Everywhere she turned, doors slammed at her face.

Her vision blurred. She would never come back here. Olootu didn't represent hope, and she couldn't bear the thought of returning to Kuta either. Jomiloju loved her, Tope did, too, and Ewa had so firmly pushed them aside after Ogele's passing. She didn't want to consider that she'd made a mistake leaving Kuta when she'd been sure there was no future for her there.

A loud sob escaped her lips. A hand clamped over her mouth, she walked haphazardly until she reached where the tavern's lights shimmered in the distance. She waded through the water not bothering to lift the edges of her clothes. The gentle waves nipping at her ankles brought a crumb of calmness. On the opposite bank, she marched towards the torches then made her way up short wooden stairs to the platform where benches and stools were arranged around an open stage. Landing on the closest seat, she motioned to one of the barmaids.

"Get me your strongest brew," she said.

THERE WAS NO JUSTIFICATION for Makinde's actions. He told himself that everything he touched crumbled to ash. Any attempt he made to be useful backfired. He had no right to Ewa. Pushing her away was the only solution even if it made her detest him. All that mattered was that she faced the future ahead of her.

He had no destiny. Someone as beautiful and delicate as Ewa deserved a partner who wasn't tainted. It had been less than a day, but he missed her smiles and affection. He had to constantly remind himself he was doing the right thing. Yet, when he'd returned to the clearing with a gourd filled with water and Wuu behind him to find her gone, all the energy had fled from his body. The gourd had fallen from his hands and smashed to the ground. Black spots had popped in the edges of his vision as he'd searched for her in a panic.

The land had been clear with only a few trees and Ewa nowhere to be seen. Thoughts of bandits or wild animals had set his pulse racing. Each inhale he'd drawn had stabbed his lungs, but he had to calm down and come up with a plan. Then Wuu had whined, drawing his attention to the fire where her basket and bags had vanished while his own pack remained.

Ewa had left him. *It's for the best*, he'd decided. Olootu was only a few miles ahead and easily covered by walking. He'd completed the task shoved on him, and there was no longer any excuse to remain by her side. He'd slapped the back of his neck where an insect buzzed. But what if in the absence of light, she slipped and fell into the river? What if she did encounter bandits? He'd already been striding north when Wuu had barked at him. The dog had appeared to censure him, warning him against searching for Ewa if he was going to keep floundering. He'd perched in front of Wuu.

"I know," he'd said. "I will find her, and I will explain. Everything. If she will hear me."

When he'd got up, Wuu had whined.

"Guard the horse for me till we return."

Dragging the animals along would only slow him down. He'd taken off into the night. He'd sprinted until he saw houses and stopped the first person he encountered on the barren streets.

"Have you seen a woman wearing brown wrappers?" he's asked the boy. "She is about this tall."

"Is she good-looking?"

The boy's question had been unexpected, but Makinde had nodded eagerly. "Did you see her?"

"She is at Iya Lapade's place, but I won't go back there."

"Tell me where to find it."

He'd listened to the boy's description and taken off. He'd skidded to a stop before two humble bungalows. As he'd rounded the corner, his eyes had bulged at the scene before him. Ewa knelt down on the ground. He'd stopped in his tracks.

"...you will remember this day," she'd said.

The rest of her words had been eaten by the night. His chest had heaved with the physical exertion. If this had been her destination, why was she prostrating outside the house rather than welcomed in?

She'd stomped off into the dark, passing by and not noticing him. He'd heard her sob, seen her wipe at her face, and anger had jolted through him. His head had snapped in the direction of the bungalow. In the blink of an eye, he'd barged into the house uninvited.

Two women sat on stools while a man snored away in a tilted back chair. Makinde barely registered the children playing with dolls in a corner of the courtyard. The older of the two women immediately leapt to her feet. She eyed him carefully, taking in the fine quality of his clothes and his beaded boots.

"Welcome to our home, esteemed one." The woman lowered her head in greeting.

A younger woman who had to be her daughter echoed the welcome. He glared at them with cold, hard eyes.

"I am Lapade, and this is my daughter, Atitebi. To what do we owe this illustrious visit?"

"I am Makinde, son of Latilu of Kuta."

He gritted his teeth as the women gasped. They tumbled to the ground in greeting with renewed vigour. The movement drew his gaze to a familiar basket on the floor between them. The scene spread out before him came to him in flashes—Ewa's belongings were spread over the bench, the box Jobayo had given him opened and its contents exposed.

"A grand warrior like you in our humble home," Lapade said. "Quickly, fetch some water, Atitebi."

"I have no need for water. I am here to see my wife." His chest ached at the words he wished were true.

"Your wife?" Lapade frowned.

"I sent her ahead of me."

Realisation dawned on Lapade. She clasped her hands before her, a supplicant before their deity.

"Whatever she told you, it is a misunderstanding."

"Tell me what happened, then." He didn't truly care to know. Ewa was nothing but kind to all who encountered her. She could do no wrong. His hands were clenched into fists. His body thrummed with anger and wanting to punish those responsible for hurting her. That he was no better than these people made him all the more furious.

Lapade lowered herself to her knees with difficulty. "Have mercy on an old woman. We couldn't verify her identity. Go and summon her back, Atitebi."

Makinde lifted a hand, and the younger woman shrank.

"My wife wanted to visit her home, and the welcome is reserved for her husband? A stranger?"

"No, it isn't like that. You see, I am old, and my memory fails me."

"Yet, you know of Makinde."

"Your name is celebrated across the region. Who ever heard of a Ewadunni?"

"You know her name. You have opened her belongings."

"That was left here by the boy Ojo. He told us that it was a gift from his mother."

"Lies." Makinde spat. "Who is the head of this family? Where is your town's council of elders?"

If he had a weapon, he would have started swinging it. Better yet, he preferred to deal justice the way he'd taken to in the recent years in a way that would draw no blood but bring a sense of rightness to Ewa.

Atitebi threw herself on the floor beside her mother. "Please forgive us. Don't report us. It was a mistake. We didn't mean to abandon her. The warriors would have—"

"Shut up," Lapade cut in.

Makinde's stomach hardened. Forest. Abandon. Warriors. It had to be the Odan-Eripa war. What had happened to Ewa there? His head swam as he recalled her haunted appearance the day after they'd left Kuta. *Were you at Odan?* she'd asked. He'd been unable to provide a satisfactory response. Or perhaps he'd chosen not to.

"Rise." He shook his head in disgust. Not all of it was aimed at these women; the sight of Lapade grovelling was an eyesore, but the fact that wherever he went, better treatment was accorded to him because of his name and station sickened him.

"Thank you, son." Lapade rubbed her palms in supplication. "Atitebi, put her things back together right now."

Atitebi made hasty work of repacking the basket. She prostrated as she placed the pack at his feet before slinking away.

"I shall return with her, and you will make amends."

"Anything, my lord," Lapade said. "We will prepare for your arrival. Our daughter has returned."

He clicked his tongue as he hurried out. Ewa could be anywhere. He doubted she would return to the clearing where Wuu and the horse waited, not after his behaviour this morning. He had no grounds on which to face her, but it didn't stop him from walking the length and breadth of the town.

He was guided by flaming lamps scattered few and far between compounds. He knocked on doors, asking occupants if they'd noticed Ewa. No one had. Olootu wasn't large, and too soon, he had visited all the homesteads. He was close to losing his sense. It was the hour of sleep, and the night had swallowed her.

He paused to rethink. He thought of returning to have Wuu track her by scent. It would take even more time, but he had no choice. As he retraced his steps to the main road, he noticed two men stumbling across the ground. They had their arms wrapped around their shoulders as they walked a crooked path. He caught them mid-stride.

"Have you encountered a woman wearing brown clothing?" he demanded. "She is a stranger to this area."

"Haa!" one man shouted, obviously drunk.

"It sounds like you're looking for the nymph at the tavern," his less inebriated companion replied.

"Nymph?"

Makinde took a threatening step forward. The men careened back. The drunker of the two fell on his bottom and started chuckling loudly.

"If she is your woman, you better hurry there before someone takes her home."

Makinde grabbed the collar of the more sober man. "Where is she?"

"The tavern, across the river. You can walk across it."

"A man that can't control his woman, we have a term for that." The drunk laughed as he rolled on his back over the dirt road like a child.

Makinde didn't linger to hear more. He sprinted in the direction of the river then splashed through the water. When he reached the tavern, he found Ewa on the wooden podium. She was spread across a table with one arm outstretched and the other holding a calabash cup. Two gourds sat in front of her.

"Ewadunni."

She lifted her head drowsily, her head wrap askew with one end hanging low over her brow. She scoffed when their eyes locked.

"What is this one doing here?"

He landed on his knees next to her. "Ewadunni, let me take you home."

"Stop calling my name like that." She swatted at his chest with the hand holding the calabash cup, splashing beer on his tunic. "What a waste."

As she reached for the gourd, he placed a hand over hers, stopping her from refilling her cup.

"Your mother and sister want to speak with you."

He was ignorant of the specifics, but he thought he'd done what he could to mend the strained relationship she had with her family. She laughed in his face and snatched the gourd away.

"Those women are neither mother nor sister. Besides, what do you care?"

Her eyes glistened. This close, he saw how her lashes were wet. If ten thousand and one needles were driven into his flesh one by one, it wouldn't compare to the anguish ripping through him at this moment. The other patrons at the bar pretended to look away, but their bodies were inclined in

their direction, eager to catch what they could of this lovers'
quarrel.

"I know you deserve better. This isn't like you."

"And what do you know about me?" Her voice raised.

"Get up, let's go."

He grasped her upper arm and made to stand up, but she
tugged. Not wanting to hurt her, he released his hold.

"You don't tell me what to do," she spat. "Why don't you
leave me alone as you have all these years, husband?"

That last word pinched his jugular. When he'd dreamt of
Ewa calling him husband, he'd envisioned it endearingly. She
might have well as called him a good for nothing bastard. He
stared down at her, and she met his gaze head on for a few
beats before kissing her teeth.

"Me, I know my wife dare not speak to me like that," one
of the onlookers quipped.

"It is intolerable."

"The flood cannot steal the river."

He needed to get her out of here. Tongues wagged, and
stories were heavily peppered with exaggeration, and before
one knew it, their life was the plot of a tale told by moon-
light. Ewa planned on making a life for herself in Olootu,
and this wasn't a good start.

"Excuse me," he said. Without much ado, he swooped
and lifted her over his shoulder. She was stunned then started struggling. The audience cheered. He couldn't wait to be
rid of them.

"Put me down immediately." She pounded his back.

"Soon, I promise." He wrapped one arm around the back
of her thighs and ignored the pummelling she was giving

him. He lowered his knees to scoop up her bags and dropped a string of cowries on the low table. Ewa lurched as he rose again, but he kept his grip tight on her.

"I am warning you."

"What a warning." The audience jeered.

"Soon," he reassured her, patting the back of her legs.

The touch quieted her. Makinde rushed down the steps and past the river. Once they were both safely in the shadows and far away from any building, he set her gently on her feet.

"You brute!" She launched at him, pounding at his chest with her hands.

"I didn't want you to—"

"You're the reason I have lost everything," she cried. "It is your fault my fate in life is rotten."

Her voice broke, and she crumbled to the ground. Her shoulders shook violently as she wept. The pain weighing so heavily on her dragged him down, too. He sat cross-legged on spiky grass near the riverbank. They were close enough that he wanted to touch her, to hold her. She shrugged off his embrace.

"It's my fault." She brushed at her face with her hands. "I should have just died in the forest."

"Ewa—"

"Don't say my name! Why can't you let me be?"

"I promised to take you home safely. They are waiting for you," he said evenly.

She laughed without mirth. "You rejected me for years. My own family rejected me even more times. I'm not going back there. Leave me."

"Ewadunni..."

"Go back to your forest. I don't need you. I never have. I will find my way."

Makinde tugged her to his chest. His arms were unyielding as she fought him off. Eventually, she relented, softening in his embrace. Then the tears started falling in earnest. Ewa poured out the pain, frustration, and disappointment gathered over the years on his body. After an eternity, her weeping turned into sniffles. He held her under the night sky with nothing but the river and stars for company. He felt her inhale deeply then release the breath slow.

"What do you want with me?"

He rubbed circles on her back. "I don't want to see you hurt."

It was the simple and honest. It was the truth. Relief flooded him at this honesty. It was a positive step on a stairwell that had no end but which he was ready to ascend. He would tell her everything. He would keep progressing until he'd exhausted his secrets. This was a new promise.

"How interesting! Didn't you tell me that we were a mistake earlier today? Makinde, you inflicted the first wound."

"I was frightened."

She reared her head back, her surprise evident. The honey-brown depths of her eyes appeared to twinkle in the starlight.

"Makinde, son of the brave man, firm like a mountain."

He often shied from the heavy mantle his life as a warrior had placed on him, yet his panegyrics always triggered a sensitive string inside him. His praise names from her lips raised sweetness in his soul.

He dipped his head wanting to claim that mouth, but she evaded him. His lips brushed her cheek.

"What are you scared of?" she asked.

"Any blessing that comes my way quickly departs. Anytime I have tried to do good in my name, I only created evil. I don't want to lose you, Dunni, and my mistake was concluding that it was better never to have you in the first place."

In the silence that followed, insects of the night chirped loudly while the dancing river gurgled. Makinde craved Ewa; he longed for her. No one else had evoked such emotions in him. She always faced him head on. He wanted to secret her far away from the world that had been cruel to her. He wanted to open his heart to her and prayed she rewarded him with the same.

"No one calls me Dunni," she said softly.

"Don't you like it?"

"I like it. You haven't apologised."

"Forgive me, Dunni." He tightened his hands on her hips and pulled her even closer. "I will seek your forgiveness in every way that pleases you."

She laid her face on his shoulder and clung to him. "I suppose that works for a start, but I refuse to remain in Olootu."

"Will you return to Kuta?"

"No." She shook her head. "You said in your name..."

"Pardon?"

"Just now, you said every good attempted in your name was a failure. My spirit tells me there is more to that."

This particular side of him was never explored, but he remembered he was plying the route of openness and revelation. "Have you heard talk of Ojiji?"

"Only a visitor from another land hasn't. Ojiji, the spirit that goes about at night tackling community issues. Why mention it?"

He sighed. "I was in exile, but Onigbaoje and Iya Ogele brought news—"

"No! You are Ojiji? You fixed the bridge on the eastern moat and set insects to bite that philandering husband."

Her excitement made him chuckle. He could never explain why he needed to intervene in the community's affairs after he'd removed himself from everyone. Onigbaoje couldn't understand, but having those good deeds assigned to the mysterious Ojiji meant they wouldn't turn sour.

As she recounted more of Ojiji's exploits, he realised where they could go. He stood up, pulling her along with him. She swayed lightly on her feet.

"Let us retrieve your belongings," he said, interlacing his fingers with hers. "You won't have to see them."

"Where are we going to from here?" she asked.

"You will know when we get there."

She chortled in reply.

Chapter Fourteen

The early birdsong spilled into Ewa's ears. She squinted her eyes open to a grey sky—it wasn't quite yet dawn. The back of her head protested as she tried to sit up. It felt as though a bird was trapped within her skull.

She shielded her eyes with her hands at the sight of the fire. What was she doing sleeping outside? Then she saw Makinde sitting across her, the flames making his skin shine. Everything came crashing down. They were in Olootu; she'd confronted Lapade, the tavern...

Groaning, she fell back to the blanket. Her quick movements made her stomach lurch, and she closed her eyes. She heard leaves crunch as Makinde approached her. She felt his calloused palm on her forehead, massaging away the creases that'd formed with her grimace.

Her pulse beat rapidly in her throat. Last night wasn't a nightmare she'd emerged from. It was real. The things she'd said, the fact she'd broken down and cried—something she'd never done in front of living human being in her adulthood. She kept her eyes closed and tried to ignore the gentle caresses he drew on her face. Soon, she drifted back to sleep.

When she opened her eyes next, he was lifting her into his arms.

"Where are you taking me to?" she asked, nestling against the expanse of his chest.

"The farm." His voice sounded deeper.

"What farm?"

Sleep reclaimed her once more. As she dozed, she dreamt she was on a boat. It cut through calm waters, causing her to move up and down. Another boat glided in her direction. When it was close enough, she saw Ogele standing in it. She appeared without any wrinkles on her and was slimmer than when Ewa knew her.

Ewa tried to stand up but was firmly glued to her own vessel. When she opened her lips to call out to Ogele, no sound emerged. But Ogele stared at her as their boats grew closer. They were going to collide at this rate. She couldn't swim.

Ogele's boat bumped noses with hers and then scraped its side. Leaves cascaded down her head. She looked down at her lap and saw three distinct shapes: oval, reed-like, and flat with five points. When she glanced up, she was alone in the boat that rose and fell gently on the water.

EWA kept her eyes closed even after she'd awakened. She hadn't dreamt of Ogele since leaving Kuta, and now that she had, she was perturbed by the lack of sound in the dream-scape. Could it have been because they were far from Ogele's home? She'd memorised every detail of the leaves that had landed on her lap. There had to be a purpose to them she would investigate later.

She sighed deeper into the crook of her elbow. She lay on a hard surface. Wherever she was carried warmth and smelled of soap. She heard the incessant splatter of rain, but she was dry, indicating she was in a dwelling of some kind. She wasn't ready to risk sitting up and examining the place.

She was mortified by her actions and what had transpired between Makinde and her the night before. They'd reached an understanding, but this didn't mean she was happy at the display of her vulnerability. She was concerned she'd acted untowardly. After all, even in her anger, she'd felt the heat of him so close to her. Her body had cried for his touch.

It was terrible how badly she wanted him. Was it reality or in one of the dreams that had come as she winked in and out of rest where she had kissed him and pulled his body over hers before he vanished like the mist?

A gust of chilly air rushed at her back and was gone the next second as the door was closed. Makinde's presence filled everywhere, just like the aroma of spices, meat, and palm oil suffused the space. Her stomach clenched, but she remained curled on the mat. He barely made a sound when he walked so she didn't know he was near until his shadow fell over her.

"I know you're awake."

His voice raised goosebumps on her skin. She squeezed her eyes shut.

"I'm not the best of cooks, but I made a stew." He placed a large hand on her shoulder then ran it down her arm.

She released a shuddering moan. There was no use pretending. She dragged herself up and angled away from him, her gaze averted.

"If I did anything untoward last night," she started. "I would like to apologise."

He intertwined their fingers. "You have nothing to apologise for."

There had to be a medicine to cure the rapid beat of her heart. This was the same Makinde who looked like he'd been crafted from gold, but he appeared different. It was in the way he openly regarded her, like he adored her. Her head felt light.

"Eat with me," he said.

"I have to clean my teeth," she stalled.

"I can wait."

The dynamic between them had changed drastically. She needed air. Ewa found her belongings placed near the entrance. She rummaged through her bags for a chewing stick and her pouch of charcoal, then she pushed aside the mat covering the entrance and exited the hut despite the rain drizzling.

Farmland stretched all around, row after row of packed earth shaped into mounds in every direction. There were tall palm trees dotting the landscape, standing alert as the scarecrows planted among the fields.

"It's the farm."

She jumped when he spoke behind her. Had his voice always been so deep? She tilted her head to look back at him. Solid arms crept around her middle in an embrace. His hard length came up behind her. It took everything she had not to melt against him.

"Ore and Tundun," he added.

Her eyes widened in understanding. Ore had offered them foodstuff, but she had no recollection of what else he'd said. The farm stretched for miles of what looked like good land. The couple had appeared so humble, she wondered if they owned so much land outright or if they worked under a chief.

She tore herself away from Makinde, her bare feet slushed in the mud as she rounded the hut. She put the stick in her mouth and began cleaning. Light drops of water touched her head and shoulders. She touched her hair plaited in cornrows. When had her head wrap fallen off? She began scrubbing her teeth vigorously. She had made poor judgements, and she wanted to do better but...was she seeing the reflection of her own tumultuous emotions in Makinde's eyes? He radiated regard and care, and underneath it all lurked a hunger that terrified her even as she longed to immerse herself in it. She regretted drinking all that beer at the tavern.

She ambled around the hut's perimeter. It was crafted of bamboo and mud bricks, the thatch roof a cone stretched to the earth on one side of the building hiding the cooking area. She tucked herself in the long space between the roof and the wall.

A covered pot rested on a hearth comprised of three stones containing burning firewood. The white horse was tethered to a tree near the grain store. A well sat behind the hut, but there was no need to draw water because the large clay pots set beside the wall were full.

Ewa used one of the bowls stacked close to rinse her face. She lowered herself before the fire and lifted the pot's cover with the edge of her wrapper. The stew simmered and appeared to be done. She found rags which she used to lift the pot off the hearth.

Inside the hut, Makinde was seated on a stool, waiting. He stood as soon as she re-entered, mouth cleaned and bearing supper. Being outside had helped. She had nothing to be ashamed of, not with him.

This time when he eyed her, she didn't shy away but absorbed the sight of him. She placed the pot on the floor. Her arms needed to be empty so she could reach for him. He reached her first, crashing her into an embrace that made her heart soar. Having Makinde hold and kiss her wasn't enough—she wanted to step inside his skin.

"What are you scared of?" he whispered in her ear.

"Hm," she murmured. She'd asked him the same question. "They say the night before one embarks on a great journey is beset with terrors."

He caressed her cheek. "You won't navigate this journey alone."

"I know. That is what scares me. I have been on my own for too long and believed I will always be."

"Not any more. I am here."

She beamed. "And I am here."

MAKINDE had thrown together yams, smoked fish from days before, palm oil, pepper pods, and vegetables in the stew. It didn't appear appetising but tasted heavenly. They ate from the pot together, a new intimacy that was only the start of more tender moments like this. Makinde scooped a morsel of soft yam and offered it to Ewa. She opened her lips eagerly.

"You're always feeding me."

His smile was boyish. "Living alone, a man has to take care of himself."

"That doesn't necessarily mean he can take care of someone else," she said. "Tell me about the forest."

She half-expected him to tense up or give his usual grunt or curt answer. But he spoke of his exile in low tones.

"I was trying to find peace initially. The ghosts of war surrounded me. I thought being home and among family would put an end to that, but it didn't. The elders considered me weak. No one in the family thought I'd excel at warring. Iya Ogele revealed to me that when my life path was read as a child, the priests advised that I don't become a warrior. My father was affronted. No son of his had the option of rejecting what all Kuta is known for."

"You must be aware of the options for healing," she said softly. "Why haven't you made use of them?"

He gave a self-deprecating laugh. "Those won't work for me. The silence of the woods, sitting in meditation with nature, now that has been beneficial to me."

"You think you don't deserve it."

"I was raised and trained to be a warrior. The war never ended for me."

"Yet, Ojiji appeared in a period of peace."

"It was a way to help others without my name attached. The life of a recluse is monotonous. I would go into Kuta and neighbouring towns to settle quarrels, repair infrastructure..."

Not even a month ago, she wouldn't have conceived speaking to him in this manner. She suspected he felt the same way. It was surprising and new, like a seed first germinating from the soil, but it felt right.

After they finished their meal, she placed her head on his shoulder and closed her eyes.

"Usiade told me you helped her escape from Odan. What happened?"

This time, she felt him stiffen. He didn't break contact, but each of his breaths came shallower.

"Who is Usiade?" he asked.

"The Oba's wife at Ibukun. She came to visit you and met me."

"You're yet to ask me what I saw at Ibukun," he said.

That question had its place in the queue. She threaded her arm through his.

"What did you see?"

"A girl who lost her life because of me."

Her grip on him tightened.

"I swore to keep her safe and then led her to danger," he continued. "She wasn't the only one."

"What do you mean?"

She'd been approaching her twentieth year when the ruler of her hometown committed a grave sin. One of the brides from their neighbouring ruler's harem travelled through Odan to get home to Eripa when a passing storm stranded her. Eripa's Olori must have been unbothered because Odan had a monarch who was brother to her husband. She'd been wrong.

Far removed from the happenings at the palace, Ewa had only become aware war being in the air when it arrived. First, the Odan defence cadre was eliminated. Anyone would have thought that spelt the end of the clash, but Eripa's warriors were operating under more nefarious orders.

Ogele was the person who'd told her the entire story. She'd revealed what sparked the war—the violence the Oba of Odan had meted on a woman who had sought refuge in his palace. Eripa's Oba summoned warriors from across the region ostensibly to defend what he saw as an affront to his person. It had been a sunny day when Ogele had led Ewa through the forest, but her words had chilled her core. "*Rumours whispered that the Oba of Eripa gave warriors the license to treat Odan's maidens the way his wife was treated.*"

"I was recruited to fight," Makinde said, drawing her to the present. "It seemed just. Many men from Kuta responded to Eripa's call. We fought and we won, then warriors breached the town, and mayhem descended. I did what I could, and I failed."

"You tried to stop it."

He shook his head, his jaw clenched. "It wasn't enough. The men in my unit...I need to pay for our sins. I spent those years in preparation."

Every warrior in Kuta became a suspect when she learned the truth. How could they commit such evil and walk through life unscathed? Kuta's warriors settled back into normalcy after violent campaigns while their victims carried physical and mental scars forever. She had swept her anger and distrust to cover all warriors, including Makinde.

To Ogele, life was composed of right and wrong in a delicate balance. On the times they bickered, the elder woman would stress how the warriors of Kuta often had no choice. They fought to protect what they knew, and often, the families were maintained on the bounty forming their reward after war. The enemy wouldn't hesitate to do the same to protect theirs. Ewa felt humanity would keep failing if at least one party didn't take the high road. Both women agreed on the excessive violence of the Odan-Eripa war.

Makinde took a shaky breath. "I've said too much."

"No, you haven't. What have you been preparing?"

"Revenge."

"Revenge?"

"For the innocent faces I see, the lives I couldn't save. I will find the men responsible."

Before she could object, before she could let him know this wasn't the way to go about making amends, he stood up.

"I told myself to tell you everything," he said. "And I will. But let's stop here tonight."

"Of course." She nodded.

The weight of his words kept her on the floor as he took out the now-empty pot. She chewed her lip. She had to find a way to dissuade Makinde against his search for revenge. Even with murky details, she knew spilling more blood would wound him deeper. She had to stop him from hurtling himself off a figurative cliff.

Chapter Fifteen

Honesty and openness were traits Makinde never got the chance to enjoy. Until now, he hadn't realised how much he was missing. Ewa now knew more about him than anyone else. They were like everyday lovers, a rite of passage he was yet to enjoy despite his age.

As a young warrior, female attention was inevitable. Returning from successful campaigns often happened with women eagerly waiting to fall into the arms of the nearest virile warrior. Many of these women were older, some married and uncaring of the social implications that came with having an affair.

He'd entertained a few liaisons, but even then, there'd been a hollowness in his chest that only widened as his years advanced. Glancing down at Ewa, he wondered if all his experiences had been leading him to this moment. She'd drifted off to sleep. Her head rested on his chest, and her gentle dozing breaths tickled his shoulder.

They'd talked about the war, their families, childhood memories...but there was one thing still a mystery to him. Only she could reveal how exactly they came to be married. He'd been at war and then returned to find his family congratulating him not just for making it home alive but also for selecting a beautiful woman to be his bride.

Between attempts at keeping his mates in order and shielding all the maidens he encountered, he hadn't seen Ewa. Surely, he would have recalled her face. The ones belonging to the women he'd failed were as fresh in his mind as if he'd seen them this morning. As the son of an enslaved woman, keeping a woman against her will was against his nature. He wouldn't wish any child witnessing what he did, with the understanding to come later that his mother abandoned him for freedom—as was her right.

When morning came, his eyes were on the ceiling. Ewa stirred, murmuring as she propped herself up. Her face glowed with a good rest, a soft sheen to her skin as though she were a flower bathed in morning dew. He resolved to ask for more of her brew so he could sleep beside her like a true lover.

She smiled at him, and he nodded in understanding. By now, he was certain she engaged in the same rituals every morning. The closest he'd come to spirituality as an adult was his quiet moments with nature. He missed that tree with its blue flowers and magnificent scent, had forgotten he'd meant to locate another of its kind to settle nearby. None of it mattered with her.

Before he made to rise, she stilled him with a hand on his bare chest. She shook her head and got up, leaving the hut instead. He watched her go, amused by their ability to silently communicate. He waited a few moments before stepping out himself.

The dawn sky was tinged blue. His dog was curled beside the horse, fast asleep. Makinde took in Wuu's muddy coat and shook his head. The dog was prone to his own adven-

tures and often needed a bath. He stretched his legs by walking around the fields. When he'd ferried a sleeping Ewa here,
they'd passed palm fronds attached to a stick planted into
the ground—a warning to keep off. He'd trudged on because
they'd had an invitation, but that hadn't stopped the farmers
in the neighbouring fields from investigating.

Ewa had been sequestered in the hut when the men and
women had come to demand what strangers were doing on
Ore's farm. They'd left only when they were satisfied with the
details Makinde gave them about Ore, Tundun, and Gbala.
Here, being a decorated warrior didn't matter, not when an
associate's livelihood was at stake.

Ewa found him after completing her ablutions. With the
earliest rays of the sun reaching for the earth, she foraged
with him. They'd eaten a modest meal of fruits when she suggested a walk. He was happy to go with her anywhere. This
trust they were building was tenuous, but with both of them
tending and caring to it, it was sure to flourish.

"I want to offer you something," she said.

They crushed dried leaves underneath their feet, holding
hands as they walked unhurriedly. She was glued to his side,
no longer walking ahead desperate to be free of him.

"You being here with me is enough."

"And I want—" her voice cracked so she cleared her
throat. "I want you here with me, wholly. Allow me to perform a ritual."

"Is that why we're here?"

The woods near the farm were light, a few skinny tall
trees making the canopy while shorter shrubs and plants
comprised most of the greenery. Two squirrels bounded past

them. Ewa paused so the animals crossed the dirt road, but only one was brave enough to scurry before them.

"I've been seeing Iya Ogele," she said. "In my dreams."

"I saw her, too, just before her passing. She knew she was going to die on that journey, and she took it."

"She's still here." Ewa placed her right hand on her heart. "What did she tell you?"

"She gave me an earful for hiding myself. I never listened. Iya Ogele wanted me in the homestead. She would have dragged me to you if she could. What did she tell you in your dreams?"

"The same thing she did you."

They both chuckled and resumed their leisurely stroll. Makinde saw Ewa as he had that first time, through the bush with leaves framing her beautiful face. His throat clogged at what he'd almost missed. If he'd refused to accompany her, this moment would have never come to pass. He would have missed the opportunity to be embraced in the peace he now currently felt.

"In the most recent dream, Iya showed me some leaves. And I believe they are for you."

He grew apprehensive. Although he trusted Ogele's abilities as a healer and he knew Ewa wouldn't hurt him, there was only one thing both women would want to remove from his system, and he wasn't quite ready to let go of it. Ewa didn't have to agree with him, but some form of justice needed to be meted out on behalf the women of Odan.

"This is one," she said suddenly.

She squatted in front of an unremarkable bush and pushed her hand through leaves shaped like a palm with five short fingers. He watched, amused, as she greeted the plant and asked for permission to collect its gifts before plucking ten leaves.

"Did you see this while you slept?" he asked.

"It is exactly as I saw it." She brandished the handful in a flourish before sliding them into the small cloth sack slung over her shoulder. "But I will admit I didn't understand everything then."

"I don't dream."

"That is because you don't sleep."

"Even before then. What people see in dreams, I see in reality."

"I believe this will help," she said, concerned. "I think this is what Iya Ogele wants."

They repeated the motions, walking without any direction or so it appeared until she recognised a plant from her subconscious.

"It just occurred to me," she said, adjusting her carrier bag. "You saw Iya Ogele when she was alive? Did she visit you often?"

"In the early years, yes," he replied. "But most recently, I came down to see her."

She clicked her tongue. "That woman! She denied ever seeing you. She knew I would have hated her if she'd been honest with me."

The more they discussed Ogele, the more he warmed up to the idea of this ritual. He'd refused his mother and denied himself Ewa all this while. Perhaps this was a step in the process of making up for the lost time. The future remained uncertain, but he was assured that even in the next life, the only woman he'd desire was Ewa.

"Before we left Kuta for Olootu, I was thinking of relocating myself."

She stared at him with wide eyes. "How come? Where to?"

"I was looking for a tree. The one with the blue flowers."

"It was magnificent."

They reached a slow-paced river. She pointed to the thin long plants beside it. "That's the last one. And just in time."

He found a dry patch of land and lowered himself while she went to commune with the plants. She rinsed her collection of leaves while chanting in low whispers. After returning the leaves to her medicine bag, she joined him by the bank.

"Why don't we go somewhere new? What do you think about the riverine area Iya Ogele called home for years?"

"I prefer the forest." He cleared his throat. "Will you stay in a forest?"

"Well," she replied, putting her hands on her full hips. "The forest is a gift, and if you are there to keep me safe...why not?"

He leapt up and carried her, spinning her around, and was rewarded by her peals of laughter. The true gift as far as he was concerned would always be Ewa. Her presence and the joy she instilled in his life were a balm to his soul. This was a part of life he'd assumed he didn't need or want. She was showing him he was deserving.

EWA knew instinctively it had to be done at nighttime when the earth was cooler. She left the gathered herbs to soak in water and returned to Makinde. When she'd confessed she wasn't skilled in cooking, he once more took charge of their meal. There were more yams in the store and plantains from the western perimeter of the farm. She had spices remaining from the batch Tope had prepared for her, and Makinde went hunting for fowl to add some flavour to the soup. All this promised a delicious meal.

After the cascade of emotions of the past weeks, she was glad for the respite. She was content to simply engage in undemanding tasks, to send Wuu chasing after a stick, to converse. Her feet thanked her for not putting them to work by walking throughout the day. While Makinde hunted, she soaked them in a basin of water and fragrant flowers that had caught her eye on the way back from foraging earlier. She counted the hours until sundown in anticipation of the positive change she would be bringing to his life.

She wasn't delusional—it was impossible for one to completely change another soul. This was a step in the right direction because he was ready. She felt it in her bones. She stood firm in her connection with Ogele and her belief. That he stood with her moved her deeply.

After they'd eaten, she started preparations. She called out to him when she was ready. It was dusk, and the sky blended orange with blue. Heat rushed to her cheeks as he emerged from the hut naked save for a small cloth around his waist and the protective amulets he wore around his arm. His long legs corded with muscle, his bare chest appeared sculpted from metal.

Her thighs pulsed remembering the feel of him. They'd spent more than a day exchanging words and were yet to do the other, more intimate kind of conversation. She sighed in appreciation then tampered her lust down for later. She needed focus.

Behind the hut, she set a basin carrying the water-logged leaves she'd prayed over. Makinde was before her like a statue. She caught his uncertain gaze and gave an encouraging smile. She started first by gliding her hand through the water in the basin. With more prayers on her lips, she grabbed a handful of herbs and wrung them over his head, stretching her arms up to do so.

The energy in the air shifted. Makinde wheezed, closing his eyes as water ran down his face. The same water trailed down her upraised arms, eliciting a shudder. As she washed him using the sodden leaves as a sponge, the tips of her fingers and toes tingled.

He landed on his knees in front of her. His head bowed, and his shoulders heaved. He gasped for air as if he were drowning. Her heart twisted in response, but she kept on washing him and praying. She was swaying on her feet by the time she'd emptied the basin over his head.

"It's done." She gingerly placed her hands on his shoulders.

He responded by throwing his arms around her hips and pressing his head against her lower belly. She ran her hands over his damp coils. They stood this way for an eternity. Her wrapper was sodden with herbal water and his tears. The night was silent and heavy like it'd carried on their burdens.

"Come in with me," he said. The expression on his face was vulnerable, but there was no shame in his need for her.

She traced her fingers down his cheeks. "I will. Go in first."

When he stood up, she used the edge of her clothes to remove the dirt on his knees. She rubbed off the green bits of leaves lingering on his skin. As he disappeared, she blinked in the direction of the farmland. The outline of a shadowy figure darker than night hovered near the palm trees at the edge of the fields. She shivered. Was this what Makinde endured?

She stripped out of her clothes and poured water from a second basin over herself. She whispered supplications for strength and protection. The ends of her plaits glistened with moisture as she waited for the air to dry her skin. She found an oil lamp and lit it the way Makinde had taught her to, chuckling when the wick caught.

When she stepped into the hut, she placed the lamp on the floor for Ogele who never slept in darkness. Makinde was fast asleep on the mat in the corner. He lay peacefully on his back, his chest rising and falling with each breath. She located her oil and massaged her skin all while observing him. She prayed this would take. She didn't know how long the cleansing would last— sooner or later, he needed to visit a priest who would determine the proper prescription to be offered.

Tying a clean wrapper around her, she sat on the floor beside him and placed a hand on the light sprinkling of hair on his chest. His skin was dry and carried the bitter yet fragrant scent of the plants. She observed his steady heartbeat. He was probably sleeping the best he had in years.

Satisfied, she massaged her body oil onto his limbs. With every minute that passed, her heart swelled with gratitude and an emotion stronger than anything she'd felt before. She laid down on the mat to sleep and gasped when he pulled her close.

"You're here," he said, his voice hoarse as he cuddled her from behind.

Her hands reached for his arms around her, holding him tighter. "I am here."

His hands shifted up. He pulled her wrapper down with urgency and cupped her breasts. She tossed her head back as he teased her nipples into hardened points. She covered his hands with hers. She wanted to hold him in place so he could continue pleasuring her this way.

"You should be sleeping."

"I've slept two nights already." He kissed behind her neck.

"It was barely a nap."

"Let me love you, Dunni."

The way he said her name made her crumble. Makinde turned her around and covered her lips with his. He consumed her with unrestrained hunger. His kisses were soft but insistent, different from that night in Ibukun. He was going to eat her up, she was sure of it. She had no interest in objecting.

Her heart thumped a fast rhythm in expectation. Her head rolled back as he licked a path down her chin, tasting her neck and finally settling on her small breasts. His tongue drew tight circles on her breast. She cried out when he wrapped his lips around her nipple and sucked firmly. His hands pulled her wrapper farther down, caressing her with the beads around her waist. She bucked beneath him, tossing her head along the floor. The feel of the beads pressing and dragging against her sensitive skin and his mouth on her breasts drove her wild.

Makinde sat back.

"Don't..."

He chuckled before ripping her wrapper away from her. She watched him take her in. His eyes roamed every inch of her skin. She grew shy unexpectedly and sent her hands down to cover the curls at the juncture of her thighs. He shook his head as he gripped her wrists and exposed her to his regard.

"You're perfect," he said, lowering his head to her stomach.

Partly hidden by her beads on her right side was her tattoo. He kissed each ink-filled spot before tracing the raised skin with his tongue. She was slowly running out of her mind. Her memories of pain at the tattooist's compound would forever be replaced with this. This type of pleasure exceeded her fantasies, and she wanted more.

Makinde nuzzled his nose against the hairs on her pubic mound. His breath was so close to her private spot, her heart lodged in her throat.

"Makinde," she keened.

At the contact of his mouth enclosed on her nether lips, she screamed. He held down her twitching hips.

"Comfortable?"

"Yes! Don't stop."

He lapped at her wetness, consuming her pleasure and regenerating it tenfold. It felt like she'd been struck by lightning, but instead of pain, currents of intense pleasure slithered through her.

Ewa spread her legs wider and began thrusting her hips against his face. His hum encouraged her to throw away the last of her reservations. Her skin grew hot as tension built within her body, concentrated on that one spot he attended to so expertly. This was what drove otherwise sane individuals wild, and now she understood why many spent their lives searching for such rapture.

A loud moan escaped from her lips as she shuddered her release. But it was only the beginning. Makinde slipped a finger into her wet tightness. His intrusion caused spasms to shudder through her. She clawed at his arms as he slowly pleasured her with his fingers. Each push triggered wetness that gushed out of her like a spring. She rolled her hips in tandem, uncaring that he had leaned back to observe her. She needed to be one with him.

Sensing her readiness, he threw an arm about her waist and pulled her atop him. She glanced down and gasped at the size of his erect manhood. It angled up his stomach creating a tent with the blanket tangled around his hips. She buried her face in his shoulder.

"Look at me, Dunni."

"I can't."

He held the back of her neck and massaged it gently. She drew back with his support and saw his expression was nothing but passion. He took her left hand and placed it on his length. She gingerly dragged her fingers along his girthy member and was rewarded by his grunt.

Many years ago, she'd assumed she would go through life without experiencing copulation. But here was Makinde below her and yearning terribly for her. All of this was for her. She pushed aside the blanket and held his member firmer, eliciting another groan from him. It jerked eagerly towards her inner thigh.

He kept his eyes glued to hers. "Take me, Ewa. I am yours."

She bit her lip and nodded. She shifted against his folded legs, positioning his member against her wet slit. She sat on it with a sigh. He stretched her in a way that was intensely gratifying. She had to remember to breathe as she rose up and down on his shaft taking more of him each time.

Each motion of her waist with delicate precision sent him groaning. She wrapped her legs around him as she rode him in the sensual dance of ages. Their foreheads pressed together, and their breaths mingled. His hands played with her waist beads, gripping them as her tempo increased.

When he started thrusting against her, she couldn't take any more. She wrapped her arms around his shoulders, her shouts of pleasure right against his ear. The feel of him inside her, of his arms clutching her waist, of his own sounds of love drove her over the precipice. She was dying of pleasure, but he didn't relent. His hold snapped one of her waist beads, sending the oval shapes across the floor.

Without a care, he shifted her so she was on her back. He drastically slowed down, grinding his hips against hers so tenderly. She moved along with him, her throat hoarse from her screaming. Ewa clawed at his chest and upper arms as the ultimate source of pleasure unfurled through her, and she kept pace as he thrust faster and harder.

Just as the world crumbled around her for the third time that night, he grunted his release. As they struggled to catch their breaths, she laughed.

"This is what you denied me for ten years," she said.

"I don't plan on denying you ever again."

Chapter Sixteen

I f the recent days had taught Ewa anything, it was that she knew nothing. A proverb stated that what an elder could see seated, a child wouldn't see standing. She was a child who hadn't anticipated how joyful Makinde's company was. In hindsight, the many divinations she'd sat in through the years gained more clarity. So, too, did Ogele's constant encouragement. It'd irritated her in the past, and now, she wished she could have exhibited more patience towards the older woman.

For whatever reason, her destiny had set her on this course. She supposed ten years was better than waiting forty years to witness him reveal himself to her. Being together came so easily; they cooked and ate, went on walks, chatted with the farmers nearby, and any spare moment between was spent making love.

She lost track of the days as she wrung freshly laundered clothes by the stream located half a day's walk from the farm. It had been a stunning sight when they'd first come across it. Four rivulets of water cascaded in small droplets from an elevated point, emptying into the stream below. Shrubs hung over the cliff with a few adventurous vines dangling in imitation of the waterfalls. The rocky shore provided space to spread the laundry.

Behind her, Makinde sat cross-legged with his back pressed against a tree. His eyelids were lowered, and save for his chest rising and falling with each breath, he appeared like a statue. Though she was more inclined to singing and talking to nature than sitting in silence, she appreciated his attempts to connect to the universe. She'd now had the occasion to sit with him and found his meditations very much like prayer. It'd also not gone unnoticed that he had been sleeping well since the bath.

When she'd finished with the clothes, she settled on a large blackened rock. She preferred not to disturb Makinde in his moment of peace and decided to loosen her cornrows. She'd barely touched one plait when he opened his eyes and unfurled his legs. She let go of her hair as he approached.

"Dunni, I didn't know you to be a hypocrite." The grin on his lips took any edge off his words.

"What do you mean?" she replied, a pretend scowl on her face.

"You didn't wash this, too?" he asked, gesturing at her middle.

The sparkle in his eye said it all. She clapped her hands as she laughed and glanced down at the green wrapper around her. She'd washed most of their clothing and kept this one for modesty. She had collected all of his tunics and trousers. The man only had two pairs his friend—who she now knew was called Onigbaoje—had lent to him. Makinde was to spend the afternoon in a loincloth fashioned out of one of her shawls. It did a poor job covering his magnificent form much to her delight.

He tugged at the knot holding her wrapper. Her body responded to the possessive move, and warmth flooded from her centre almost immediately. She and him weren't only speaking with words or coded glances, not any more. Their communication extended to the physical—their hearts beat in tandem, their most secret parts hungered for the other. Even their blood flowed in alignment. To her, the connection with him went even deeper to otherworldly places where they must have been fated to each other, too.

Still in a playful mood, she held her wrapper up. "Is this how it was in your forest sanctuary? Was everyone naked?"

He grunted, the sound an affirmation. She glanced at his beaming face and then away, up to where the water tumbled from.

"Is that why the maidens of Kuta were always coming up to search for you?"

"Indeed. They must have heard of my skill."

Her head snapped back. She glared at Makinde who was chuckling, beside himself. She shook her head and stormed off to the water's edge. He was close behind her. He touched her arm lightly, and it was enough to cause goosebumps to sprout everywhere on her body. Her nipples hardened while the nectar he was so skilled at milking from her continued pooling between her thighs.

"You're the first woman I've touched in years," he said.

"Is that so?"

"Of course. I won't lie about this."

Ewa lowered herself, only to scoop water in her hands that she splashed at his surprised face.

"Y-you were not upset."

She laughed raucously in response. He lunged for her, and she dashed away. Lukewarm water hit her back as he got his repayment, but he was unsatisfied until he'd caught her in his arms. She squealed as the sky tilted. He lifted her up, his arms strong and sure around her as he carried her back to land. He laid her down on it. She spread her legs so he could see her eagerness in the light of the day. She was no longer the shy woman of before. She giggled in feminine delight at the way he ate her up with his eyes.

"Did you bring the honey?"

She pointed to the spot where they'd left their pack in the shade. "Why?"

"You'll see."

Makinde leapt off her. Ewa propped herself up on her elbows to watch his actions. Her brows creased. Why was he suddenly interested in eating honey when she was here?

She didn't rest in confusion for too long. He returned and took no time drizzling the honey on her midriff.

"What—"

Her objection turned into a moan when he began licking the honey off her.

"I have wanted to do this since fetching this honey," he murmured, his teeth clamping her nipple.

She gasped. "Since then!"

"Even before."

"When?"

She lost her senses then as his honey-dipped fingers pressed into her. She threw her head back and grasped his shoulder. The sun was on her face. She closed her eyes and saw red as he took her to the heights of pleasure. They'd journeyed this delectable path frequently now, and the honey brought a new addition.

Wanting to please him, too, she pushed him onto his back. He looked at her eagerly as she took some honey on her fingers and trailed it from his throat down to circle his belly button. Her mouth replaced her fingers but ventured lower. She wrapped her lips around his turgid member, tasting honey and his own essence. He stiffened, his hands gripping the fabric beneath them.

"Dunni," he shouted hoarsely.

Emboldened, she took more of him into her mouth. She stroked him with her hand as she sucked. His stomach was taut, the muscles in his legs tense. His reaction to her was a new kind of pleasure. Her wetness trailed down the back of her thighs. Makinde grunted her name again.

"Come to me."

She needed no further encouragement to climb on him, taking him in her damp warmth. He gripped her waist and pumped upwards without preamble. He was in complete control and unrelenting in his mission to bring her to rapture. She moaned loudly and dug her fingernails into his unyielding shoulders.

"Don't dare stop," she urged him on.

His upward movements caused her beads to jingle as they clashed against each other. She was aware of the way her breasts moved with each thrust. She felt the sun on her shoulders, a cool breeze from the water on her back, everything serving to heighten her pleasure.

Makinde sat up and brought their rapid motion to a pause. Her pleasure-clouded mind was ready to protest when he lifted her up and placed her in a new position. She was on her knees and he was behind her. A jolt shocked her body at the feel of his tongue on her nether lips. Before she could reacquaint herself with the sensation of his mouth on her, he slid his manhood into her once more.

They both groaned. She leaned forward on her elbows, giving herself more leverage to push back. Her behind was one of her best assets, and she made it jiggle for him. Bliss rose within her in waves like the waterfall feeding the stream behind them. Sweat covered her back, her sensitive nipples brushing against the cloth beneath her as he pushed and pushed till she shrieked continuously. She stretched a hand behind and he caught it, holding onto him as his love poured into her tightness.

Afterwards, they lay on cloth-covered grass following a brief dip in the stream.

"You have ruined my cloth." Her chin was propped on his chest, and she felt his chuckle deep in him.

"I will buy more for you, Dunni." His hand cupped her bottom, scuttling her closer to him.

"You owe me beads for my waist, too."

"I will buy you twenty more."

She purred as he started drawing circles from her bottom to her lower back. "Since you're so agreeable, you should meet a priest soon."

As far as she was concerned, he needed deeper spiritual intervention to be free of the ghosts of his past. She wanted these days of joy and laughter to last for eternity and felt strongly that Ogele's remedy was temporary. But to her frustration, he laughed off her concern.

"I have you to thank for bringing me peace," he said. "You're enough, Dunni."

"While I appreciate your faith in me, I don't believe it is enough. You need someone like Fadahunsi."

His roaming hands stilled. "You mean that man?"

She caught the dark cloud passing over his face even though he kept his tone light.

"Are you jealous of my friend?"

He pursed his lips. "If you thought I was meeting maidens in the forest...perhaps I thought you were entertaining the priest."

It seemed like a lifetime ago when she had carried a flame for Fadahunsi. Whatever she'd felt for him was nothing compared to Makinde. If Fadahunsi lit anything in her, it was a lamp with a quivering wick while Makinde easily set her world ablaze like fields after a harvest.

"Fadahunsi wasn't my lover," she said at his raised eyebrow. It felt good to pay him back for earlier, to know their jealousy was mutual. "My Makinde, we can't stay here forever. It won't do for Tundun to return to an empty store."

"Indeed."

He continued caressing her back much to her pleasure. She snuggled against him. "Where shall we go?"

"Why don't we travel the land like Iya Ogele?" he suggested. "When we see land that pleases us, we will set our roots."

"I will be happy as long as we don't travel forever."

He gave her a reassuring squeeze. "We won't."

MAKINDE'S fate had been selected before he was born. While he wasn't familiar with what was predetermined for him and thus couldn't read the future, he knew a lot about patterns. Those dictated that nothing good ever lasted—the naivety of childhood snatched the day he witnessed his mother's escape; the friendship he'd found in like-minded men ended with the slaying of innocent lives. Now, the love he'd come to share with Ewa was going to be dashed. He felt it approaching in his bones even before the runner appeared at the farm.

He had been in the hut with Ewa, having spent hours of slow love-play when they heard Wuu's barking.

"Leave him," Ewa said. "That dog does what he wants. Disappearing then returning to demand our affection."

"He is used to the wilderness," he replied. Wuu would never be domesticated and loved to remind him he didn't need them to survive. But he had lived with the dog as his companion for long enough to know this warranted attention. He stood up and fetched one of her wrappers to cover his nudity.

She grinned. "That's one more wrapper you'll have to buy for me."

"I will hire a weaver to stay by your side and spin clothes for you nonstop."

"As expected of my Makinde. My husband who bathed me with honey."

He chuckled at the new praise names she gave him. He planted a kiss on her nose before leaving the hut. He ducked his head as he stepped out. He found Wuu barking at a stranger standing at the farm's boundary. They were well acquainted with the farmers tending to fields within reach by now, and he observed this wasn't a familiar face. The fine quality of his clothes and half-shaved head pointed the stranger out as a messenger in the employ of a palace. His mouth went dry.

"Greetings to Makinde of Kuta." The runner prostrated as he approached.

There was a log in Makinde's throat as he directed the man to stand up with the flick of a wrist. Introductions weren't necessary.

"Great warrior. The Oba of Jaku requests your service."

As they stood in the shade of palm trees, his vision swam. When he lifted a hand to his forehead, he found it was doused in sweat. Thunder rumbled in the distance even though the sky remained clear. He cleared his throat.

"Tell me."

"Our previous Oba passed away..." the messenger began.

It was the same information Onigbaoje had brought to him in Kuta months ago. A monarch deceased and his sons squabbling for the throne in open disrespect of the selected crown prince. This crown prince had done all he could to appease his brothers—offering titles and land—and ensure a peaceful start of his reign, but they'd banded against him.

"Our spies tell us that an army grows to remove the rightful ruler of Jaku," the messenger said. "In response, the Oba asks for the assistance of the best warriors from across the region."

Onigbaoje would surely be there. Arole, too—he was connected to Jaku. The end of this decade-old nightmare was finally within reach.

"Will Arole of Kuta be there?" he asked.

His voice was calm and collected, the hand on his forehead projecting concentration instead of the dismay simmering in his stomach.

Three wrinkles appeared between the messenger's brows. He appeared ruffled and took his time responding. The worst blunder for one in his profession was to have his message misinterpreted. Especially one that came directly from a monarch.

"I was sent to find you and cannot speak on other warriors. The Oba has promised to reward all who answer his call handsomely. However, Jaku won't wait like fowls in the open field before a hawk swoops in."

Makinde was separated from himself—on one hand was the loving husband devoted to reinventing himself, and on the other was the seasoned veteran. Sweat dripped down his bare back. This might be his chance to make amends, to confront Arole and other members of their unit. Arole had always been his target because he was a close friend, but the man had all but disappeared.

The adrenaline coursing through his veins at the thought of a fight was a betrayal, not only to himself but to the fragile bond he was building with Ewa. Even considering that, it made no sense to let this opportunity go. He thought of returning to her from Jaku. He instinctively knew she would be displeased, but perhaps this might be their relationship's first test.

He dragged a hand down his face then pressed his thumb against his lower lip. A scream welled up inside him, and he needed to ensure it didn't escape. Even before leaving

Kuta, he'd suspected his encounter with Arole would be his last. Facing Arole would differ from the chastisement he secretly dealt to bad elements in Kuta's environs. Arole matched his skill with weapons, but even if Makinde succeeded, he would have lost all the same—in this at least, Ewa was right.

The messenger eyed him warily as the silence extended.

"When?" he asked.

"As soon as possible. I can lead you there."

"I will prepare."

In a few short words, everything he had been trying to achieve lately unravelled. An ugly shadow shifted in the corner of his eye, a reminder carried through the gentle breeze that shook the leaves overhead. *You are a murderer.*

He spun around and froze. Ewa stood behind him, her features sombre and her mouth downcast. A pulse started beating in his head. He needed refuge from the disappointment etched on her face. He marched past her towards the hut knowing she was behind him. She waited until they were indoors to descend on him.

"What is happening?"

"You must have heard it," he said.

"I want to confirm what I witnessed from your lips."

He found his pack and patted the dust off the beaded leather. He sighed. "The crown of Jaku is at stake, and I am to defend it."

"By whose order?"

"The legitimate monarch's."

He stuffed the other pair of clothes Onigbaoje had given him next to the short spears and knife in his bag.

"Don't do it." Ewa's tone shifted from confrontational to pleading. "My Makinde, don't engage in warfare."

Her words tugged at his heart. She touched his back, trailing his skin as she moved to stand in front him. The contact shattered him although he remained standing. He could barely look at her, instead staring at a spot over her shoulder to keep his resolve from vanishing like mist in the afternoon. She touched his clenched jaw.

"It is Arole..." he murmured. "For ten years, I have waited."

"Makinde, please." She held his face in her hands and lowered it down, forcing him to regard her. "Shedding more blood isn't the answer. Makinde, we choose a path of healing."

He made a frustrated sound between a grunt and a groan. He lowered his lids, shielding himself from her concern.

"Arole killed an innocent woman in front of me. He has to pay."

He saw her then, limp on the floor as life bled out from the gashes in her chest and neck. Arole gloated over her fading body. What made killing on the battlefield any different from this? There was one tale he was yet to tell Ewa in its entirety. During the Odan-Eripa war, he'd trusted his friend with the safety of two maidens and their families while he ran through the woods searching for more people to rescue. As far as he was concerned, the war had ended on the battlefield with Eripa's repugnant command notwithstanding. They were trained to defend, not to molest.

Yet, fleeing families screamed, running faster when he approached them. Only a few accepted his offer of aid. Upon returning to the secluded cave where he'd left Arole, he crossed paths with his younger brother. He recalled telling Togun to lead the families he'd herded out to safety. "Let no harm befall them. I will join you shortly with Arole," he'd said, unprepared for the horror waiting for him.

If he'd known Arole was no different from the other marauding warriors, he would have never left the women in his care. He would never understand the action of men who snatched and caused needless violence. They'd been called to defend a ruler, to meet with other trained men on equal grounds. The slaughter of anyone outside this specific circumstance was what separated warriors from murderers.

In his exile, he'd often considered how there was nothing noble about taking a life even when justifiable. He was no better than his brothers at arms in Odan-Eripa, and he was no better now in Jaku.

Ewa massaged his temples, bringing him back to the present.

"All these years, you settled abusers and oppressors in the shadows. People thought you were a spirit and called you Ojiji, but you are human, of flesh and bone. There are other ways to deal justice, Makinde. You could have tracked down her family and sought forgiveness there. You could have asked the deities to intercede. You aren't interested in justice. You are more inclined to torture yourself—"

"You're not a warrior, hence your lack of understanding," he said, stepping back. It was true he'd never considered those options, but it was what made him separate from Ewa.

He clenched the leather strap of his bag. "You can be too naive about the ways of the world."

"Pardon?"

"Karma isn't real. The universe doesn't mete out any justice."

Ewa drew in a sharp breath. He didn't wait to witness her reaction to his words. He snatched the saddle and exited the hut. His skin itched as though he'd stepped into a termite mound and was covered in the tiny biting insects. He was destroying everything, as usual.

He untied the horse from where he'd secured it. The animal skittered away, sensing his inner turmoil. He tried to calm it by petting its withers. He heard a twig snap as Ewa caught up with him. The horse was positioned between them, and he focused on it.

"You never asked me how I made it to Kuta," she said. "You still are yet to ask how I became your wife."

He didn't want to hear it. He turned around, but she circled ahead of him. She blocked his path, her arms outstretched and her face blazing in anger.

"I was surrounded by warriors who fought beside you for Eripa."

His jaw clenched. "Ewa, enough."

"Naïve, you say. I fought with all the power I could muster. Imagine me against warriors. It was my Creator that aided me. I'll never know I escaped."

"Ewa—"

"They chased me like I was prey, but the forest aided me. It sifted a path for me that led right to your friend, old Onigbaoje. I was desperate. He was an elder and seemed kind.

I-I told him the name of the valiant warrior, the one we'd all heard during the siege. It was your name, Makinde. I'd forgotten Onigbaoje's face until he came with you to meet Baale Semore. He must have known you, known that no warrior was keeping a maiden captive for you, but he saved me. He brought me to Kuta."

The atmosphere went deadly quiet save for her ragged breathing. His arms begged to hold her and his tongue to give her comfort. It was so easy to forget about the others that demanded his honour long before he knew her. His body, led by his heart, wanted to.

"I never knew," he said, head bowed and voice low.

"How could you have? I planned to flee, but the moment never arrived, and...well, here I am. Makinde, the little decisions we make define our lives forever. If you choose to follow that man, you choose vengeance, but you deserve so much more."

"I have to do this."

"Please!"

"I will return," he promised.

"How easily you throw away everything we've shared."

"Wait for me in Olootu." He saddled the horse.

Ewa raised her voice. "Didn't you hear what I said? I opened up to you because you walked away from the past. Even if you return, it will be with more blood on your hands, more ghosts, and more pain hovering around you."

"Dunni, the past is who we are."

"Don't you dare call me that."

"I will meet you at Olootu," he repeated.

She laughed bitterly as he climbed astride the horse. "I am no warrior's wife that will polish her husband's weapons and cheer when he brings the enemy's head home. You hear me?"

She snatched the reins from his hands and glared at him. He felt the burn on the side of his face and neck.

"I support life and the spirit." Then her voice cracked. "Makinde, won't you listen?"

He swallowed. Overhead, the sky darkened with rain clouds. The messenger waited for him across the field. If they rode day and night, they would get to Jaku in no time, then he would be back to plead forgiveness from her. His mind had already been decided ten years ago. This was one oath he couldn't escape. Ewa would eventually understand. She'd said so herself—these past few days were a fantasy, and reality had come calling.

When he tugged the reins from her grip, she let them go. He urged the horse forward then pulled it to a stop. He glanced behind him at her downcast face and quivering chin.

"I have a duty," he said, one last attempt to explain his actions.

"You could have said no," she replied.

His chest was hollow as she inhaled shakily and stormed off in the direction of the forest.

Things never went the way he wanted them to, no matter how much he longed for it. He urged the horse to where the messenger lingered.

EWA buried her face in her elbow. She sat in a corner of the modest hut, her arms propped up on her knees. Walking in nature hadn't calmed the roaring in her chest. When she'd caught herself lashing out at the wide fan leaves of a plantain tree, she'd retreated to the hut.

The man was indecipherable. How could Makinde go back to the life he claimed to have been running away from for so long? She concluded that perhaps he'd never wanted to change. It must have been why he avoided any deep ritual cleansing. It made no other sense for a human being to torture themselves so thoroughly unless they gained twisted pleasure from it.

Wuu sneezed outside the hut. The dog carefully padded through the open door and nudged at Ewa in her corner. She sobbed as she wrapped her arms around his neck and stroked his flank.

"He abandoned you, too," she said.

His one companion through the years, and Makinde had left Wuu behind. If he hadn't fetched her from the tavern in Olootu, she would have drunk herself to a stupor and then found a way forward later. Too much had occurred in such little time—she'd gone from hating him to loving him, her dreams of reuniting with her family dashed, Makinde betrayed the promise they made, and not just once.

Bile filled her mouth when she recalled their plans to live together far away from politics and assumptions. She was a fool. She'd spent all those years in Kuta hating him, but the truth was that what drove this emotion was her hatred for herself. She couldn't run away—she was scared of starting afresh and being on her own. Despite her desperate attempts at clinging to others—her birth mother, Ogele, and now Makinde—she was alone.

Wiping her tears with more vigour than required, she cradled Wuu's face.

"Won't you come with me?"

She took the dog's bark as an affirmation. She refused to return to Olootu. Makinde had no right to dictate her movements. The fact he'd asked her to return to her family and not to his irritated her.

A small voice inside her whispered that he didn't want his family in Kuta to know of their reunion. He was hiding her. For the past weeks, they'd lived as husband and wife, and she'd granted herself permission to imagine living this way for the rest of their lives. Now, it was clear he had never cared about her. The irresponsible side of her that insisted on making excuses for him pushed back. Olootu was closer than Kuta, and besides, he'd said he would return.

"Quiet," she said out loud in warning to herself.

When had she become one of the legions of men and women partial to Makinde? Ewa leaned against the adobe wall. She shifted the dog on her lap, cradling him like a child. She'd had enough with the self-pity. The fact of the matter was that she was alone. She'd been on her own for many years now.

She willed herself to be stronger. She would need to fend for herself henceforth. She took stock of her skills in healing and the kindness she offered and had found in others—she would excel anywhere she was planted.

As the first drops of rain fell, she allowed herself to savour the painful emotions. She was hurt and dejected, this was true. Her sense of faith pushed back, reminding her she was never truly alone. A court of otherworldly mates supported her, and her Creator was always by her side. Although she failed to fathom what kind of destiny she'd chosen before coming to Earth to require such challenges, she needed patience.

She drew in a grounding breath and closed her eyes. She listened to the rain, the howl of the wind, and the far clap of thunder. She felt herself become the rain, floating up the clouds then dropping back down to earth and snaking inside the hut where a section of the thatch roof leaked.

When she came back into herself, she rubbed at her arms, missing Makinde's warmth as the room grew cold. Then she remembered Usiade.

"We're going to Ibukun," she said as she petted Wuu.

The next day, she swept the hut clean. She refilled water pots, leaving some her purifying stones in them. She rolled up the mat and slipped two brass bracelets within the raffia folds then hid long glass beads in pots of uncooked grain.

When Ore, Tundun, or their daughter discovered these gifts, they would know she had left them. With this, she walked in search of the neighbours. She needed an escort to Ibukun.

Chapter Seventeen

It took two days to get to Jaku. The town was situated in the grasslands with nothing but short shrubs and a thin river surrounding it. Jaku was a sitting target. The messenger led Makinde past men digging a trench around the perimeter of the town—the first sign of impending war after the relative quietness of the trip here.

After they'd passed the first couple of houses, he observed the men milling about the area, their gait and amulets announcing them as warriors. They swaggered about the town with swords, axes, and clubs weighing down their shoulders and waists. Around the central palace was a wall as thick as he was tall. Right in front of the palace's portico, more men were engaged in mock battle. He dismounted, handing the reins to a steward.

"I will lead you to the Oba," the messenger said, motioning with his hands.

He followed. Before stepping under the magnificent roof, he spied a familiar face. Onigbaoje squinted in his direction, then his jaw fell open as Makinde was ushered into the palace.

He met Jaku's legitimate heir to the throne in a meeting with his council. This was a good sign. The man wasn't cowering in a dark room or shielding himself with the finery that came with his station while sending others off to fight on his behalf.

He waited outside a hall wide enough to ensure that the whispered words of the dignitaries didn't carry over to his ears. In the empty lull, he could no longer distract his mind from reaching for Ewa. His gut twisted as memories of their parting filled his mind. He shouldn't have left her in distress, but he'd failed to think of any other option. He needed to be here, and she refused to understand.

When he was called in at last, he prostrated before the Oba. The monarch's youth was glaring upon closer inspection. He lowered his gaze so as not to stare at the five whiskers on the Oba's face and his smooth, unmarked skin. He wondered how old the brothers who wanted the throne were if the crown price was barely out of babyhood.

When the Oba spoke, his voice was high-pitched.

"Makinde of Kuta. I am grateful that you accepted my invitation."

Makinde bowed in response, his lowered head protecting the room from seeing the doubt in his eyes as he replied, "It is my honour to serve you."

"Then you will swear to fight for the rightful ruler of Jaku."

From his downcast position, he saw the Oba's robes flutter as he motioned to an attendant. He'd been in this position enough times to know what came next. He would pledge his allegiance before the deities. And although he was here for personal reasons, he had no compunctions keeping up appearances.

He placed a hand on the iron sword the Oba proffered and swore not to betray the interests of the ruler before him. Only then was he free to locate Onigbaoje. He found his old friend sitting in the western corner of the courtyard under the shade of dried-brown palm fronds. The men had taken a break from their exercises to eat a meal of fried millet balls, a source of strength for warriors.

Makinde nodded as greetings erupted. He recognized some familiar faces but elected to sit beside Onigbaoje who eyed him warily.

"I didn't expect to see you here," Onigbaoje whispered, a cup of water hovering over his mouth.

"And yet, here I am," he replied. "You ought to know why."

Onigbaoje's scoff put an end to the conversation. Makinde accepted a bowl of the fritters and dug in. Afterwards, he joined the others in training. By the end of the day, his aching body reminded him it'd been too long since he'd engaged in combat. He was fit, but his skill at parrying blows from weapons meant the dulled machetes and sticks they used to practice left him bruised.

With the explosion of warriors in the town, accommodation was scarce. Four to six men stayed in the rooms provided by the palace while citizens opened up their doors to warriors. Despite these measures, other men slept under open-sided tents fashioned from wide leaves and withered blankets.

As night approached, he was led to one of the makeshift tents. His body—drained from the journey and the exercises—lulled him to sleep. He spread on the ground with only a thin sheet separating his body from the cold earth. He closed his eyes and saw darkness.

She materialised behind his lids, the individual sections of her threaded hair appearing like thorns. Her tearful eyes blazed in anger, and this time when her lips moved, he heard her words clearly.

"I knew you were evil through and through. Are you going to keep slaughtering innocents?"

He kicked as he jerked up from the floor. His heart thundered in his chest, cold fingers raking across his skin. The spectres were back. Leaving Ewa had nullified the protections that allowed him to rest well at night. As he fought to bring his raging breath under control, his eyes darted back and forth in the tight dim space. Despite the terror, he was grateful there was no other human being there to witness his weakness.

The men around him in the training ground appeared primed to do what was needed. A question that had needled him since childhood arose in his brain. Why couldn't he be like his mates?

The front of the tent was open to the elements, yet he failed to notice Onigbaoje's approach until the man stooped to enter the space. Onigbaoje carried a lamp in his left hand. He set it down on the floor as he sat cross-legged in front of him.

"You should be enjoying your honeymoon, my friend," Onigbaoje said in lieu of a greeting. His words were barely above a murmur in acknowledgement of the many ears surrounding a camp like this one.

"I should be calling Arole to justice." He was unprepared to talk about Ewa or to deal with his friend's meddling. Then he recalled her pleas. "Onigbaoje, you brought Ewa to Kuta. You are the one that married her for me."

"It was a good match."

When he didn't laugh at his attempt at a joke, Onigbaoje covered his face with both hands and sighed loudly.

"Ewa's people must have taken to the wilderness when the war entered the city. The boys who attacked her said they came across her family but wanted her as their bounty. And instead of defending their daughter, her family fled. I assume you know the rest."

"Those warriors..."

"All disciplined." Onigbaoje dropped his hands to his thighs and tilted his head, regarding him with barely restrained pity. "You aren't meant for this, Makinde."

"So, I am a coward?"

"Listen to me. You were...are a great warrior, but your destiny calls for another path. I am certain your mother Ogele has told you this. Why don't you heed it?"

"Is Arole here?"

Onigbaoje sucked his teeth sharply. "I haven't thought to ask. That boy isn't among the warriors gathered."

"Are you sure?"

"I've been here for a week."

"Could he be on the other side? It is just like him to offer support to those who don't deserve the throne."

Without warning, Onigbaoje clutched Makinde's sweaty shoulders and shook him. It was his age and the respect it demanded that prevented him from shrugging the old man off.

"You are always doing the wrong thing," Onigbaoje said.

"I am well aware—"

"Must you always resist?"

There was a harshness in Onigbaoje's tone that confounded him. Onigbaoje shuffled closer. His steady hands gripped Makinde's shoulders again as though the contact would compel him to listen.

"The deities gifted you a wife. They gifted you the resilience to start anew where even trained royal spies can't reach you."

Onigbaoje couldn't be aware he and Ewa had considered moving away and establishing themselves somewhere, yet his words hinted at a hidden awareness.

Makinde's eyes widened with understanding. This time, he shrugged off Onigbaoje's hands and rubbed at the dullness in his chest. The longing he'd dammed successfully over the past two days broke. He missed Ewa. He saw her smile, felt her touch and her warmth. He wished to share a plate with her as they'd grown accustomed to. If she bathed him once more, his ghosts would dissipate. Ewa had never shown fear at anything, but she hated war. She'd told him why, and he'd run off to the first war that came calling for him.

"Traitors are killed." His fingers recollected the cool touch of the metal he'd sworn his allegiance on. It would be metal that sliced him down if he dared back away now as Onigbaoje subtly proposed.

"You aren't listening to me. Anyone can retire, and I thought you did. Look around. Is everyone you know here?

Your own brother Togun remained in Kuta to be with his wife and child. Moyero is alive and well in Ofa. He chose not to be here."

Makinde shook his head. None of these men had a bone to pick with Arole. "It is too late. The fact that I am already here means this is my destiny. I must find Arole to make things right."

His speech didn't convince either of them. Onigbaoje rolled his eyes to the heavens.

"My Creator help me, you are as stubborn as a goat." Onigbaoje dusted his trousers as he rose. "We can't look for Arole now. Give me some time."

JOBAYO danced a quick dance while singing a welcome song for Ewa. Despite her sour mood, she smiled at the way the man shuffled his feet and moved his shoulders.

"Welcome back," he sang. "Ewadunni of Odan, welcome back!"

When she'd arrived at Ibukun, she'd kept an eye out for Jobayo at the palace but hadn't seen him. Another attendant had taken her to reintroduce herself to Ibukun's monarch, and it seemed word had spread. Jobayo met her in the palace's primary courtyard.

"Enough, Jobayo! People are staring."

"Let them," he replied between pants. He ended his dance with a flourish, and she cheered for him. "Where is your warrior?"

Her smile fell. It was amazing how two words could foul her mood. "I am here on my own."

"No matter." Jobayo didn't seem to notice the frown on her face. "We must take you to the Olori."

"Shouldn't I go to the guesthouse first?"

"Forget that," he said, pulling her away. "I am certain Olori will want you to stay with her."

She allowed him to lead her to Usiade's quarters. They skipped the main entrance with its queuing guests and veered right where stone steps led down to an opening in the mud wall. She walked between columns carved with the likeness of women engaged in different activities—some cooked and others carried babies while others pounded into mortars and plaited hair.

They emerged in a lush garden of brilliant colourful flowers. Plants in varying stages of bloom crowded the pavement Jobayo traversed. Ewa paused to appreciate a sculpture of stone and iron set in a small clearing before Jobayo dragged her away. They turned this way and that before stopping at a bas-relief door. While he knocked gently on it, she lifted her head and noticed the palace's tall thatch roof and guessed they'd travelled a convoluted path leading them behind the palace.

They were let into an open courtyard before Usiade's quarters. The kitchen was on the far end opposite the entrance, and a bungalow housing a series of rooms opened up to the right. On the left was a high wall.

Usiade sat under the thatched awning in front of her quarters. She beamed as Ewa approached and rose to her feet.

"Ewa," she said, stretching out her arms.

Ewa gripped Usiade's hands in greeting. "I had to accept your invitation."

"And I am all the more happier for it. And your husband?"

"He is out on a campaign," she replied, a forced smile on her face.

"You must miss him."

She remained silent. Usiade led them to the shade where two toddlers wrapped in silk slept soundly. Observing the imperceptible rise and fall of their tiny chests lifted her mood.

"Taiye and Kehinde." Usiade pointed to her twins with her chin.

Ewa couldn't tell them apart. They were identical down to the matching coral bracelets on their tiny wrists. She waited for Usiade to retake her seat before settling on a stool carved from dark ebony.

"Lover's quarrel?" Usiade asked, eyes narrowed.

She sighed. What was it about her that encouraged people to read through her as though she were a bowl of scrying water?

"Not at all." She ignored Usiade's cocked brow and continued. "I see myself settling in Ibukun."

Her distraction worked. Usiade clapped her hands in glee. "You will live here with me."

"I can't impose—"

"I insist. My husband is either at court or with his other wives. My first son is away at Ipondo. I arrived here a stranger with no ties so my only friends are my attendants."

"Won't the Oba oppose?"

"I will speak to him. Besides, you're only here at the palace till your husband returns. We can work towards building a house for you when that day comes. Tell me, what are you skilled at?"

"I..." Ewa paused. She was primed to continue objecting to Usiade's offer, but the woman had already made up her mind. "I am a healer."

"Did you train formally?"

"My mentor Ogele is late. She was an esteemed healer in Kuta."

"In that case, I will have Jobayo introduce you to our guild here."

"Thank you." She knelt down in appreciation, but Usiade didn't let her remain in the position for a second. As she reclaimed her seat, Ewa asked, "Wouldn't it be more prudent for me to lodge with the healers?"

"Meet with them first, but you must return. I'm better company."

It wasn't an easy task extracting herself from Usiade's generosity, but she managed it. At dusk, she found the temple housing the healers' guild surrounded by greenery. From miles away, she smelled the herbal infusions brewing.

Familiarity hastened her footsteps, and she soon stood in front of a bungalow. She followed her nose, entering the building and walking down the short corridor to the open door behind. The backyard was buzzing with activity—women prepared herbs, milled powders on grinding stones, and peered into simmering pots carefully propped

on coal. There were larger pots where a meal was being prepared. A trio of older women sat under a plum tree observing
it all.

"Can I be of help?"

A young girl appeared in front of Ewa. She appeared to
be Tope's age with burnished dark skin and small almond-
shaped eyes.

"I am looking for work," she said, smiling at the girl.

"You need to speak to the elders then."

Ewa wasn't surprised when she was taken to the three old
women. After greetings were exchanged, the girl relayed her
request. The first pangs of doubt hit her belly as the women
exchanged loaded glances. That they didn't bid her to stand
up from the kneeling position she'd adopted to greet them
was also concerning.

"We will leave this to you, Iya Aloyo," one said.

"As usual," Aloyo replied with a wince, as if tasting bitter
medicine. She was the plump woman sat on the far left of the
group wearing a head wrap and a shawl over her shoulders. A
permanent crease on her forehead and the downward curve
of her lips gave her an air of unfriendliness.

"You don't sound like you're from around here," Aloyo
said, taking on the task of interrogating her.

"I am from Ku...Odan," she replied. Her nervousness
caused this careless mistake, and Aloyo homed in on it.

"You don't know where you're from?"

"I was born in Odan but came here from Kuta, where m-
my husband is from."

Aloyo scratched at her upper arm. "So what brings you
here?"

"I am looking for greener pastures."

One of the other two women who were pretending not to listen snorted. Ewa's optimism quickly evaporated.

"I was a healer in Kuta. I trained under one of my husband's mothers. She taught me how to heal with herbs. Iya Ogele was renowned in Kuta."

"Eh." Aloyo sounded unimpressed. She leaned back in her chair and crossed her hands over her breasts. "Have you been initiated into the order of healing?"

Ewa swallowed. Ogele was a wild card, and most of Kuta had overlooked it because her remedies worked. "I haven't."

"It shows on her," one of Aloyo's companions said while the other women snickered.

"In that case, how are we expected to entrust you with the lives of others?" Aloyo asked.

Ewa clenched her teeth and lifted her chin. Kuta might not be as grand as Ibukun, but her skill remained the same. Regardless of whether these women doubted her skill, she'd facilitated more births than she could count.

"Try me," she said. "Put me to a test, and I will surely excel."

Aloyo shook her head. "Absolutely not. To catch a monkey, you must act like one. Have you heard that saying before?"

"I have."

They wanted her to learn their ways. She wiped the sweat from her hands on her skirt. The reason Ogele eschewed associations wasn't only because of their formality—guilds held a strict hierarchy, and she would be at the lowest rung. It wasn't unheard of for guild mates to have newcomers engage in menial tasks like washing the outhouse or eating leftovers.

"Do you agree?"

She had no other means of earning a living. She briefly considered fishing and dismissed it as she wasn't skilled at the bargaining that went with entrepreneurship. Back in her youthful days, it was her girlfriends who fixed prices. She was good at working with her hands, and she was outstanding when it came to making medicines.

"I agree."

"Wonderful," Aloyo said. Then she called, "Nifemi!"

The young girl who'd welcomed her earlier came running.

"This is our newest student. What did you say your name was?"

"I am Ewadunni."

"Ewadunni," Aloyo repeated. "Take her under your wing. Show her what is required."

Ewa looked at the girl who could be her daughter. Fate had turned Nifemi into her superior. Gritting her teeth, she thanked the elder as she rose.

"There is a fee that must be paid," Aloyo said.

"How much will that be?"

"We accept cowrie strings, livestock, foodstuff, and precious metals..."

Patience, she reminded herself as Aloyo hashed out the guild's terms. With time, she would show these women the error of underestimating her.

WAGING war was for the patient. Makinde had forgotten it.

Just as warriors arrived in Jaku daily, the enemy camp was growing their own numbers. Once the trench around Jaku was built, the waiting game would launch. Each side hovered between defence and offence, strategizing as to how best to begin the skirmish. Intelligence poured in feeding both parties. If they were lucky, the aggrieved brothers would attack first. Otherwise, warriors would be required to leave Jaku in search of the enemy, leaving the exposed town even more vulnerable. And amidst all the intrigue, he wouldn't be able to confront his past.

Day bled into night, expanding the emptiness inside him. The lack of sleep hit him hard, his body having grown accustomed to the luxury that was only due to Ewa's influence. Shapes transformed into faces, discarded branches into disembodied arms. The maiden of Odan taunted him at will.

He threw himself into mock battles, sparring with mates but seeing Arole's face before him. Arole and Makinde had trained together from boyhood, and as adults, the man knew all his weaknesses. He sidestepped Makinde's blows and evaded the thrust of his club. With each day of training, it dawned on him again that he might not walk away from a fight with Arole. Was this why he'd hesitated over the years? What made killing on the battlefield any different from this? Arole's taunt haunted him as much as the maiden.

Back then, he'd been rooted to the spot, confused at the carnage he was witnessing. There was Arole and there on the ground were dead bodies. It took him longer than needed to register the bodies were of the families he'd left in Arole's care. Arole had slaughtered elders for no apparent reason other than because they attempted to prevent him from raping their daughters.

Those moments of inaction had proven deadly. There was the lady with the threaded hair, and there was Arole tossing a spear at her as she ran for the exit. Makinde launched and saw the terror on the young woman's face, the certainty he was going to stop her escape. He'd stepped between the bloodied weapon and the young woman. The scar in his side from where that wound had healed pulsed at the memory.

Everything after that was a blur. He must have clashed swords with Arole, but all he knew for certain was that the people he'd tried to save had died due to his own naïveté while Arole walked unscathed. It was Onigbaoje who brought him back to Kuta, and like before, Onigbaoje remained his buoy in Jaku.

One afternoon, he drew Makinde away from practice. Makinde scanned the surroundings with distrust as Onigbaoje let him down a maze of clustered homes.

"Did you find him?"

"When last did you sleep?"

"You know I can't sleep."

"Well, you certainly appeared well-rested on your first day at Jaku. A bit frazzled from the journey here, but mostly refreshed."

A pained expression pinched his features. He'd made a grave mistake leaving her in anger and by now knew she wasn't waiting for him.

"My friend," Onigbaoje said. "Do you intend to fight Arole before the war or surreptitiously wound him in battle?"

He frowned. "We will fight one on one."

"And what if he refuses?"

"He can't."

"I see."

Onigbaoje drew to a sudden stop. They were in a section of the town Makinde hadn't ventured to before, the noise of the practising grounds replaced with that of household activities. It was as though this part of Jaku was unaware of the war. Onigbaoje glanced up at the crowd of trees with hanging fruits resembling long thick pods to their left. He reached for a tree and pushed it, testing its weight.

"Let's climb," he said.

"Pardon?"

"I suppose I'll go first."

Despite his advancement in years, Onigbaoje scaled the tree nimbly. Makinde stared up at him in confusion.

"The air smells different up here."

"I'm heading back to camp." He was tired and at his wits' end. Where his future had once appeared hazy but certain, it was now covered in shadows. He had no time to play Onigbaoje's games.

"You won't know Arole's whereabouts if you don't come up."

He froze mid-turn and groaned at Onigbaoje's eccentricities and began climbing the tree. Onigbaoje shifted so Makinde sat beside him on a sturdy branch. Their position provided an excellent view of a homestead. Framed by the leaves and hanging fruit, he saw into a walled compound where several people were engaged in dyeing cloth, indigo lengths of fabric spread to dry on bamboo poles.

"Did you bring me here to spy?"

Onigbaoje didn't respond. A jolt of alertness shot through Makinde. Arole was here. He leaned forward at risk of tumbling to the ground. Most of the people in the compound were women which made sense because every able-bodied man was preparing for war.

Then he saw a small boy below the age of ten. He gripped the branch beneath him with trembling hands. The boy played with a doll, unconcerned with the commercial activity around him.

His head swam, and he felt himself tilting backwards. He was going to split his head open when he fell on the ground.

Onigbaoje seized him around the shoulders.

"Arole is dead," Onigbaoje said. "Will you exact revenge on his son?"

Makinde couldn't blink. He couldn't tear his eyes away from the child who resembled Arole down to the dimple in his chin. If he closed his eyes, he might be a young boy once more playing with this child unaware of what the future had in store for them.

An ethereal roar popped his ears.

"You knew," he said.

Onigbaoje didn't shrink back from the accusation. "Yes."

"How long?"

"Five or six years."

Below them, Arole's son laughed as one of the women ushered him indoors. Makinde tore his gaze away. His hands gripped the branch so tight, wood embedded in his skin.

"Don't you dare accuse me of not telling you," Onigbaoje said. "Your mother and I never stopped advising you to give up on your reckless mission. You—"

"I never listened."

Tremors shook him with such force, Onigbaoje held him firm.

"You were wounded and unconscious. We didn't count Arole among the dead we buried, yet he didn't return home. While you were nursing in Eripa, news of the skirmish spread far and wide of a ruler who commanded his hired warriors to attack innocents even after winning on the front. Eventually, it reaching Oyo. The Alaafin had to intervene. Eripa lost its Oba, and guilty warriors were tried before the Ogboni council. Again, Arole was nowhere to be seen."

"I know..."

"I believe he avoided returning home to Kuta because of you, Makinde. And it was due to your insistence that we searched and found him here in Jaku."

"You should have told me then."

"You went down in Odan-Eripa but not before inflicting damage of your own," Onigbaoje continued as if he hadn't spoken. "Arole had lost use of his legs. Would you have challenged him to a duel?"

"That's his son." Whatever his disability, Arole had lived well according to societal standards. He'd had a family, a child—both had been denied to Makinde.

"Arole spent the last days here in this compound. I hear he suffered from a bout of illness. The conclusion remains the same, Makinde. You've been chasing a ghost."

Ghosts. He lived fleeing and in pursuit of several of them. He'd gone in exile, denied himself love. He began pounding at his chest with his fist. Onigbaoje embraced him.

"What have I done?" Tears sprung from his eyes as he repeated the question. He beat his chest hard. "What have I done, Dunni?"

Chapter Eighteen

E wa no longer counted the weeks separating her from Makinde. She'd blocked him from her mind, evading all questions from Usiade and any mention of Jaku. Choosing wilful ignorance, she dedicated herself to Ibukun's guild of healers with zeal. She cleaned, fetched water, and went to the market on behalf of her seniors.

Where she'd had her own clients in Kuta, she was limited to observing Ibukun's healers taking care of theirs. For all intents and purposes, it was a demotion, but she considered her new position a boon. She was learning new things. The healers at Ibukun worked closely with the religious class of the town. Many knew how to divine with cowries and could diagnose sicknesses without even seeing the client. There was also a unique massaging technique healers here gave pregnant women.

She shaped her hands in the air as she watched Aloyo knead flesh because no one would let her touch a client. A chance to impress the guild came when an elder suggested a test. She was blindfolded and given a variety of plants to identify by taste. She recognised all of them but remained a junior regardless. She was thirsty for new knowledge, and if she had to pay for it by engaging in menial tasks, so be it. Cooking however remained Nifemi's task after Ewa burnt moi-moi. Her new guild mates had teased her for days even after she'd bought a sackful of beans and spices to make up for her error.

After a long day observing and cleaning, she tended to the evening's batch of brewing herbs. She got on all fours and blew at the firewood under a pot of herbs. When the coals continued burning hot, she turned to the granite stone where herbs shrivelled after drying under the sun waited to be ground. She passed the grinder back and forth over the stone.

Within minutes, she felt a stitch between her shoulders. She remembered eons ago, when she'd sat by while watching Jomiloju exert herself in this manner. Too much had taken place since then. Her lips parted in a yawn. She paused grinding to cover her mouth.

A shadow fell over her. She looked up and met Aloyo's upside-down smile.

"Hm," Aloyo sounded.

"Good day, Iya." Inwardly, she wondered what her mentor wanted this time.

"Hmm."

Ewa stretched her lips to force a smile disguising her irritation. The truth she had come to admit to herself was that she was used to older women coddling her. Her father's mother had spoiled her rotten, and later in life, Ogele had greatly favoured her. She'd come to associate such care from mentors with her profession. However, Ibukun was different. She was worried Aloyo was another Lapade at first, but the woman was never sadistic despite her curt ways.

"Shall I fetch some water for you?" she asked.

Aloyo hmmed again, and this time, Ewa couldn't stop her left eye from twitching. She was very close to telling the older woman to leave her be so she could concentrate on the task at hand.

"So it is true what they say," Aloyo said. "The expert at casting the divining chain will still have to consult another Ifa priest to know the future."

Ewa's brows knitted. "I don't understand."

"Come. Sit."

She followed Aloyo, bewildered. The elder made her sit on one of the low chairs scattered around the courtyard. She felt everyone's attention on them even though they pretended not to look.

"Give me your hand."

She did so reluctantly. Aloyo rested Ewa's arm on her lap with a tenderness that belied her usual brusqueness. As Ewa summoned up the words to ask what the older woman was doing without appearing rude, Aloyo started feeling for her pulse.

"I'm not unwell," she gasped.

What kind of test was this? Now, the other women in the yard openly regarded them. She tugged, but Aloyo's hold was unyielding. She didn't release her until she'd deciphered what she was looking for.

"Walk with me," Aloyo said.

Ewa massaged her wrist. She glared at the ground rather than at the elder society demanded she respect. They walked out to the exterior of the temple where plants grew haphazardly. When they were away from prying ears, Aloyo turned to regard her.

"Count yourself lucky," she said. "Few women can boast of not having symptoms in the early days of their pregnancy."

Ewa's mouth grew wide. She raised her hands to stop from screaming. This was her specialty, and she'd failed to recognise her own pregnancy. She'd ensured her monthly bleeding had ended before her departure from Kuta to avoid any inconvenience. She was unbothered when her courses took their time appearing in Ibukun. Having travelled on foot through forest and grassland before, she was aware the stress of the journey often led to missed menses. It was true that after they'd first made love, neither she nor Makinde could keep away from each other.

For years, both the Oracle and Ogele had foreseen the blessings of children for her. She'd desired motherhood herself. So why did her mouth feel like it was filled with ash? She should have been rushing to the nearest Ifa temple to arrange for a thanksgiving. She ought to praise her Creator and her ancestors. Instead, she wanted to cry.

Aloyo leaned forward. "I heard you first came here with your husband. He will be overjoyed on his return. You should take it easy until then."

"I had no idea."

"It is often that way," Aloyo replied. A rare smile touched her face. "That's why we're here. We will take care of you and the life within you."

"I am grateful, Iya."

"Take the rest of the day off. I know this revelation comes as a surprise."

Ewa was thankful for the break. As she rushed to the palace with her arms wrapped around her middle, a new consciousness dawned on her. She was going to be a mother, and Makinde a father. The very stubborn man who had rushed into war despite her pleas had left not just her but their child.

Her throat felt swollen. Rather than retreat to Usiade's quarters, she found Wuu in the stables where he'd been entrusted in Jobayo's care as dogs were forbidden in the inner palace. Wuu was excited to see her and wagged his tail nonstop. She petted his fur.

"We're going for a walk," she announced.

Then, she led Wuu to the outer gardens surrounding the palace's southern walls. There, guarded by trees and with the dog that loved her unconditionally, she unspooled. She cried and then she laughed, concern morphing to exhilaration.

IT was a blessing to return to the comfort of Usiade's palace quarters later in the evening. Although she sometimes spent the night at the guild, Usiade kept an open invitation for her. Usiade was a woman of her word and didn't call her sister in jest. She sat for dinner with the Olori. On some days, they ate accompanied by their own voices, but on other days, Usiade hired performers to provide entertainment.

A band composed of drummers, a flutist, and percussionist played melodious tunes while the dancers spun. Ewa and Usiade were seated in the porch, a variety of dishes spread between them. There were trays containing three different types of roasted meats, vegetable and okra stews, seasoned yam porridge, steamed beans, and kola nuts. With the entertainers at play and Usiade's bevy of attendants either eating or keeping her children occupied, Ewa whispered the news in her ear.

"Congratulations!" Usiade tossed her arms around Ewa's shoulders and swayed them both from side to side.

"Thank you." She beamed.

When they sat apart again, Usiade said, "I pray this means the guild takes it easier on you."

"Iya Aloyo promised to, but I have no plans to turn to laziness. I'm barely showing."

"Do you have plans to tell your husband?" Usiade asked. "We could send a messenger to Jaku."

Usiade looked at the dancers and patted the curved edge of her head wrap when Ewa glared at her. By now, she knew Makinde and her weren't on good terms. Usiade knew the bare bones of the matter as Ewa didn't know where to start confiding in her friend. How could she explain that when they were together at Ibukun, she and Makinde had essentially been strangers? Trying to tell her of their unconventional marriage was more work than she was willing to undertake.

"You are suggesting we send someone to a war zone," she said.

"Eh." Usiade clicked her tongue. "So you were listening when I said that the war for Jaku's throne is turning out to be a bloody one."

Eight nights prior, she had been trying to sleep when Usiade had come with news of a battle she didn't want to follow. On a good day, when she was kept busy, she navigated the time without thinking about Makinde. On other days, however, every part of her ached for him.

"Don't send a messenger," she warned.

"But—"

"Don't. Please."

Usiade sniffed. "I suppose it is a good sign that you can now speak so informally with a queen."

Ewa spluttered into the cup of water she held to her lips.

"I am teasing you, Ewa." Usiade giggled as she coughed. She rubbed delicate circles on Ewa's shoulder.

The performers were now casting tricks. Fire erupted from a pot balanced on the head of one of the dancers. It was enough to grab the attention of everyone in the porch and yard. Despite her fast-moving feet, the pot didn't crash. When the dancers moved on to safer moves, Usiade turned to her.

"You pretend not to care. But I know you do. It is okay to show more concern."

Usiade's words were true. It was a challenge to pretend everything was fine, but she didn't plan on stopping. She placed a palm over her stomach. "My only concern is for the child in here."

In the outer gardens with Wuu, she had considered her situation. Good parents ensured their children lived better lives than they did. Her child should never know what happened when states went to war. Even if the world were burning, she would guarantee peace for this being who had chosen her as a mother.

Marrying again was out of the question as she'd witnessed the cruelty of step-parents firsthand. No child of hers would shed tears over family turning their backs on them or a father who chose war over love.

She'd concluded she would have her child here at Ibukun. This would grant her a minimum of three more years in this community. She needed to get on Aloyo's good side.

THE will to fight evaded Makinde. After swearing his loyalty, leaving Jaku spelled death—the only punishment suitable for cowardly traitors. It felt like he was dying regardless.

A chasm had opened inside him, consuming everything that made him a person. After two months waiting for the enemy to strike, the Jaku army was split into two, with one sent to fight in the plains and the other remaining in the defence of the town.

Onigbaoje had arranged it so Makinde remained in the town, but he couldn't fight. Old warriors taught boys to sing songs about longevity before stepping into battle. If one showed fear, one welcomed death. Makinde didn't sing—his lips were sealed shut. The spectres glued down his arms, mocking him as they rooted him to the spot. They'd shifted from calling him a murderer to mocking him for wasting his adult years for nothing.

When the enemy came inevitably, he was ill-prepared. Rather than thrust his sword through flesh, he evaded, swinging weapons and throwing feeble punches. He manoeuvred the battlefield in a daze until he was brought down by arrows. He lay on the earth, bleeding from the holes piercing his back and left side, the sounds of the skirmish around him becoming his dirge.

Is this the end? he wondered. The last word echoed in his mind as feet dashed to and fro, slinging dirt into his widened eyes. He choked, a gush of warm liquid parting from his lips. His mouth tasted blood. He needed to see Ewa, but it was a frigid darkness that claimed him. He'd faced death enough times to imagine what it would feel like. Some elders said that when one died, their true family in the otherworld celebrated their return with a feast.

What he didn't expect was to hear Onigbaoje's insistent voice.

"Your wife? Where is she?"

"Olootu."

Grey swept over the night and sucked him in. Blurry figures hovered at the edges of his vision. Pain touched every pore from his scalp to his toes. When the shadows claimed his consciousness once more, he was grateful for it.

USIADE was hiding something, and Ewa suspected what it was. She'd stopped her from going to the temple this morning, insisting they go for a walk together. The walk led them through the main thoroughfare road in Ibukun that went from the palace to the houses of important dignitaries.

Most likely, Usiade had ignored her and sent a messenger out to Jaku anyway. This was what she expected her friend to reveal. However, the way Usiade squeezed her hand as they walked through Ibukun's main street was troubling.

"Won't you tell me where you're taking me to?" she asked.

Usiade smiled with her entire face at any given time. This wasn't one of those moments. The upward tilt of her lips didn't cause her cheeks to plumpen or her eyes to sparkle.

"We are almost there," she replied.

The hairs on the back of Ewa's neck rose. The day was moderately warm, but an aura of coldness enveloped her. Usiade held her hand. They moved slowly with her entourage following behind them. Their procession stopped frequently as Usiade exchanged greetings with the women of the marketplace near the palace environs. The snail-like pace caused Ewa's stomach to somersault and spin like one of the performers from the troop the Olori favoured.

Eventually, they reached their destination. Set apart from the road, three buildings sat adjacent to each other. They had high roofs rivalling the crowns of the tall trees gracing the yard. A familiar bitter smell graced her nostrils.

"A healer lives here," she stated.

Usiade nodded. "This is Iya Aloyo's home."

Ewa frequently encountered her mentor in the professional arena of the guild's temple and had no business at her home. Judging by the well-kept state of the compound, Aloyo had done well for herself. The yard was empty of any soul apart from the few trees for shade. She imagined everyone in the compound was working elsewhere. There was only one reason to be at Aloyo's house.

She took a calming breath. The elders had found her skills worthy and were ready to initiate her into their mysteries. This awareness didn't bring her peace of mind. As they moved towards the central hut, her chest heaved. The front door, although kept open, revealed nothing but shadows. From outside, there was no way to tell what lay past the threshold.

"Why did you keep this a secret? You had me worried."

"It wasn't my intention to." Usiade paused and turned to face her. The corner of her eyes crinkled in concern, and she held both of Ewa's hands. "Ewa, before we enter, I want to re-assure you that everything is fine."

"I hear you."

Usiade was treating her like an egg. Footsteps at her side drew her attention. Aloyo appeared in the doorframe, the frown on her face deeper than usual. She prostrated in greet-ing to her mentor.

"Welcome to my home, Ewa," Aloyo said. "I apologise that it was under these circumstances."

"Circumstances?"

Aloyo exchanged a weighty look with Usiade. She smacked her lips before jerking her head behind her.

"Come."

Ewa shot a quick glance at Usiade then walked into the building. As she waited for her eyes to adjust to the poorly lit interior, she felt pinpricks along the back of her legs. The air around them was wrong.

Aloyo was halfway down the hall when she caught up with her. An older man sat on a chair close by one of the rooms at the back of the house, a hat pulled low on his face. He lifted his head at their approach. It was Onigbaoje, a face she had no reason to imagine seeing ever again.

Pulse racing, she pushed past Aloyo, disregarding Onig-baoje who was standing up. She barged into the room and

saw Makinde lying stone-like, face up on the bed. She let out
a sharp cry and felt Aloyo grasp her arms from behind.

"He is alive," Aloyo said. "He will make it."

Yet, as she stared at Makinde's chest, she failed to make
out the rise and fall signalling life. Her knees crumbled beneath her. Aloyo groaned under her weight.

"Pull yourself together. And listen to what I'm saying.
He is well."

The older woman guided her to his side. He appeared to
be sleeping. The expression on his face was serene, with even
a lopsided smile gracing his lips. Ewa put a trembling hand
on his bare chest. It was hot to the touch. She closed her eyes
to better concentrate on the motion of her hand rising and
falling with each breath he took.

"When?" she demanded.

"He was brought to me last night," Aloyo said. "The messenger the Olori sent to Jaku brought them here."

She swallowed. Her fingers grazed the bandages
wrapped around his midriff and over his right shoulder.

"Was he in pain?"

"He has been in and out of consciousness. It appears he
hasn't rested in a very long time."

She slid to the mat-covered floor. Her face was level with
Makinde's. She pushed her hand into his bushy hair. There
were a hundred and one questions she wanted to ask, but she
kept silent. Although she trusted Aloyo's skills as a healer, she
was filled with the urge to check his wounds herself.

Out of respect, she waited until her mentor had left
them alone before lifting the bandages and probing the poul-

tice-covered gashes. As she secured the wraps once more, her initial shock gave way to a frustration laced with anger.

This was the fate of women who partnered with warriors—they tended to wounded and broken men while constantly carrying the fear every campaign would be the one to render them widows. At the same time, seeing Makinde in this condition disabused her of the notion that she'd moved on from him. It was impossible, when her heart pounded as though it were him controlling every rhythm even in his insentient state.

She stayed in the room, taking breaks to eat and freshen up, changing the bandages and dressing his wounds herself. She poured her hope in believing her presence would revive him. And when it did, when she noticed the first signs of him stirring, she beat a hasty retreat from the room.

MAKINDE EMITTED A GROAN as he was shoved into the land of the living. His eyes snapped open to take in a sparsely furnished room with a stool in one corner. Layers of mats covered the clay floor. It was as though he saw clearly for the first time in years. Everything appeared brighter. The burden that came with the quest for vengeance appeared to have evaporated at death's gates. There were no ghostly shadows gliding along the walls.

"You're really awake," Onigbaoje said, cackling as he moved into the room. His concerned eyes surveyed Makinde's prone body.

He shifted in an attempt to prop himself up. His head was light as air. Agony stabbed at his side and back, pushing him back down faster than Onigbaoje's hands could.

"Take it easy," his friend said. "You were a disgrace in battle."

He chuckled then cleared his dry throat. The atmosphere was tinged with warmth, and even though the only other person in the room was Onigbaoje, the scent of coconut oil and soft flowers told him Ewa had been with him. She was the reason he still lived.

"Water," he said, his voice rough with disuse.

"I'll get it. Just stay still."

Onigbaoje left the room to return shortly after. Makinde's eyes craned over the man's shoulder in search of her. Disappointed, he sipped at the water being offered.

"I suspect storytellers will share tales of the great Makinde's fall from might," Onigbaoje continued once he had drunk his fill. "I don't see anyone calling you for future campaigns."

"Wonderful," he replied to his friend's amusement.

"The crown prince retained his hold on Jaku, but I know you don't want to hear of politics now."

"Dunni?"

"Your wife? She fled from here as though she'd seen a snake."

His heart sank. Ewa remained upset with him. He couldn't blame her when he'd caused her undue agony. Sighing, he closed his eyes as if to sleep.

ALOYO met her pacing in the front yard.

"What exactly is the issue?" she asked brusquely.

Ewa came to a stop and didn't say a word.

"You love this man. Why do you run from it?"

"Elder," she began. She shifted her gaze to the point where the roof met the sky and swallowed. "You have seen how I've been at my wits' end for days. This is what it means to be a warrior's wife. I can't bear it. What will happen when he's wounded again?"

To her horror, her eyes pricked with tears. She'd wept too often lately after years of considering herself too strong to cry. She didn't want Aloyo to see her in such a state. She licked her bottom lip then sank her teeth into the soft flesh.

"Hush, don't speak evil into being. The part of you that is a healer should at least be moved to attend when a client calls out for you."

"Calls for me?" Her head snapped in the direction of the bungalow. She hadn't heard a sound.

"In his heart." Aloyo raised a palm to her chest. "In here. Answer him unless you want me to drag you to where he lays."

She held back a groan. "I will do my best, Iya."

Because Aloyo was staring her down like a leopard watching an antelope, she retraced her steps indoors. She passed by Onigbaoje and seized the opportunity to tarry. However, greeting the man only took so long.

"We must prepare a feast," Onigbaoje said, stalking away. "Makinde has returned to the land of the living."

Ewa rubbed at her temples. She righted her clothes and ran quivering fingers over wrinkles. She stepped into the room that appeared as it did the first time she was here.

Makinde reclined on the bed, his eyelids resting closed. She exhaled in relief. Their confrontation had been delayed. She moved into the room quietly and touched his forehead. She checked wounds she knew were healing nicely. Then it occurred to her he would need water when he next awakened.

She turned to exit the room, but the edge of her wrapper caught on something. She glanced down and followed the trail of the blue fabric to his outstretched hand. Her face grew hot.

"You were pretending," she breathed.

"Would you have stayed otherwise?"

With Aloyo breathing down her back, she probably would have. She shifted so she was facing him. He was drained. His skin had a greyish cast, and his lips were chapped. Yet, he was as striking as she remembered. She tightened her hands into fists to refrain from touching him again.

"How do you feel?"

"Like I almost died." He coughed. "Thank you, Ewa. You saved me."

"I didn't. Olori Usiade sent the runner to Jaku. Ba Onigbaoje brought you here, and Iya Aloyo administered the treatment. There were probably other healers that attended to you between Jaku and here."

"Dunni."

Hearing her pet name on his familiar lips stung. She wanted to leap onto the bed and fling her arms around him, but she remained standing. Her posture was rigid, her shoulders tight.

"I am sorry. You were right."

His admission doused some of the tension in her, but she needed more.

"I visited an Ifa priest at Jaku. Do you know what he said?"

Her brows lifted. She took one step forward as if compelled. "What did he say?"

"'What are you doing fighting a war?' That was his first question. He said my destiny was elsewhere."

"You already knew that."

He nodded. His gaze was fixed at the ceiling rafters. "Why are you so far away, Dunni? Won't you hold me?"

"I'm frightened," she whispered.

Her breath was shaking. She noticed water fill his eyes and trail down the sides of his face into his ears.

"I refused to leave this world without telling you. Dunni, you are the one my heart chooses. You are my heart entirely, the light of my life. You are my partner in this journey of life."

His declarations pulled her like a magnet. She eased her trembling body on the bed and lay her head gingerly on his unwounded shoulder. Makinde took hold of her with a strength contradicting his weakened state. He squeezed her, and it eased her heart.

"I will never leave your side," he said.

There was a mountain of discussions to wade through in order to regain their trust. There were more secrets to be revealed, including the news of their impending parenthood. The future remained uncertain.

But in this moment, Ewa had found belonging. She allowed herself to be held as Makinde's words of love filled her head.

Epilogue

Six years later
    Ifelaja

S Ewa shifted her bag of tools and herbs over her shoulder. In her left hand, she held a wrought iron staff adored with small birds. The dirt road she treaded was a thin red gash cutting through the verdant forest. Red clay dusted her throbbing feet and the ends of her wrapper.

"Iya!"

She kept walking as Laaro hurried to catch up with her. She heard his pants in her ear.

"Did you say you were only going to ease yourself?" she asked.

Laaro, the young man who'd accompanied her on this healing campaign, flustered behind her.

"I did," he objected. "But then, there was a very pretty butterfly with golden wings. I wish you'd seen it, Iya."

"Your mentor will be very upset to know you left me alone."

"Please don't!"

As her escort, Laaro was to keep his eyes on her at all times. According to Makinde's instructions, even if he was pressed, Laaro ought to have held it until they stopped for the day. In reality, she tolerated the young man's distractions.

Laaro's stories kept her laughing for many nights on the road she plied frequently from Ifelaja to Ibukun.

As they drew closer to the iroko tree, her face lifted in recognition of Nifemi tapping her foot as she waited under the canopy.

"Did you bring it?" she demanded without preamble.

Laaro shouted, "I hope you aren't talking to our mother like that?"

"This doesn't concern you." Nifemi flicked her wrist in his direction as though Laaro was a pesky insect. "Sister Ewa, did you bring it?"

"It is Mother," Laaro corrected. "Iya Ewadunni isn't your sister."

Ewa clicked her tongue in good nature. These two bickered yet clearly seemed to like each other. She slipped a hand into her pack and brought out a tightly-packed parcel of spicy smoked meat prepared by Nifemi's elder sister. Nifemi jumped in glee as she snatched the package from her.

"Thank you!" she said, running to the village ahead of them.

"That girl likes food too much," Laaro said.

"And you like her just as much. Close your mouth, Laaro. Everyone knows. Let's proceed."

Usually, Nifemi travelled to Ibukun with her in order to reconnect with the family she'd left behind, but this time, Ewa had left her in charge after one of their citizens fell sick. They'd settled here two years ago, but to her, land belonged to Earth herself. It was strange to claim Ifelaja as theirs.

As the path widened, Laaro sped ahead of her. He was first to pass through the ivory obelisk announcing the entrance to Ifelaja.

"We're home." He spun and walked backwards so his gaze remained on her.

"Hm, that's why you're now pretending to take your job seriously."

"It isn't like that, Iya." He stumbled on a rock.

"Just watch where you're going."

There was a renewed eagerness to their movements. When they'd left Ibukun slightly over two year ago, the Oba had blessed their ventures while Usiade pouted. Makinde's treks to find a new home for them had finally been successful.

Ewa had hired priests to bless the area and fortify it spiritually. The priests had spoken of good fortune—Ifelaja was blessed with resources that would lead to wealth. Their Oracle advised them to be respectful of a certain tree with vivid blue flowers and to never cut any part of it down.

Word was spread far and wide. Slowly, people began to trickle in. Jomiloju came with Togun, their children, and Tope—all longing to be close to Makinde. When Ewa had left Kuta, Tope had been a girl clinging to her wrapper, but the Tope she met was a sulking young girl. Jide now had a younger brother who followed him around. Ore and Tundun relocated their farm to Ifelaja's environs, supplying the growing town with delicious staples. Makinde had taken to farming as the priest he saw in Jaku had predicted. He joined Ore and Tundun in feeding his people. When planting season passed, he hunted. He'd managed to generate a sizeable income from the pelts of the leopards that had terrorised the settlement in the past year.

The ramshackle hut Laaro had built for himself was their first stop. The young man kept walking with her.

"We're already home," she said.

"But—"

"He won't object. Find time to visit us during the week for your reward."

Laaro grinned and bowed to her before slipping away. The pace of her heart quickened as she neared home. There were roughly six families who called the forested area home. Makinde had grand plans for Ifelaja. He dreamt of a future where the town was grander, boasting high walls and a moat. For now, Ifelaja was a much smaller version of Kuta.

She made out the triangle of the thatch roofs between the thin trunks of trees. The two bungalows were made from the whitish clay found in the river bed bordering the south. Looming between the buildings was the majestic tree with blue flowers. It was the same tree in the clearing where Makinde used to meditate when he lived roughly in the forest. That part of him was ancient history—although he still sat in silence every few days.

A grin spread across her face as she stepped into the empty front yard. Her return was earlier than predicted. When she'd received a message that Aloyo needed her aid in eliminating an infectious disease that claimed a village on Ibukun's outskirts, she'd packed her bags immediately. The Ibukun healers' guild had managed to reclaim the community's health, saving the lives they could.

After weeks away, she had chosen not to send word ahead that she was returning to Ifelaja soon. She wanted to surprise her family. With no one at home, she set her tool bag hanging on a post by the front door and placed her staff standing upright in front of the house. She then rinsed her hands and face.

She was swishing water from the cooling pot in her mouth when Makinde strode towards the yard with their daughter, Ogele, bouncing on his neck. Wuu panted at their heels. Ewa tried to conceal herself round the wall of the house, but the dog revealed her spot by dashing straight to her.

Ogele squealed at the sight of her mother. Makinde carried her down carefully before she jumped from his shoulders into Ewa's awaiting arms. Ewa hugged her and swung her around.

"Yaya," Ogele said. "There was a big lizard on the farm."

"Is that so?" She set her daughter down on her feet. The resemblance between daughter and father amazed her—from their bronzed skin to their long noses, no one would doubt Ogele was Makinde's daughter.

"I asked Baba if I could keep it as a pet, and he said no."

"Ha!"

Makinde chuckled as he scooped her up in his arms. He lifted her so her toes grazed the earth as he rubbed his nose along the curve of her neck.

"Where is your escort?" he asked.

"Me, too, Baba!" Ogele inserted herself between them.

"I sent him home."

"Baba!" Ogele reached up for a hug.

Makinde bent down and carried Ogele up high. "He should have brought you to the door and waited for me."

Ewa pressed a kiss on his arm. As Ogele found to tell them more about her day, Jomiloju approached from the distance carrying a tray.

"Welcome home," she said, waving wildly. "I brought food."

Ewa collected the tray from her. It was warm under her hands as she carried it into the main house with Jomiloju trailing behind her.

"I pounded yams with plantains. And I made egusi soup. There's also a bottle of plantain wine."

"Thank you, my darling Jomiloju. It is as though you were expecting me." Ewa placed the tray on a bench resting against a wall in the inner courtyard. Jomiloju wasn't an expert at making and selling alcohol.

"How was it?" Jomiloju asked eagerly.

"Challenging. We will discuss that later."

Makinde joined them with Ogele. "My precious girl, will you like to visit with your aunt tonight?"

Ogele shrieked in delight, clearly eager to play with her cousins.

"Wait, wait," Ewa objected. "You aren't visiting anywhere."

"Come on, Sister Dunni," Jomiloju crooned, holding on to Ogele's hand.

"Please, Yaya."

Ewa quirked a brow at Makinde, and he winked at her. The expression in his hooded eyes sent a jolt of awareness through her. She turned to the tray of food. It was a terrible weakness the way he easily readied her body for his member with just a look. They'd spent every day making up for the decade they'd lived apart, so much so, they'd named this town after the love they shared. She felt when he wrapped his arms around her waist.

"I've missed my wife so." His breath raised goosebumps on her neck. "Shouldn't we send our daughter to sleep at To-gun's? We both know you can't help but scream when I make love to you."

Her knees turned to honey as he told her the ways he was going to pleasure her when they were alone.

"Aburo," she croaked. "Please take Ogele with you for a few days."

When she glanced over her shoulder, she found she was alone with Makinde in the courtyard. Arching her back, she reached for his neck and pulled his face down so his lips met hers.

"Let's start right away," she murmured against his kiss.

Author's Note

Thank you for reading Sweetest Fortune! Writing historical fiction has been a challenge for me, and I am thrilled that I have accomplished it here. I had so much fun writing this that there will be a follow-up series set in Ifelaja involving Ewa and Makinde's descendants sometime in the future (hopefully!).

When I set out to write Ewa and Makinde's story, I wanted it to take place in the 14th century. Written sources on Yoruba history from that period are few, and I drew a lot of inspiration from the Ifa corpus. While I did a lot of research for this story (and have included part of my reading list below), I have taken liberties in many details. Some town names mentioned in this novel are real and remain today, but I have situated them in random locations here. And while the wars may have been inspired by true events, I used my creative license to make them fit with my story.

I have tried my best to depict Yoruba spirituality with the respect and care it deserves. Any error or misrepresentation within these pages is entirely my fault.

References

Anatomy of Love by Helen Fisher (1992)

"Divorce among the Yoruba." by Peter C. Lloyd; American Anthropologist 70, no. 1 (1968): 67–81

Ewe: The use of plants in Yoruba Society by Pierre Fatumbi Verger (1995)

Ibolo: A History of the Ibolo People of Kwara State by Rahaman Adetunji Lateef

Ifá: A Forest of Mystery by Nicholaj De Mattos Frisvold (2016)

Ifism: The Complete Works of Orunmila by C. Osamaro Ibie (1986)

Iwure: Efficacious Prayer to Olodumare, The Supreme Force by Fayemi Fatunde Fakayode (2011)

Iwure Owuro: Morning Prayer in Isese Way by Ifagbenusola Owomide Popoola (2020)

Journey in the Yóruba and Núpe Countries in 1858 by Daniel J. May (1890)

A History of the Yoruba People by Stephen Adebanji Akintoye (2010)

The History of the Yorubas by Samuel Johnson (1997).

History of Yoruba Land by Gbade Aladeojebi (2016)

Hugh Clapperton Into The Interior Of Africa Records Of The Second Expedition 1825-1827, edited by Jamie Bruce Lockhart and Paul E. Lovejoy (2005)

Iwa Rere: Morality In Yoruba Traditional Religion by Lloyd Weaver And Ademola Fabunmi (2016)

"Iwuré: Medium Of Communicating The Desires Of Men To The Gods In Yorubaland" by Ayo Opefeyitimi; Journal of Religion in Africa XVIII, 1 (1988)

"The Ogunda Meji Temple Apata, Ibadan, As A Model For Modern Trends In Yoruba Traditional Worship" by Aderemi Ayotunde Davies (University Of Ibadan)

Orunmila's Healing Spaces by Oluwo Ifakolade Obafemi and Iyanifa Fayomi Falade Aworeni Obafemi (2011)

"Yoruba Folk-Lore" by John Parkinson; Journal of the Royal African Society, vol. 8, no. 30, 1909, pp. 165–86

"Yoruba Pottery" by Georgina Beier; African Arts 13, no. 3 (1980): 48–92

The Yoruba Traditional Healers of Nigeria by Mary Olufunmilayo Adekson (2003)

Yoruba Myths by Ulli Beier (1980)

Thank you for reading Sweetest Fortune by Bambo Deen. If you enjoyed this story, support the author by leaving a review at the site of purchase.

Books by Bambo Deen

Sweetest Fortune
How To Fix A Broken Heart[1]
A Little Bit of Love's Magic[2]
Enchanted Vol 2 Anthology[3]

About the author

Bambo Deen is a writer telling stories of all kinds of Black love set in Africa. *How to Fix A Broken Heart* is her first novel-length romance publication. Her previously published works from Love Africa Press are *A Little Bit of Love's Magic* and *Enchanted Volume Two*. *Sweetest Fortune* is her latest book.

---

1. https://www.loveafricapress.com/product-page/how-to-fix-a-broken-heart-by-bambo-deen-ebook

2. https://www.loveafricapress.com/product-page/a-little-bit-of-love-s-magic-bambo-deen

3. https://www.loveafricapress.com/product-page/enchanted-vol-2-anthology-ebook

OTHER BOOKS BY LOVE AFRICA PRESS

Fugitive Heart by Mathitu Wairimu
Mistletoe Mafia by Kiru Taye
Her Golden Touch by Holly March
Betting on Love by Kani Sey
Like Whirlwind by Feyi Aina
Schemes N Love by Jomi Oyel

CONNECT WITH US
Facebook.com/LoveAfricaPress
X.com/LoveAfricaPress
Instagram.com/LoveAfricaPress
Threads.com/LoveAfricaPress
www.loveafricapress.com[1]

---

1. http://www.loveafricapress.com

BAMBO DEEN

LOVE AFRICA
PRESS
African Love Stories

www.ingramcontent.com/pod-product-compliance
Lightning Source LLC
Chambersburg PA
CBHW050549190726
48283CB00007B/2066